# THE SACRIFICE

# THE SACRIFICE

## Yearning for Messiah

### JACK A. TAYLOR

THE SACRIFICE
Copyright © 2024 by Jack A. Taylor

Soft cover ISBN: 978-1-4866-2638-0
Hard cover ISBN: 978-1-4866-2640-3
eBook ISBN: 978-1-4866-2639-7

Word Alive Press
119 De Baets Street Winnipeg, MB  R2J 3R9
www.wordalivepress.ca

WORD ALIVE
—PRESS—

Cataloguing in Publication information can be obtained from Library and Archives Canada.

*This book is dedicated to all faithful servants of God
who have embraced his sacrifice as their own.*

CONTENTS

When the time came for the purification rites required by the Law of Moses, Joseph and Mary took him to Jerusalem to present him to the Lord (as it is written in the Law of the Lord, "Every firstborn male is to be consecrated to the Lord"), and to offer a sacrifice in keeping with what is said in the Law of the Lord: "a pair of doves or two young pigeons."

Now there was a man in Jerusalem called Simeon, who was righteous and devout. He was waiting for the consolation of Israel, and the Holy Spirit was on him. It had been revealed to him by the Holy Spirit that he would not die before he had seen the Lord's Messiah. Moved by the Spirit, he went into the temple courts. When the parents brought in the child Jesus to do for him what the custom of the Law required, Simeon took him in his arms and praised God, saying: "Sovereign Lord, as you have promised, you may now dismiss your servant in peace. For my eyes have seen your salvation, which you have prepared in the sight of all nations: a light for revelation to the Gentiles, and the glory of your people Israel."

The child's father and mother marveled at what was said about him. Then Simeon blessed them and said to Mary, his mother: "This child is destined to cause the falling and rising of many in Israel, and to be a sign that will be spoken against, so that the thoughts of many hearts will be revealed. And a sword will pierce your own soul too."

There was also a prophet, Anna, the daughter of Penuel, of the tribe of Asher. She was very old; she had lived with her husband seven years after her marriage, and then was a widow until she was eighty-four. She never left the temple but worshiped night and day, fasting and praying. Coming up to them at that very moment, she gave thanks to God and spoke about the child to all who were looking forward to the redemption of Jerusalem. (Luke 2:22–38)

Given the history of bloodshed, intrigue, international turmoil, and chaos around the building of the Temple in the years before the Messiah, how did these Hannah and Simeon survive as they waited for the ultimate sacrifice? Here is one version of their story.

CHAPTER ONE

# THE LOSS

*74 years until Messiah (80 BC)*

The sizzling sun had already sucked the dew off the blades of grass and chased the night creatures back into their dens and hiding places. Simeon ben Samuel turned his face toward the source of warmth, shook a pebble out of his sandal, and plucked a thistle from the edge of his knee-length tunic.

"Bokor Tov, Ha'Shem," he pronounced.[1]

The faintest whisper of a breeze brought something else into his nostrils. The aroma of sacrifice? But this wasn't the time or place for sacrifice.

Something was wrong. He detected no birdsong. Children's voices were absent. The stench of smoke seemed stronger.

A deer darted by. Had something startled it?

The smell of fresh horse dung rose up as he stepped forward. Where had all this come from? His small village of Pharisees had only one horse. Perhaps traders had come by to share their wealth.

The acrid tang launched a memory of his own first sacrifice. He'd raised the lamb from birth for a year and coddled it all the way to Yerushalayim. Fresh from his bar mitzvah, he'd relished the promptings to act the man and do what a man must do. The line to the altar had been long and the lamb grew heavy and restless. Without hesitation, he had handed over his pet to the priest and watched as it was tied. He'd stretched his hand for one last pat.

The slice across his lamb's neck was swift. As blood spurted onto his hand, the lamb looked to him in desperation. It struggled, then weakened as its life flowed into a cup.

Simeon stepped back, wiping the blood on his tunic as the dead lamb was dragged to the butchery table and nearby fire. What a terrible price to be a sinful

---

[1] "Good morning, Lord."

man. The invisible stain hid under his skin; he wiped at that which could never be wiped away.

He selected five smooth stones and busied himself slinging them at the olive trees lining the neighbor's field.

"Take that, Goliath," he murmured as he selected a few more. He squared his shoulders and set his jaw firm as each dull thud echoed from their target. He aimed at a scurrying hare and missed. Guilt and relief flooded him. "Kill only what you need."

It was a strange morning. The rabbi Penuel, from his tribe of Asher, hadn't shown up to give the lesson. This was the lesson on the coming of the Messiah and the importance of sacrifice. Simeon had been waiting all week for the details.

Soon after dawn he had anchored himself in place at the learning tree until his legs needed to dance, run, or chase something.

"Until you understand the sacrifice, you can never understand the Torah," the rabbi had warned on the last Sabbath.

The words swarmed through Simeon's mind like bats in an orchard. His hand rubbed again against his tunic. Would the stain ever go away?

The usual vendors, traders, and workmen were vacant from the road. Even the sunrise spotted the cloud bellies with a strange mix of crimson, pink, and orange, as if the divine artist had emptied his palate at random across the heavens.

The dead dog stopped Simeon in his tracks. He'd hurled a stick for this very animal a few hours before. It wasn't his, just a village mutt surviving off the trash heap at the edge of the settlement. The aroma of the carcass was strong, the foul remnant of rotting food it had eaten, or rolled in. The dog had been friendly enough. Now its jaws hung open in a soundless bark. Its tongue licked at the dust as flies buzzed around sightless eyes. The coagulating patch of red on its neck betrayed a spear or dagger at play.

A dark swirling cloud of smoke rose from his village—not just the plumes of a backyard fire but the spiral of an angry, consuming devourer. His gut twisted and without hesitation he ducked into the cover of a copse of oak trees, doffed his sandals at the base, and climbed. It was cool here, near the trunk.

At five times his height, he settled on a branch and scanned the village. Horsemen in armored vests tossed torches onto the flat roofs filled with drying sheaves of wheat. The straw mats, wattling, and wooden trusses provided lasting life to the flames.

Kneeling facedown in the middle of the town square, the villagers lay like piles of discarded rags, six men with swords surrounding them. The rabbi stood bowed with two ropes around his neck, one rope attached to a horse facing north and the other tied to a horse facing south. The riders gave a shout, the horses leapt forward, and Simeon looked away. When he dared to look back, every person remained flat on the ground as the attackers marched on. This family's fate was clear.

Marauders stepped into formation like a trail of ants and quick-stepped past Simeon's hiding place. Two riders stopped beneath him as he pressed hard against the trunk of the tree. If they noticed his sandals lying abandoned a few steps away, his death would be certain.

Their language and accent marked them as kin. Nothing was making sense. Why would they kill their own?

"Two more villages under the torch and we'll see how Queen Salome Alexandra dares to prove her strength," one said. "These Pharisees are a plague on the land. King Jannaeus wants us to stomp them out for a reason."

"She will probably poison the old goat," the other rider remarked. "Who marries two brothers and outlives them both? As long as we leave no witnesses, we can blame this on the Parthians, the Romans, or bandits." He urged his horse forward. "The blood of this Pharisaic cult boils in the queen's blood. When her husband crucified eight hundred of the vermin, what do you expect her to do? All we have to do is to wait for her to appoint her son. Then we will rise again."

The two rode off after the rest of their band and Simeon slid down the tree, stepped into his sandals, and sat against the trunk. His stomach churned and he swallowed hard against the urge to retch.

His uncle and grandfather had perished in the crucifixion of the eight hundred. From the time he was young, his family had been on the run. The queen herself had sheltered them in caves and fed them from the royal reserves. Once her second husband had died, she'd ascended to power and urged the surviving Pharisees to retake their place of privilege. The villages had been built based on this assurance.

The chill of evening breezes stirred the leaves and the first shadows of dusk slid across the land, smothering the vibrancy of color. Despite what lay ahead, Simeon pushed himself toward the devastation he had seen. His stomach rumbled and growled. Only the village could quell his hunger pangs.

Nearing the village, he heard the wailing of a lone griever. A woman. Young. The cry was mesmerizing, drawing him toward the theatre of death. No one should have to endure such agony alone. His ears guided him when his eyes fought to look away. The girl sat, her mother's body still beside her, the head nestled in her lap. The older woman's scarf lay crumpled in the dust like a discarded rag.

The girl's jaw slackened open when she saw Simeon stumbling toward her, as if the living in such a macabre scenario were the real ghosts. Her wail ceased and her eyes grew wide. Bloodied hands covered her mouth.

When he stopped a few strides away, she looked down at her mother and then back at him.

She was the rabbi's daughter, Hannah—and from the looks of it, the lone survivor.

"I was going for water when they came," she stuttered. "I hid in the bushes. There was nothing I could do."

Simeon crouched, focusing on her deep hazel eyes. "I went for lessons with your Abba. He never came. I hid in a tree." Dismembered bodies lay like crumpled dolls all around them. "We have to bury them all. Ha'Shem has given us life to live. We must work and then eat. Is there anyone else?"

Hannah shook her head. "No one. They did terrible things to my Abba and Ima. Ha'Shem has looked away from his pious ones. Not even the queen can save us now."

"We await the promised one. One day we will see him and he will set us free to worship as we should."

"I await no one until the blood of my family is avenged," she said. "For too long we have been running, hiding, slinking about in the shadows as if we were rodents inviting extermination. You bury them. I cannot leave my Ima like this."

Four clay lamps set the perimeters of the gravesite. No one had designated a space for death since the village was fresh and everyone focused on life.

The blacksmith's hut had a digging tool and Simeon borrowed it for the task. He slashed at the earth until blisters tore his hands. Two of the lamps flickered out. Still he dug.

When he could lift his arms no more, he knelt and sobbed. Hannah found him there and gently stroked his back.

"Shalom, shalom," she said. "Shalom. Shalom."

He rolled onto his side, exhausted. The cool night air set him shivering as it sucked at his sweat. Hannah set a fresh lamp and a wooden tray of goat cheese, crackers, olives, dates, and figs before him.

"It is time to eat. The hole is deep enough. We must bury the dead before the wolves come. But first, you must eat." Hannah took his hands and pried open his fingers. The blood and ooze gave witness to the blisters and lack of skin. "I will find some ointment and a rag for you. You must rise and say prayers for the dead. You are the oldest in our village now."

"I don't know what to say," he said.

"My father used to stand under the stars and call out to the King of the universe," she said. "He used to just talk like he was talking to his own Abba. I don't know what good it did, but it seemed to give him peace. Maybe right now you can just ask for help."

* * *

Hannah portioned out the food bit by bit for seven days until the Sabbath passed. Their routine was simple: rise for prayers, prepare tea and flatbread, scavenge through a home for whatever they could pile onto the village cart, eat, tidy up the home they had ravished, and scour the forest for useful fruit, roots or berries before collecting water from the stream. They would eat again.

Out of propriety, they had separated into their family homes for sleep, but hours into the first night, after burying the village, Hannah knocked lightly on his door.

"Shalom, Simeon," she whispered into the dark. "I am afraid on my own."

Simeon removed the basket that covered the clay lamp he had been burning. He was huddled, back against the wall, facing the door. "Nothing will hurt you here."

She shuffled inside, still in her goatskin slippers. "You have two rooms. Let me stay in one. We don't even have the dog to warn us if someone or something comes." She knelt beside his reed mat. "I'm sure I heard the leopard and wolf outside looking for the bodies."

"They're probably eating the dead dog," he said. "I should have buried it as well."

"It smelled so bad," she said, raising a perfumed wrist under her nose. "You don't think the wolf will dig everyone up?"

He motioned her to the next room where his parents had slept. "I'll put stones over the pit tomorrow."

"I have my own bedding and will cause you no trouble."

"What will other Pharisees say if they hear we are unwed and sleeping in the same house?"

Rising, Hannah bowed and backed toward the bedroom door. "I have not yet reached my womanhood and I will keep my distance," she promised. "We are like the first man and woman in the garden. We will leave this place and find others like ourselves. I need your protection and provision." At his silence, she moved into the other room. "I will prepare your meals, wash your clothes, and wash your feet."

"You are not my mother," he said. "We will leave as soon as possible and you will be free to find your own way with another family."

Hannah moved back into the room and sat against the wall. "Who were those men and why would they kill people who only want to follow the word of the Almighty?" She lit a second clay lamp. "I like it better in the light. You can sleep and I will stay here watching."

Simeon sighed and released the images haunting his heart. "I'll sit up with you."

* * *

Seven sunrises and sunsets came and went and not a soul passed the devastated scene. The birds sang again. Deer and rabbits wandered by as if no world-shattering event had happened. The breeze rustled the leaves and spiders spun their webs. Not a drop of rain fell for them to collect.

Hannah changed the wrap around Simeon's hands each morning and applied new cream. She claimed to have no idea what the soothing white ointment was meant to do, but it eased his discomfort and gave him the courage to gather firewood and useful items from other homes.

"Are you going to be okay to move on?" he asked.

"I'm ready if you are."

Simeon dragged out the cart from behind the carpenter's shop, but with no horses or donkeys left behind it was clear they would have to push and pull the contraption if they chose to take more than a pack on their backs.

Once they had finished loading everything of use they could find, Simeon set himself between the yoke and Hannah pushed. Puffs of dust arose from each step down the road.

Their throats were parched well before noon. Still, they continued. Twice they unloaded sacks of grain to lighten the weight. Highlands towered to the north, west, and far south. The land sloped slightly toward the east and it seemed easiest to roll the cart in that direction.

Simeon tied a rope from the cart around his chest, grabbed the yoke, and left Hannah to push again. Together, they evacuated this place of death. Their sweat left no reservoir for tears under the blistering sun.

The sun reached its zenith and was rapidly reaching for the horizon when they saw their first person. It was a man, sitting on a horse, moving slowly in their direction. He was broad-shouldered, big-bearded, and sat tall in his saddle.

"Shalom, children," the man called. "Where is your home and why are you pulling that cart?"

"Let me talk," Simeon urged Hannah. Without waiting, he released the yoke and stepped toward the rider. "Shalom, I am not a child. My bar mitzvah is past. We come from a village of people who follow the God of Abraham, Isaac, and Jacob. Everyone else was murdered by invaders. We seek a peaceful place to stay."

The man dismounted and approached. "Have you travelled far? Do you know where you are?"

Simeon looked around and pointed west. "We left at dawn and have pushed hard. We haven't been in these parts before, but we are ready to settle and re-establish our people."

The man chuckled, his generous belly jiggling. "The valley in front of you is Jezreel. To the south is Egypt and to the east is Mesopotamia. The best place to live is up on that ridge where the settlement is. You're not going to get your cart up there, so you better use my horse to pull it."

He didn't wait for a response but set his horse in the yoke and tied it securely. He looked through the heap of supplies in the back.

"I'm surprised the two of you got this cart anywhere with all this stuff in it," the man continued. "I'll trade you the services of my horse for two bags of grain. You look tired, so you both might as well take a ride."

"The cart is heavy enough without us straining the horse," Simeon said. "We'll walk and give you one bag of grain in exchange for the use of your horse. Is this the valley where Gideon defeated the Midianites?"

"I see we have a barterer and a scholar. Gideon also defeated the Amalekites and kings of the east. As far as you can see in this valley, we raise barley, wheat, flax, and whatever the gods provide. Over on that ridge is where the people of Philistia overthrew the yoke of Saul and restored the hope of our people."

Simeon fell into step beside Hannah, who looked ready to drop. "You can ride, if you like," he told her. "This man is a pagan and we can't defile ourselves by taking hospitality from him. Guard yourself. We have already seen what it's like to fall under the wrath of enemies who hate our people."

"He stinks," Hannah whispered.

"We probably don't smell much better to him. Hide your nose in the grain bags if you need to."

"What will we do when we get to his house? We can't anger him, or he may do worse to us because of the disrespect."

"Sit in the cart and I'll figure something out." Simeon helped Hannah into the cart and strode up to where the farmer led his horse by the bridle. "One and a half bags, so the girl can ride."

The animal resisted the strain and weight of the cart as they ascended toward the village on the hill.

The farmer waved an arm over the vast sea of green undulating in the gentle breeze. "The gods have heard our prayers and accepted our sacrifices. The wheat and barley are sprouting perfectly. Legend says that the Great Sea once rested all across here to the Jordan River valley and even filled up the Salt Sea."

"The Almighty is wise in the way he cares for his own," Simeon said.

"You will stay with us tonight and we will find a home for the two of you in the morning," the farmer said. "My wife has some pigeon pie and pig's feet pudding, which will double your weight in one sitting. This is also the new moon festival and you will learn how to dance like you've never danced before."

Simeon prepared to launch into a diatribe as to why they needed to find their own space, but the farmer's eyes grew wide.

"Watch out!" he warned. "Warriors are riding hard this way."

The man untied his horse and allowed the cart to roll back under its own weight.

"Stop!" Simeon yelled, desperately hanging onto the yoke as he bumped down the road. His foot caught a stone, and before he could say anything he tumbled down an embankment. Another blow to the head left him dazed and staring up at a dozen ravens circling overhead.

* * *

The comfortable nest Hannah had built for herself soon became a chaotic pile of shifting weights falling over her. She had seen the armored warriors, javelins poised, riding hard toward them.

When the cart bumped down the hill, she yanked a blanket over herself as the bags of grain pinned her in place. She held her tongue and waited for the terror to pass. Where was Simeon?

All movement ceased and she heard strange voices chattering. The cart swung around and started a slow, controlled descent. Perhaps Simeon had worked out a deal with the newcomers to avoid the pagan farmer's hospitality. Her legs cramped, but she held still. Simeon would tell her when the time was right.

Finally, the cart stopped. Someone climbed on and moved the sacks of grain. Simeon was finally here.

Hannah threw off the blanket and stared into the face of a fiery-eyed warrior. A tangled bush sprouted from his chin, but his upper lip was bare. His snarl exposed even more terrifying brown teeth. She screamed as he reached for her, attempting to scramble out of his reach. He called excitedly to the other seven men and grabbed her foot, holding her upside-down over the cart. She secured a fistful of the hem of her tunic and shoved it between her legs, desperate to regain a fragment of modesty.

The seven grinned mischievously and sidled up to their prey. More chatter erupted in what seemed like an argument. One of those on the ground grabbed and pulled at her. The one in the cart pulled back hard. Another warrior ran his hand over her face while another tugged at her tunic.

Simeon was nowhere to be seen.

The warrior in the cart carried some form of authority, for he shouted and pulled hard enough to cause Hannah to tumble back into the middle of the cart. The warrior grinned, pounded his chest, and tied her arms and legs tightly with a strip of cloth he had kept around his waist.

Sitting beside her, he waved his arms and gave orders which got the others moving again north. When she ducked her eyes to look away from her captor, he grabbed her chin and forced her face skyward. He continued to chatter and chuckle.

She had no idea why in the world Ha'Shem would curse her so terribly. Without Simeon, she had lost everything.

# CHAPTER TWO
# THE QUEEN

*69 years until Messiah (75 BC)*

Simeon prostrated himself with the others as the queen stepped onto the marble platform in the outdoor theatre. The glories of her womanhood were on full display. The sun glistened off the jewels on her silver scepter and gave a sheen to the golden crown on her head. Her strength and dignity flowed as she paced in front of her subjects.

The cheers of the crowd echoed like thundering waves against a breaker and their vibrations filtered to the core of his bones. Hundreds of soldiers lined the perimeter of the enclosure with javelins and swords ready for a disturbance.

A scarlet-robed judicious figure took his place beside the monarch and held up his hands. Silence fell like a curtain.

It had been five years since Simeon had crawled out of the scree on the slopes of Jezreel to watch the marauders disappear with Hannah. He'd turned his back on the pagan farmer and headed north. A large stone arch had provided shelter as the sun descended.

A shepherd had awakened him in the morning with a gentle hand on his shoulder. The kindly folk of Shunem had proceeded to provide him shelter until a group of Pharisees stopped by on their way to hear the new monarch. A patriarch named Baruch had welcomed him as an aide. Simeon had joined them, relieved to find his own people again.

"Queen Salome Alexandra wishes to speak to her subjects," the robed figure declared. "Let her be heard. Let her be exalted."

"Shalom to my friends in the Galilee," she said. "You people of the book have been under great pressure from my husband during these past years as he tried to expand our territory and keep peace at home." She looked compassionately at the ragged band on their knees. "You know I have tried to provide for you as you hid in the caves of Mount Merob, Mount Hermon, and Mount Carmel.

It's time for you to take your place of leadership and enjoy once again the harvests of the land, the wildflowers of our hilly slopes, and the birdlife in abundance. It's time for your children to run free without fear and for your places of study to thrive again in our villages and towns."

The cheers echoed off the marble walls until the scarlet-robed figure held up his hand again. "Hear the queen!"

She held up her scepter. "This symbol of our strength was held by Judas Maccabee himself and it was handed to me by my husband to bring peace to our nation. Two generations ago, when the Greek overlords burned our Torahs, banned our Sabbaths and feasts, outlawed the mark of our covenant, and substituted our holy sacrifice with swine, Judas and his four brothers led the rebellion to restore our rights and rituals. They founded our Hasmonean dynasty, which endures to this day. The fight continues. The fortress of Ragaba on the other side of the Jordan has fallen and the rebellion in our land is quenched. I value your assent as we work together to help our land flourish again." She stepped down, drawing closer to the crowd. "My Hebrew name, Shlomzion, shows that I am a queen committed to peace." She pointed to two young men standing to the side. "My two sons, Hyrcanus and Aristobulus, will continue to manage the high priesthood and assist me in the transformations we need to make. The Almighty reigns in this land, which is at the crossroads of empires. Traders from east, west, north, and south surge through our roads and fill our coffers with treasure. If you can take your place in our government, judiciary, and training centers, we may yet rival Solomon with glory."

Instead of a raucous cheer, the men on their knees broke into a rumble of prayer. Simeon joined in the uttering of recitations and psalms, which carried on until the queen's assistant made himself known.

"The queen honors your prayers on her behalf and asks you to continue this noble practice while she is busy with her rule," he intoned. "She also requests prayers for her health and wisdom."

Simeon was too busy praying on behalf of Hannah to consider the queen's health.

Rather than returning to Shunem, he soon joined a group comprised of Baruch and six others, all older than himself. They headed south and settled on the outskirts of Jericho where they would busy themselves in their study of the Messiah.

"He is coming soon," Baruch assured Simeon. "We must bide our time."

\* \* \*

Hannah's journey had been a nightmare. The warrior who had claimed her on the outskirts of Jezreel ravaged her like a hungry wolf day after day, unleashing indecipherable tirades while demanding meals which never seemed to satisfy. Her initial cries to Ha'Shem died with her whimpers through the night.

An older woman, dragged into the dark hut one day by Hannah's captor, set about to train her in how to prepare proper meals—and how to satisfy her man.

By listening carefully, the man's garbled utterings began to take on meaning and life became more predictable.

It was months before she discovered that she had become part of village life in Alexandrium, west of the confluence of the Jabbok and Jordan rivers. Mount Sartaba rose around her and the locals referred to its fortress, erected on a pointy barren hill overlooking the Jordan, as Sartaba. The precipitous slopes left them vulnerable to desert winds and winter rains.

The path up the mountainside was steep and the fortress seemed impenetrable. Large limestone ashlars formed thick walls that blocked the winds but hardly blocked the cold. The Hasmoneans had built it as a tribute to Alexander Jannaeus, the queen's former husband. Captives from the fall of Ragaba crowded into the dungeons until their bodies failed to withstand interrogation and were unceremoniously discarded into a pit whose fire never ceased.

She recalled childhood dreams of holding butterflies on her finger, picking petals from wildflowers, sprinkling them in a shower over her mother's head, and throwing sticks for the village dog. They all evaporated, leaving only dreams of escape.

There was one problem: Alexandrium was a military garrison meant to guard political prisoners.

Having grown up in a prosperous village where games, food, family, and festivals were shared without thought for who owned what, the constant fear was soul-numbing.

"I need to get out of here," she whispered to the birds. "Why can't I fly away like you?"

For a while, she imitated the prayers of her Abba.

"Oh Lord, sovereign King of the universe. You who hold the world in your hands. You who control the hearts of men, free me from this pit of terror." She would wait in the same way her father had waited, but nothing would happen. "Release me from the pain of foul-smelling men. Unbind me from the scourge of death in my dreams at night." The words fell limply from her lips. "You are the only one I can turn to. Guard Simeon from pain and fill him with peace. Amain."

The prayers grew shorter and less frequent as the days passed without change.

The beauty of nature was a constant ally. A trio of green bee-eaters joined a handful of sparrows, starlings, and black kites who dropped by for handouts. Hannah wooed them with generous crumbs and scraps outside her door. Wildflowers provided a rainbow carpet of delight. She watched the golden eagle that drifted by at least once a day, scaring away the spotted lizards who took refuge in the limestone rocks jutting out from the slopes. A pair of rock hyraxes whistled their calls to each other.

Slaves continued to refine the roadway where a constant stream of donkey carts supplied the fortress with water, food, bedding, security, support, and weapons. Traders and vendors paraded past the soldiers and family members who resided in the small village surrounding the fortress.

Her husband Jeroboam—for that is how she chose to label the warrior, as a way to diminish her guilt, shame, and fear—was tasked with overseeing the searchers assigned to pick up enemies of the state.

He grew restless when the snow melted in the spring. After animated discussions, he led his men on raids. Great delight erupted from the other residents as he shared tales of his conquests around the fire each night, reliving details such as the terror on an enemy's face just before being captured or killed.

One morning, while her husband was away, the old woman who so often served as Hannah's only companion escorted her on a day trip by donkey cart toward the Jordan River. It was the first time Hannah had been this close to the river without a significant number of male escorts. Only one young man trailed them along on this journey, and once they alighted from the cart he seemed more interested in using his sling on birds than observing the women. A small herd of gazelle and a pair of hyenas provided the perfect distraction.

When they neared the riverside, the old woman chattered at the sentry and sent him off. Once he had moved out of sight, she doffed her tunic and waded into the water, naked. She urged Hannah to do the same and soon the cool, clear water of the river flowed over her body. The older woman scrubbed her hair with scented lotion and rubbed sand over her skin. Hannah followed her lead.

The two were enjoying themselves so much that Hannah didn't at first notice the sentry, Rezim, gawking from the bushes. When she did, she turned her back and lowered herself into the water; the old woman shook her fist at the man but made no attempt to hide herself.

A short time later, as they were dressing, Rezim appeared and made a grab for Hannah. The old woman clawed at him, but he elbowed her in the jaw and threw her limp body into the river.

As the old woman floated away with the current, Rezim turned his attention fully on Hannah. There was nothing she could do.

When Jeroboam returned, he questioned Hannah about the absence of the older woman and Hannah admitted that she had seen the woman floating in the river.

"How could you go without an escort?" he demanded.

"We had one!"

"Who?"

"Rezim!"

"How did the old woman die if you had an escort?"

"She fell in the river."

"And this Rezim failed to save her?"

"He was away while we bathed."

Jeroboam's mouth hung open. He marched toward her, finger pointing. "The old woman died in the river and you said nothing?" He paced the room. "You bathed in the river. Then you returned alone with this Rezim? And you want me to believe nothing happened?"

His fury at her for taking a trip to the river without his permission was clear. His passions were rough and demanding and she flinched at the smell of his breath as he pressed his foul body against her.

Later, at the community meal, Hannah noticed Rezim staring at her. The young man was dressed like a prince and carried himself like one. She stared back and smiled.

Soon her husband grabbed her by the hair and threw her to the ground. He yanked out his dagger and gutted the unsuspecting Rezim. No one attempted to help the dying man, who groaned in the shadows; Rezim had crossed the line.

In that moment, Hannah learned of her power over men. The realization sent a shiver up her spine. It was a good thing Simeon wasn't around to see her now.

With the queen firmly in control of the land, more and more captives arrived to fill the garrison chambers. In the early days, Hannah often covered her ears to block out the blood-curdling screams of torture victims. As the months passed, it became a routine feature of the night, the horrifying sounds drifting by in the wind.

\* \* \*

Simeon's first vision of the Temple was hardly memorable. Rubble cluttered the paths and plazas around it and only a few pilgrims pushed their way through the crowded streets of the capital to engage in the sacrifices offered by white-robed priests. The Greeks and Syrians had renamed this hilltop metropolis, calling it Antioch, but Baruch and his compatriots still genuflected toward the house of the Almighty in Yerushalayim.

Baruch pointed toward the high ground ahead of them as seven pilgrims reached the top of the Mount of Olives.

"You see how the city resembles the two humps of a camel?" Baruch said. "The hump where the Temple sits is Mount Carmel, where Avraham offered up Yitzak on the altar. It is the place where King David purchased the land from Araunah to stop the plague killing the people. It has always been the place of sacrifice." He pointed toward the other hump. "That is Mount Zion. It is the city of David, which he took from the Jebusites. You can see the royal palace still used to this day by visiting dignitaries."

"Will the Messiah come to the Temple to claim his crown?" Simeon asked. "What will happen to the queen? How will we choose one over the other without causing a war among our own people?"

Baruch chuckled. "You ask good questions. We will study the books when we return to our shelter. I don't recall any passage speaking about a conflict between the King of kings and the queen of queens."

"Talk of a battle may be unnecessary," a nearby man said. "It seems the queen is sick with distemper and in need of care. Her sons grow restless to take their place on the throne. The fate of every monarch seems to be short, with others ending their reign through poison or a dagger."

"No doubt she will declare for Hyrcanus, her eldest," still another noted. "I don't trust the youngest, with that Idumean advisor he has taken on. What is his name? Antipater, I think."

"Let that be a lesson to you," Baruch said. "It isn't the enemies without you have to fear but the false friends within. Guard your heart, mind, and soul and brandish the word of Ha'Shem like a sword."

While walking through the Temple courts, a strong sense of destiny surged in Simeon. He stood atop a large limestone block resting at the edge of the courtyard.

"One day I shall meet the Messiah in this very place," he said.

Baruch waved him down. "Don't exalt yourself above those who have journeyed this path for many years longer than you. We all have declared that one day we will hail the Messiah, yet no Messiah has come. Perhaps this queen will pave the way for the true Prince of our Nation, but the holy books speak of Elijah's return in the wilderness and no voice has sounded for as long as anyone can remember."

"And yet I shall see him," Simeon muttered.

*  *  *

Two years into Hannah's relationship with Jeroboam, she developed fluency in the local languages. She had grown up with Hebrew but came to learn Aramaic, Greek, and a smattering of Parthian. By her fifth year as a wife, she passed easily as a native speaker.

One day her husband entertained a small group of emissaries of unknown alliance. As she served the meal, one of the newcomers stated plainly in Greek, "Side with us, with Aristobulus and the Nabateans. The queen won't last long. We will prevail for the throne and the high priesthood."

Jeroboam rubbed his beard with his knuckles thoughtfully. "You speak of rebellion and yet the very place we sit is where rebels come to die. Antipater, you have no loyalty to our people. And the reward you promise our nation doesn't seem worth the risk. What treasures would there be for someone like me if I joined you?"

Antipater, the Idumean, smiled as if triumphant. He pounded Jeroboam on the back with enthusiasm.

"Why, the treasures of the Temple would be yours! A room full of gold awaits the man willing to liberate the Holy Place and all its riches." Antipater stood and spread his hands. "Perhaps the famed treasures of Solomon still lie hidden in the caves and rooms guarded by those self-righteous servants of the faceless deity."

"I will see this treasure house for myself, and then I will speak with you," Jeroboam said. "When Antiochus invaded the city and sacrificed a swine on the altar, he saw nothing of distinction. The Maccabees cleansed the place for worship but said nothing of gold."

"Then it is hidden, ready for liberation!" Antipater crowed in triumph. "Together we will unite the role of king and priest and shape the future of our nation. With wealth will come power. No one will tell us what to do anymore. We will be the advisors in robes, like the Parthians."

Jeroboam began to spin a plan. "I will go tomorrow in disguise," he said. "I will travel with my woman like a pilgrim and survey the courts and hidden places for myself. I'll let you know what I discover. Together we will change the world, like the great Alexander of Greece."

In the morning, Jeroboam roused Hannah before the roosters began to crow. He wrestled the blankets off her and dropped a gown overtop of her outstretched form.

"Put that on," he said. "Today we will be wealthy pilgrims visiting the Temple. No one will wonder why we roam about. If you try to run, you will regret the day you ever met me."

She already regretted that day, as well as almost every other since her capture. If Jeroboam hadn't posted guards outside her hut, she would have run long ago. At least she had food, shelter, and clothing.

But surely life was designed for more. She hoped Simeon had it better.

CHAPTER THREE

# THE STRUGGLE

*67 years until Messiah (73 BC)*

The shadows falling over the twin palaces at Jericho were darker than the clouds blotting out the sun that morning. The queen had built two identical palaces for her squabbling sons. On this day, both courtyards hosted delegations waiting for the arrival of the monarch. So far the news had been as dark as the day.

The tables were set and staff scurried around, guarding the lavish feast that had been prepared. The guests' thoughts of celebration continued to diminish as the hours passed. Representatives from the delegations in the courtyards engaged in verbal jousting, and it wasn't the first time this had happened.

The first hint of the coming struggle came at a meal designed to celebrate a border skirmish victory against the Edomites. Queen Salome Alexandra had invited the leading voices of the Pharisees to join in the feast, but she failed to appear.

Simeon accompanied Baruch to the entrance of the third palace, this one set aside for the queen herself. Simeon sat near the sentry with his back to the wall as the elder man ducked inside.

Several servants then emerged and huddled nearby.

"She has a serious fever and cough with discharge from her eyes," declared one of the servants.

"She has tremors and seizures," said another.

"Hyrcanus is ready to take his place on the throne," added the first. "He's already taken his rightful place as high priest over the Temple in Yerushalayim. All the Pharisees have risen to support him in honor of the queen. Tradition brings stability to us all."

Baruch emerged and listened to Simeon share a report of what he'd just heard.

"Someone trustworthy needs to offer the sacrifices," Baruch said after Simeon had finished.

The back of Simeon's hand throbbed. What was happening? He pressed it up against his chest. "We can't ignore the sacrifices," he said.

"Rumor has it that Hyrcanus is courting the Nabateans at Petra to back himself," a young servant was saying. "I don't trust Arabs in any form. Hyrcanus has been listening to that Idumean, Antipater. If I were backing Hyrcanus, I would eliminate that tongue wagging in his ear. Nothing but trouble brews when that Idumean is around."

A balding Egyptian, as thin as a broomstick, shuffled up to the group of servants. "The younger son, Aristobulus, has rallied the Sadducees to his cause. The nobility, the internationals, all the merchants... they'll be standing behind him."

The first servant pulled an orange from a pocket in his robe and rubbed it on his chest. "Hyrcanus can take care of himself. I wouldn't worry about some story you hear by the village well."

An elder among them sat on a stump and rubbed his chin. "Our story as Pharisees is one to be remembered. The Great Alexander built his empire on the backs of men like us. His culture now flows through our veins. Alexander's successors agreed with our leader Simon that we should not be taxed." He stood facing Yerushalayim and lifted his arm high. "Through David we say no counting us, and through Simon we say no to taxing us." He adjusted his mantle. "As those who guard the welfare of our people, we must stand for what is right and true. No taxation. No registration."

The first servant stood and waved his hands in front of his face. "It's not like the Romans or Parthians have marched into our land and tried to register and tax us. The queen has two sons, so why can't one be king and the other be high priest?"

"Blasphemy!" the second servant shouted. "The Seleucids declared generations ago that one member of Simon Maccabee's descendants would wear both the crown and the ephod. The oldest is the right choice. We must support him. Both he and his mother have given us the task of leading the people and we must choose to lead right."

The elder nodded and waited for silence. "The younger is the more ambitious of the two," he pronounced. "Cherish your position of favor for now but prepare your shelter if times change."

* * *

The fortress at Alexandrium absorbed the chill in the air and Hannah was forced to wrap her little one in a blanket. She'd stepped outside the stark stone walls to give space to the men now huddled in her dining room, eating the meal she had prepared.

When the chill was no longer bearable, she stepped back inside but hovered in the doorway without fully entering.

Jereboam and Antipater looked away from her quickly, but Hannah didn't think much of it. The two men always seemed to be planning something. Antipater, son of the governor of nearby Idumea, was a converted Arab who had more wealth and influence than he knew what to do with. For some reason, this charmer from across the Jordan had chosen to befriend her husband.

The newborn in her arms had been crying and she did her best to breastfeed and stay discreet. She was weary from getting too little sleep all week long and struggling not to abandon the child outside to the hyenas. The birth of her firstborn son had been one of her most painful experiences, even worse than the rough intimacy Jeroboam had forced on her in the early days of their marriage.

When the child had finally settled and submitted to a nap, she wrapped him warmly and headed to make tea for the men.

The whispers of their conversation didn't surprise her, but the content did. Without meaning to, she overheard the word *sacrifice*. Such a shiver gripped her spine that she nearly collapsed in the doorway. She hadn't heard the word's context.

She shook off the tremors that followed. Sacrifice was a normal part of Temple worship.

"We need to name our son," Hannah said, interrupting them as she entered. "Our people usually circumcise our sons and name them on the eighth day."

"Your people are not my people," Jeroboam said. "Our son will undergo the rites of my people when the time is right."

"We should go to the Temple. They can tell us what to do," she said.

Jeroboam shook his head. "We know what to do."

"We can talk later."

Later in the day, Hannah stepped outside to retrieve some water from the rain barrel. She turned at the sound of her husband's voice.

"Hannah!" he called. "Come on back here and tell Antipater what we saw at the Temple last time we went. How much gold do you think was in all that furniture?"

21

She went back inside just in time to see Antipater leaning in close to Jeroboam.

"Why don't you step outside and make sure there's no one around," the Idumean said to him. "We wouldn't want anyone to overhear us."

Jeroboam nodded, got up, and walked toward the door.

"Can't you stay?" Hannah asked.

Jeroboam hesitated, looking toward Antipater.

"I'm sure I can handle a little girl like her," the Idumean said.

Jeroboam gave Hannah a warning look and then stepped outside. Was he remembering the river incident?

Once they were alone, Antipater stood up and moved his chair closer to Hannah. Sitting uncomfortably close, he laid a hand on Hannah's knee.

"Now, I know you are looking for a real man in your life," he said seductively. "Say the word and I can take you away."

Was this a test? "I am chosen and will stay where I am."

Antipater inched closer and placed his hand on her wrist. "Your beauty drives me to my limits. Find a moment when he is away and we will find our own passions."

"You need to back away or I'll scream."

He stood to his feet. "You will regret this."

Jeroboam stepped back into the room and raised his eyebrows at her. "Wife, I need some tea!"

"I'll give the report you asked for, from our last visit to the Temple," she said. "Then I'll make you tea."

Hannah's report was lengthy. As he listened, Antipater moved over to a stool across the room from her. Jeroboam hovered near the doorway, watching closely.

She explained that she and Jeroboam had taken six trips to the Temple in the past two years. Jeroboam hadn't been permitted within the Temple grounds and so had pressed Hannah to explore as much as she could and report back to him.

There was nothing impressive about the limestone edifice. The shrines and high places on the other hills around the capital had received better care and upkeep. The large washbasin in the courtyard had appeared to be fashioned from brass as opposed to gold. They had noted gold thread in the large hanging curtains, but apart from this the only gold they observed came in the form of boxes containing the Temple offerings. Most pilgrims had generously emptied their leather pouches of coin and were quite happy to be noticed when giving.

"If you're looking for gold, the only place you might get it easily is from the pilgrims before they reach the Temple," Hannah continued as they began making the tea. "When Jeroboam first took me, I expected to see many more riches. We stopped by the shrine to Molech a few months ago and it had a lot of gold on display."

Antipater rose and accepted his mug of tea. "So you think Molech is more blessed than the Almighty?"

"I would lose my tongue if I said such a thing," Hannah said. "I only share my observations on the care devotees have shown to the houses of their gods."

"Perhaps it's time to put the gods to the test," Antipater said. "Jeroboam has been preparing himself ever since he knew you were with child."

Hannah froze in place like a marble statue. "What does testing the gods have to do with my newborn son?"

Antipater smiled. "Not just your son. All sons. This land is fertile because its women have paid the price to satisfy its gods. And now Judea has been given the Samaritan districts of Lydda, Aphairema, and Ramathaim to govern. What do they expect when we destroy their place of worship on Mount Gerizim? We must teach these miscreants the true way of our land."

"I used to think there was only one god in this land," she said, shuddering visibly. "I thought he would answer my prayers and save me from my pain. I'm far past that now. What is this test?"

"You'll find out at the next full moon," the Idumean told her. "Take good care of your son. Feed him well. He will need to be strong for what's ahead."

* * *

The synagogue in Jericho spoke well of the care given by its patrons. Gold glittered from the lampstands, the edging on the main rostrum, and the lettering of the Shema etched above the ark where the Torah scrolls were preserved. The large meeting hall at the side bustled with the learned.

Three rabbis sat side by side on a dais behind rostrums at the front of a hall whose walls and floors were covered in Persian carpets. Large windows let in light, but dozens of flickering torches still burned in designated alcoves.

Simeon sat in awe at his privilege. With a packed room of more than three hundred eager learners, the sages were almost shouting their wisdom.

The first of the rabbis sat like a pumpkin on his stool, overflowing the edges with his girth. The second rocked back and forth as if he were chanting and praying, his hands folded, his head bobbing up and down. The third, with the frame of a Roman legionnaire, had large tufts of hair like nests above his ears on either side of a bald skull.

"Consider the blessing of the Almighty," chanted the second rabbi. "Under this queen, in reward for her piety, we have seen rain fall only on Sabbath nights. None of the working class have been forced to suffer and the fertility of our soil is so great that our grains of wheat are as large as kidney beans, our oats as large as olives, and our lentils as large as gold coins. Consider your own obedience to the law."

"Rise and be amazed," intoned the first rabbi. "We, as the true followers of the book, have been restored to our rightful place as judges in the Sanhedrin. We will determine the administration of justice and faith for all common people. Such is the mercy of the Almighty for his own."

The third raised his fist and brought it down firmly into the palm of his other hand. "Tremble in your sleep," he bellowed. "Consider the fate of the Sadducees who sought to destroy our culture, our faith, our hope, our country. They have been banished by the queen to their own feeble cities where true light will never penetrate. Turn your face toward truth and stand firm until the righteous One comes for us all."

The first rabbi cleared his throat and the others looked his way. "Those Sadducees claim to be people of the book because they only recognize the five books of Moses. They are so tied to the Temple that without it they have no hope. Our queen has opened up learning to women in their own schools and we are set to expand truth to the people in their own homes, as Moses commanded."

He waved to a young man who brought him a scroll and set it on a rostrum in front of him.

"Now read this," whispered the large rabbi to the young assistant, who was adjusting the scroll to its proper place.

The voice of the younger man crept through the crowded room like a whisper. The learners strained to hear him.

"These are the commands, decrees and laws the LORD your God directed me to teach you to observe in the land that you are crossing the Jordan to possess, so that you, your children and their children after them may fear the LORD your God as long as you live by keeping all his decrees and commands that I give you, and so that you may enjoy long life. Hear, Israel, and be careful to obey so that it may go well with you and that you may increase greatly in a land flowing with milk and honey, just as the LORD, the God of your ancestors, promised you."[2]

---

[2] Deuteronomy 6:1–3.

The first rabbi held up his hand and the young man stopped.

"Recite the next verses with me," the rabbi said to the audience.

Simeon found his voice and joined the chant. It was a section of Scripture he had learned with his first words.

"Hear, O Israel: The LORD our God, the LORD is one. Love the LORD your God with all your heart and with all your soul and with all your strength. These commandments that I give you today are to be on your hearts. Impress them on your children. Talk about them when you sit at home and when you walk along the road, when you lie down and when you get up. Tie them as symbols on your hands and bind them on your foreheads. Write them on the doorframes of your houses and on your gates."[3]

The rabbi waved his hand in dismissal. The young man rolled up the scroll and took it back to the cupboard from which he had brought it.

"The command is clear. Both you and your sisters must learn." The rabbi held up his hand as if restraining any potential questions from being asked. "The Sadducees have sold themselves to the Greeks. They claim to be the true children of Moses, but they confine life to the few years we have on this earth. They deny the immortality of the soul, bodily resurrection after death, and the existence of angels."

He turned to the second rabbi and nodded.

The rocking rabbi took up the lecture. "It is the wealth and haughtiness of the Sadducees which had them work with our monarchs to try and destroy us. They are rightly restricted to their own small settlements while we are rightly restored to our place of influence in the land. Our leaders can easily be led astray by deceitful and scheming advisors. This is why we must maintain our place of trust with the people and teach them from infancy."

The discussions continued throughout the day with occasional breaks for the crowd to nourish and take care of their bodily needs. It was a disciplined life and Simeon relished the chance to stretch his mind with others in community. He was among the righteous, and it was clear Ha'Shem had spared him for a reason, perhaps even to see the Messiah himself.

\* \* \*

Jeroboam stepped through the door of his home and shut it firmly behind him. He leaned against the wall panting as Hannah came to him.

"Grab the boy and come!" he demanded.

---

[3] Deuteronomy 6:4–9.

"Why? What is happening?" Hannah asked.

"It is time for the test."

Hannah frowned. What was he up to? "Why are you hiding?"

"Don't ask," he replied. "Come! Time is short."

She gently lifted the babe and cradled him in her arm. With one hand, she gathered an extra blanket, a change of clothes for her son, and a food basket, setting them by the door.

"What else do I need?" she asked. "How long will we be gone?"

Jeroboam stood over the small pile of clothing and food, examining it. "It is enough."

The donkey cart ride was bumpy but didn't disturb the child from his sleep. Hannah hummed as they moved toward the unknown. As they travelled, she found the view breathtaking. A cloud of black kites darted in formation overhead. Oh, to be free as a bird! To dance the skies on wing and never have to fear the terrors below...

Antipater met them at the bottom of the hill along the Jericho Road.

"Shalom," he called cheerily. "We'll stay overnight at the inn outside Jericho and go up to our destiny in the morning. We're about to change the course of our nation and your son will be at the center of it all."

"How can a babe change a nation?" she asked.

"Wait and see," Antipater said. "Perhaps like Queen Esther, you have been brought here for such a time as this."

The two-day journey to Jericho proceeded without incident and the rocking of the cart settled the babe.

Antipater rode his horse and walked alongside Jeroboam. Twice, while Hannah was breastfeeding, Antipater dropped back and eyed her greedily. She pulled her head covering over herself and the boy, wondering if her husband would yank out his dagger and gut this man too.

Upon their arrival in Jericho, they navigated through the numerous caravans jostling for space at the caravansary, stopped for supplies at the market, and registered at the inn. The child was restless as they worked out the sleeping arrangements.

The restlessness, anxiety, and fear of the unknown kept her pacing through the night. She hummed and whispered to her little one all the while. Twice, she considered bolting, but Antipater set himself across the doorway and Jeroboam snored soundly nearby. What would Queen Esther have done at such a moment?

The first rooster crowed as dawn crept across the land. Antipater shook Jeroboam awake and then left to procure some tea and bread for the morning meal.

"Pack up," Jeroboam called to his wife. "We'll have to leave soon."

The trio joined a caravan consisting of traders, Arabs, pilgrims, and a small band of Parthian military escorts.

"Such a perfect day for travel," Antipater remarked as he watched the camels, horses, and donkeys filing by alongside them. "Ha'Shem has every opportunity to pour out his blessing on those he claims. Jeroboam, your name will be as well known as the first Jeroboam who wrestled the kingdom away from that weak monarch, Rehoboam."

"Do you mean the son of Solomon and the grandson of King David?" Hannah asked.

Antipater nodded. "There is no place for weakness in our land, only strength. Today we will overcome the weak."

Everyone else in the caravan turned off at the gates of Yerushalayim, but Antipater pushed them onward.

Hannah released a huge sigh. There would be no Temple visit today. No robbery of pilgrims to secure their gold. The test would be something else.

Within an hour, they turned off toward the shrine of Molech on the crown of the Mount of Olives. The Golden Arch glistened in the afternoon sun. There, thousands of people crowded around a priest who spoke between episodes of music and chanting. The priest, a mountain of humanity, sported a trimmed white beard that flowed over his generous belly. His golden robe, edged in rabbit fur, lay open to reveal a golden loincloth underneath. Golden sandals adorned his feet and a large ruby necklace dangled from his neck, nestling in the beard.

A band of two dozen other priests danced in a perpetual circle of twisting, turning, and gyrating. They were dressed in golden loincloths and flashed daggers in both hands.

Hannah wondered, would this be the test? Glancing over her shoulder toward the Temple of the Almighty, she felt a strange longing to turn away from what lay ahead.

Jeroboam and Antipater dismounted from the cart. When the giant priest noticed them, he instructed the crowd to form an opening.

Jeroboam helped Hannah down with the babe. What was he up to? Never before had he shown her such deference and kindness.

The priest stepped down from his dais and approached them with a smile. He held out his arms and Hannah clutched her son hard to her chest. No way would she allow her child to be taken from her.

Antipater stood behind her, gripping her elbows as Jeroboam stepped in front and made a grab for the babe. Together, the men succeeded at tugging the child from her arms. The boy screamed at the rough handling, but he was soon in the hands of the priest.

When Antipater eased his grip on her, Hannah tore herself away and charged toward the priest. The child reached for her, screaming, but Jeroboam grabbed her and placed an arm around her throat, covering her mouth with his sweaty hand.

"Stop!" he whispered harshly in her ear. "You will only bring me shame."

When she saw the golden statue of Molech billowing smoke and flames, all her terrors found their focus. The sacrifice. Her son was about to become a sacrifice.

She elbowed and squirmed, but this only resulted in a tighter embrace from Jeroboam, who continued to stifle her screams with his hand.

The dancing priests danced harder and cut themselves with daggers. Blood flowed over their bodies and splashed on the ground. The music grew louder and more intense. Meanwhile, the priest held up the babe toward the heavens, chanting, but he could not be heard above the raucous noise of the crowd as the people joined in the chant and pressed close. The jaws of the dreadful golden beast fell open and the priest surrendered the babe to the flames.

Hannah collapsed and Jeroboam carried her back to the cart.

"The test is over," her husband said to her. "There will be other sons, but our harvest is assured."

At that moment, a loud trumpet sounded behind them. Dozens of horses dressed for war trotted forward with their riders. Then a carriage arrived followed by hundreds of foot soldiers.

Nabateans.

The crowd fell silent and stood back, exposing the platform, the priests, and the smoking Molech. A royal figure in the robes of the high priest stepped out of the carriage and moved toward the platform.

"I am Hyrcanus, high priest of the Almighty in Yerushalayim." Hyrcanus turned to the giant man in the golden robe. "What has happened here today?"

"We have completed the rite of the firstborn son to ensure the harvest in our land," the man answered.

The high priest stepped onto the dais. He was a full head shorter than the giant beside him. "Who has given up his firstborn son for such a test?"

Antipater stepped forward and pointed. "It is that man, Jeroboam from the fortress at Sartaba."

"Seize him," Hyrcanus ordered.

Jeroboam gripped Hannah hard and his eyes grew wide. What had happened? He had passed the test. Or had he?

Hyrcanus raised his arm as the crowd murmured in confusion. "Under the queen's orders, we are restoring the primacy of the Temple in Yerushalayim and Molech is no longer welcome here. All those who have worshipped him will feed his belly on this day, starting with the father who sacrificed his son."

As Hannah watched from her knees in the cart, the soldiers lifted Jeroboam like a log and tossed him into the flames. His screams seared themselves in her mind, just as the screams of her son had done.

The giant priest in gold attempted to flee and ordered his followers to fight. But the soldiers' swords and javelins slashed until everyone lay dead or cowering. One by one, they hoisted the bodies and fed the furnace.

The smell of seared flesh and billowing black smoke mesmerized Hannah until she pressed her head between her knees and sobbed.

Hyrcanus himself stopped by the cart. "You are clearly the mother and have suffered enough for one day. Collect your things and then come with me in my carriage."

He walked away, surrounded by bodyguards.

Antipater stood on the dais and pointed at Hannah. "She is the mother. To the flames with that woman!"

A few of the soldiers moved toward her, but she darted toward the carriage and jumped inside.

Antipater arrived at the window. "Sire, we must purge the land and the fire is ready."

"She is with me," Hyrcanus said. "She will live under my sanctuary at the Temple."

Antipater grimaced. "If I see her outside the walls of that place, I will have no choice but to feed her to the flames."

There was a meaningful pause and then Hyrcanus nodded to Antipater. "You have served me well today. You have passed your test."

CHAPTER FOUR

# TR_ANSITION

*61 years until Messiah (67 BC)*

The purge in the land stalled when the queen's younger son, Aristobulus, pressed his advantage during the chaos and moved against his brother Hyrcanus. The queen lay prostrate, clearly in her last days despite having led a life of pious faith and diligent rule. The Sadducees cheered Aristobulus with all their wealth and influence.

Meanwhile, Simeon and the Pharisees shuddered in their positions of responsibility over the people. Several key rabbis had been captured and beheaded, despite the understood rules of civil war among the Jews.

At least the synagogue at Jericho where the Pharisees stayed, as well as the queen's palace courtyard, provided a thin veil of protection.

"The queen has jailed the wife and sons of Aristobulus to stem his ambitions," a newcomer said to Simeon as they shared a meal one day outside the synagogue's hall of study. "They're imprisoned in the Antonia Keep just north of the Temple. The act has only served to make Aristobulus more determined to take both the throne and the Temple as his own. He has called for the death of his own mother."

"The descendants of the Maccabees from King Alexander to Hyrcanus and Aristobulus, have run amok," Baruch confided. "This house of the Hasmoneans once saved our nation, but now they are returning to their practice of purge and revenge." He squeezed his beard hard in both hands. "We suffered under King Alexander for almost three decades and survived. Although his family were heroes to our people, they are not from the line of David and lack legitimacy. We have supported the queen for our own survival." The humble rabbi rubbed the back of his head and offered a faint smile. "We will bide our time until our own champion arises. As people of the book, we use our pens, not our swords. We trust in the Almighty to bring us the Teacher of righteousness in his time."

"It is my one desire to see the Messiah in my day," Simeon said. "With my own eyes, I want to see him. That will be enough to bring peace and hope."

"It's the dream that keeps our people opening the scrolls and rising each day in prayer," Baruch said. "The prophets tell us that his coming is near. The sword of the enemy may hinder us, but it cannot hinder the Mighty One."

"May he come soon." Simeon nodded and then turned back to his study.

Baruch laid a hand on his shoulder. "Since he has not yet come, may I inquire whether you will soon be seeking a bride from among our people? Some have noticed your piety and diligence but don't understand your family lineage or history."

"You can tell any inquirers that I'm an orphan with nothing to my name. Tell them that there is one woman in the back of my mind I am considering. Perhaps their daughters can find another from among the many who are among us."

"Maybe you can offer a sacrifice and ask for Ha'Shem's blessing." Baruch knit his brows together in a frown. "Why do you keep rubbing the back of your hand like that?"

"No reason."

As Baruch stepped away, another rabbi entered the room. "The queen has died," he pronounced. "Hyrcanus now has control of the sceptre and the ephod. There is agitation among the Sadducees and much talk of a coup. Aristobulus is favorable to the idea of taking both from his brother."

"We need to call the community together," Baruch said. "It won't be long until we are tested beyond what we realize."

* * *

The gate of the Temple provided an invisible lifeline for Hannah. The new king and high priest stopped in his duties as he passed next to it.

"I see you are still well." Hyrcanus then turned to one of the slaves responsible for cleaning the courtyard. "Watch over her and feed her from the Temple coffers."

It was something he always said, even if the one instructed had no power to fulfill the demand.

On this day, Hannah smiled as he left.

The servant to whom Hyrcanus had given his instructions was mute, having had his tongue cut out. Still, the man was efficient and quick to serve. A sparkle in his eye accompanied the smile on his face. He had a light step and a quick nod of greeting. The maimed or impure were limited in their access to the Temple courts, but few even noticed the man as he went about his tasks.

Hannah found herself identifying with the mute man. Her voice, too, had been taken along with her spirit.

Losing her son and husband within moments of each other six years ago had gutted her. For a week, she had curled up in a corner near an archway leading to the fortress. Temple guards and servants had walked around her without stopping. There had been one servant who stopped by twice a day with food and water, even when she hadn't eaten anything for three days. Apart from finding a secluded place to use a chamber pot a few times a day, she lay motionless.

By the fourth day, she had uncurled at dawn and reached for some of the dried figs and dates that had been brought to her. Her lips had been parched, cracked, and painful, but she sipped water from the gourd. Without thinking, she wandered toward a gate off the courtyard and came face to face with Antipater, standing outside the Temple grounds.

"Hannah," he had called. "You know it's only a matter of time before you step out from this place. One of my men will be waiting. You won't know who it is until it's too late. You should have perished in those flames."

She had turned her back and wandered the grounds to find a place to call her own. Ha'Shem had done nothing to provide for or protect her. The least he could do was share his house.

Hyrcanus had found her there on the Sabbath, listening to a rabbi.

"Come, walk with me," Hyrcanus had said. "I know it isn't appropriate for someone like me to be with someone like you, but I can't get you out of my mind. Tell me your story."

Hannah had shrugged. "My story is short. Everyone in my village was killed by marauders—that is, except one young man and me. He tried to take me to Jezreel, but we were caught by a band of soldiers from Sartaba. My husband took me as his own, we had a son, and I was tricked into giving that son up to Molech. You heard Antipater's threat; he thinks I should be sent to the flames." She opened the palms of her hands. "You are the rest of my story."

"Why does Antipater want you to perish in the flames?"

"I'm not sure. He may believe that the gods need to be satisfied to ensure the fertility of the land. Or he may believe that any woman who gives up her son to a false god should die with her offspring. Possibly he's just upset that I resisted his advances. Whatever the reason—"

"Antipater is a zealous patriot and close confidant," Hyrcanus had said. "You were caught in a test designed to secure my authority as both king and high priest. Unfortunately, I don't think my brother is impressed. Stay in the

Temple and the fortress wherever you find space and I will ensure your needs are met."

\* \* \*

Soon after the third full moon, upon Hannah's arrival in the Temple, it became known in the community that Aristobulus had vented his wrath on his brother. The result had been that Hyrcanus lost his patience, or so it was told.

While visiting a group of Pharisees on the outskirts of Jericho, Simeon met with a man who pointed toward a nearby field. Armed militants had gathered on either side of that field, shifting in and out of the trees.

"It's Hyrcanus, come to put down his younger brother's rebellion," the man said. "We need to find higher ground so we don't get caught in the skirmish."

Simeon backpedaled up the hill toward a large brick building. He and several other Pharisees gathered on the roof.

"Those are Nabatean mercenaries with Hyrcanus," Simeon noted. "If he can't find enough of our people to support his cause, what hope do we have?"

"Aristobulus has already used his influence with the wealthy to take over most of the walled cities and bastions," another Pharisee said. "The Sadducees are funding him. They want back control of the Temple and are willing to give him control of the nation to get it."

Another Pharisee joined them at the edge of the parapet. "Word is that Aristobulus has agents promising untold wealth if the mercenaries will mutiny and join his side. Soldiers who fight for pay only know one commander and one loyalty: the one who pays highest."

As if on cue, men from the left side of the field, where Hyrcanus had gathered, began drifting toward the opposite side. As Simeon watched, archers went to work unleashing a fusillade of arrows. Then Aristobulus appeared on a horse, shouting encouragement to his troops. Suddenly, the men all began to march forward in rows, javelins in front, archers behind.

By the time the two sides met hand to hand in the middle of the field, the outcome had been determined. A few men fell—and when a gap opened in Hyrcanus's lines, the others quickly fell back and ran for their lives.

Simeon was surprised to see a contingent of turncoats switch sides and gather around Aristobulus as though to collect their pay.

Simeon turned away and huddled with the others.

"It's time to secure our shelters," he said. "These Sadducees will remember that we opposed the effort of Aristobulus's father against the Samaritans. No, their Temple wasn't the right place to worship, but destroying our neighbors will only come back to haunt us."

One of the others turned with Simeon as they descended the stairs from their rooftop perch.

"Hyrcanus set up the proper rituals in the Temple," the man said. "No doubt the Sadducees will have their rites and positions restored. I'm not sure we will be welcomed back into that place of worship."

* * *

Hannah was surprised to see Hyrcanus and two of his bodyguards slip through the Temple gate in peasant robes. Their scarves were pulled over the bottom half of their faces. Their haunted eyes were no longer filled with the grace and compassion she had seen in them just a few days before.

The high priest looked past her. Something terrible was happening.

The men sheltered in the Temple and the reason soon became clear to Hannah.

Suddenly, dozens of armed men stormed through the gate and began searching the grounds. Hannah slipped behind a pillar which stood before an overgrown bush. She peeked out as more and more warriors arrived, some entering the Temple but most standing outside to prevent worshippers from entering.

Many of these warriors nodded in deference when their commander arrived. Aristobulus's gait was confident, his face stern. The younger brother's long amber hair flowed onto his shoulders and a carefully trimmed beard and mustache framed his strong cheekbones.

He stepped into the middle of the courtyard and raised his voice. "Hyrcanus, the battle is done. There is no place left to run. The people are with me and you are alone."

There was only silence in response.

A nearby servant got Aristobulus's attention and pointed toward the door where Hyrcanus had hidden.

Aristobulus moved closer and shouted again. "Hyrcanus! Your brother has come to claim what is his and negotiate for peace. The deal is your life for peace. You may negotiate for the lives of your men."

A burst of movement from above drew the attention of everyone in the courtyard.

"I am here, little brother," Hyrcanus called down from the tower of his refuge. "Spare my people. I will negotiate for peace."

"Bring down your seal and let these terms be approved by sundown," Aristobulus returned. "You will relinquish the roles of king and high priest in exchange for your life. You will go into exile in a place of your own choosing and no longer lay claim to anything that is now mine."

"Do you put me in the role of Esau while you claim Jacob?" Hyrcanus asked. "For the sake of the people, I will not contest what you have declared. All I ask is that you treat the people well, uphold the name of our family, and restore worship in the Temple."

Aristobulus lifted a scroll in his hand. "I attach my seal to these terms. Once you attach yours, you and your people are free to leave and find your own peace where you can."

Hannah watched as one of Hyrcanus's servants stepped out from the doorway of the tower and accepted the scroll. He then went back inside, conveying the document to the former king.

A short time later, Hyrcanus stepped into the open and nodded at Aristobulus.

"We have spared much blood on this day, my brother," said Hyrcanus. "See that you continue to spare it in the future."

With the tension lifted, Hannah stepped into the open. What would happen to her now that Hyrcanus, her protector, had relinquished his throne?

A moment later, she was looking on as Hyrcanus mounted his horse and galloped away from the seat of his former power.

* * *

Simeon paused his camel in reverent reflection as he looked back at the awe-inspiring sight of hundreds of the animals kneeling in the shadows of towering rocks. They looked to be the size of ants beneath the glistening red sandstone of Petra, a magnificent spot huddled halfway between the Red Sea and the Dead Sea. It provided an important waystation for travelers and traders moving between Arabia, Egypt, Syria, or Phoenicia.

"Welcome to the capital of the Nabateans," Baruch said from atop his own camel. "We'll see if the rulers here might welcome us… should things go bad under Aristobulus. We need a center from which to promote our cause and keep our traditions alive. We should find allies here."

"How do they manage their water system?" Simeon asked. "It seems so inhospitable."

"There are hidden channels, tunnels, and diversion dams combined with cisterns and reservoirs to control and collect the seasonal rains. These rocks contain tombs and temples, high places, copper mines, and gathering spaces. This winding cleft is the main entrance." Baruch stopped and pointed toward a triple-arched entrance gate. "Beyond the arch is a theatre and baths. Aaron, the brother of Moses, is said to be buried among the tombs."

Simeon pointed ahead. "Wait! Isn't that Hyrcanus and Antipater? What do you think they're doing here?"

"Probably the same thing we're doing," Baruch said. "Kings in exile have to go somewhere."

The groaning beasts knelt on command and Simeon and Baruch dismounted. They stretched and kneaded their sore muscles.

"They've seen us," Simeon said. "I'm leaving the talk up to you."

Antipater spoke first when the pair came closer. "Shalom, and welcome to my home," he said. "My father is the governor here and you can find peace while you stay. You may not find the protection you desire under that usurper Aristobulus. But if you're for Hyrcanus, join us as we discuss our future."

"Shalom to you," Baruch replied. "While we support and encourage the role of our lord, the true king, we come in peace and only desire to find a safe place for our people to study and prepare for the Messiah."

Antipater nodded. "We have seen spies from Aristobulus lingering in our shadows and suspect it's only a matter of time until he makes an attempt on the true king's life. We've come to enlist the assistance of King Aretas of Petra and his Nabatean army. He has promised fifty thousand mercenaries in exchange for some land and cities."

"Aristobulus is secure in Yerushalayim," Baruch said. "It would mean laying siege to the city. Many innocents will suffer in the process."

"It is inevitable for the innocent to suffer," Antipater said. "Some innocents will be lost so many more innocents may be saved."

Hyrcanus let out a sigh. "I fear your rage blinds you."

Antipater shook his head vigorously. "I've already spoken to the king of your good qualities and how you would be a loyal ally and trading partner if you're returned to power. You have the firstborn's birthright."

"When are you intending to act?" Simeon asked. "It is almost Passover. Many pilgrims will be on the roads and in Yerushalayim for the feast."

"That will only put more pressure on Aristobulus to capitulate," Antipater insisted. "If the people know the source of their suffering, they may revolt and join us in overthrowing the usurper." He turned to Hyrcanus. "Everyone knows you are the true king. Yet you will have to prove your royal authority with the power of a sword."

"We will pay a visit to King Aretas," Hyrcanus agreed. "Perhaps we can speak reasonably about these land concessions he would require. I believe he wants the ten cities east of the Jordan."

Antipater smiled at his king. "Command your servants to bring our gifts to Aretas. We will impress him with your sincerity. We have set a course which cannot be changed now."

Simeon watched as the deposed king and this son of a governor wandered away in animated conversation without a word of goodbye to their guests.

"We will not want to be in Yerushalayim for this Passover," Simeon mused. "How can we get a word of warning to our people there without alerting the enemy?"

"Caravans leave for there every day from Petra," Baruch said. "I'll find someone we can trust to deliver a message to the synagogue in the lower city. We may not be able to avoid warning our enemies, but we need to concern ourselves first with our own people. These Hasmoneans are not meant for the throne. They aren't of the line of David."

"We await the true king and Messiah," Simeon reminded him. "Perhaps this battle for the capital will allow the righteous One to be revealed."

"From your mouth to God's ears." Baruch turned once again to observe the impressive rock formations around them. "Anyway, do you think you might find a wife in a place like this? There are many beautiful women everywhere I look."

"Guard your eyes and your heart, old man," Simeon said. "The righteous One will be looking for righteous followers."

## CHAPTER FIVE
# CITY UNDER SIEGE

*57 years until Messiah (63 BC)*

Hannah detected the iron-tainted scent of blood in the air. It had been so strong in the early days of her stay at the Temple, but over the last few years it had woven itself into the tapestry of dust, donkeys, carts, pilgrims, incense, and sweaty feet. She knelt by the foot-washing station and carefully arranged the sandals abandoned by worshippers rushing to access the Temple's services and sacrifices. No one had asked her to fill this servant's role, but she had seen the need and bent to do it. A few worshippers had dropped a coin for her now and then. She had been sharing these proceeds with the mute servant who purchased goods from the market for her.

Over time, she had become part of the scenery for the guards, priests, servants, worshippers, and regulars who inhabited the Temple grounds. She had paced out the two hundred steps of the plaza going east, north, west, and south more times than she could imagine. She had her own alcove each evening where she unrolled her reed mat away from foot traffic, set up her blankets, and slept without fear or concern. At dawn, the roosters alerted her of the need to clean it all up and tuck it away in a gap behind one of the colonnades.

The Temple—also known as the Beit HaMikdash, the holy house—included a sanctuary where uncircumcised foreigners like Antipater could not intrude. The Temple, a destination for Hebrews around the world, was nothing special in terms of architecture, but it served its purpose.

While on her knees straightening sandals, she came across a pair with the feet still in them.

"Shalom, my friend," the man's voice said gently. "Do you understand the place in which you serve?"

Hannah sat back on her heels, shielding her eyes from the sun's rays. The golden halo around his head cast his face in shadows.

"Perhaps you are a prophet sent to tell me," she said.

The young man chuckled. "Not at all. Let me move into the shadows so we can sit. Perhaps you know more than I about this place. I've seen you here for three years now, walking the perimeter deep in thought."

She followed him to the stairs by Solomon's portico where colonnades towered more than four times the height of a man. The brass capitals atop each column featured lilies. The view overlooked a deep valley, and the porch itself was supported by a wall two hundred paces long. Four brilliant white stones, each ten paces long and two paces wide, implied the structure's invincibility.

"Forgive my intrusion into your busy day," he said as she kept watching the new arrivals kick off their sandals, step into the footbaths, and then scurry toward the inner sanctums. "Feel free to take a moment to relax and share some conversation with someone who's gripped by isolation. My name is Caiaphas."

She turned toward him. His eyes sparkled in the light. The man's generous beard grew from a young face, seeming out of place. His skin had weathered in the sun, but not excessively. His deep dark eyes drew one in toward hidden secrets. His smile was genuine, inviting, welcoming.

"Play the part of my rabbi and I'll sit at your feet until I'm full," she said.

He chuckled. "I pray that would not be too soon." He turned away from the direct sunlight and leaned against a pillar. "You doubtless know that the great King David chose this spot. It was here that Abraham tried to sacrifice his son Isaac in obedience to divine command. King Solomon then completed the task of setting up a glorious home for the ark so it would no longer be left to wander. Then Nebuchadnezzar of Babylon destroyed the city and took our people away." He paused to see her nod. "Cyrus the Great released Ezra to rebuild this Temple. Darius the Mede confirmed it later, as did Artaxerxes—twice. Zerubbabel, the new governor, dedicated it."

She adjusted her head covering and scarf. "Perhaps you should tell me about how the Temple was almost destroyed again by the arrogant Alexander of Macedonia. How he desired to be deified in this place. How our wisemen had to placate him with flattery and diplomacy. His death likely saved the place from turning back to rubble."

"Ah! So now I am the learner," Caiaphas said. "When Alexander's death resulted in the division of his empire, the Ptolemies gave us liberties until they were defeated by the Seleucids. Antiochus tried to turn us into Greeks in every way with the introduction of the pantheon of gods in our Holy Place. We rebelled, but he crushed us until his son took over."

Hannah held up her hand. "But we did not go away. When the Sabbath and circumcision were outlawed, when the statue of Zeus was erected here, when the priests sacrificed pigs on our altars, we could tolerate no more. Mattathias and his five sons led the rebellion until Judah Maccabee himself cleansed the Holy Place."

"And so we celebrate Hannukah, which is why I'm here," Caiaphas said. "I come in a dark time looking for a light that will not go out. I look for a lamp that will not run dry. I look for life that never ends."

"If you seek the Messiah, he is not here." Hannah straightened her tunic and rose. "I need to return to my work. I gave up on the Messiah many years ago. I've been here every day and he has never appeared. You may need to look elsewhere."

"One day he will be here. Stay faithful in your work and one day the feet of the righteous One will stop in front of you, ready to be washed."

Hannah could never look at the feet of pilgrims in the same way again. Perhaps one day the feet of the Messiah might come. But then, perhaps he would never come. Each pair of sandals left her wondering.

* * *

Petra's halls of learning had provided an oasis of safety for the Pharisees escaping Aristobulus's vengeful hand on the other side of the Jordan. Hyrcanus himself sat in on the lectures and debates at times, but he was preoccupied with Antipater's plans to take back the throne and high priesthood.

However, the last Passover had come and gone without a resolution on the concession of lands. Aretas was demanding that twelve cities be returned to him for his support.

The morning after a Sabbath, as the men loitered by the marketplace outside the grand amphitheater at the heart of Petra, the deposed king stopped in front of Baruch and Simeon.

"Aretas has granted us fifty thousand men," said Hyrcanus. "We will ride and march soon and need men to fight for us." He held out a sword. "Join us. I have fought for your rights. Now I need you to fight for mine."

Simeon glanced at his mentor and the two shared a knowing look. They were not men of war.

"We will help by bringing truth and hope to the people when your war is done," Baruch said. "Two Passovers ago, we urged you to avoid bloodshed when pilgrims are in the city. I issue the same plea now. We would only get in the way. The people want to rise up and serve one who can lead the living, and we will be with them. But we urge you to wait."

Hyrcanus furrowed his brow. "But my brother will be there, presiding over Passover as high priest. He cannot avoid the spectacle of being the center of attraction. This is the perfect time to strike." He backed away. "The Arabs are with us. The mercenaries have been paid. We go now or lose momentum."

Baruch and Simeon shook their heads as Hyrcanus left them, rubbing the back of his head in thought. No way would the deposed king back down again. The network still in Yerushalayim would have to be warned.

"What can we do?" Simeon asked.

"We warn and we wait," Baruch said.

Within the week, the mercenaries assembled on the outskirts of Petra. Their tents were spread across the desert as far as Simeon could see. Camels and horses were loaded and donkey carts packed. The support staff would bring up the rear, managing food, weapons, and the wounded.

When a trumpet sounded, the energy of these warriors heading to battle bubbled up from the sand. The commanders gathered for instruction and then conveyed it to their troops.

At first light, the columns of soldiers marched with shields and swords, followed by archers. Alongside, the cavalry rode with javelins poised and ready for destruction. More archers on camels nestled in behind with the support group working to keep up.

Simeon exited the lecture hall near the great synagogue to watch the sendoff.

Seated on a camel, surrounded by hundreds of armed horsemen, he watched as King Aretas III waved a banner and drank in the adulation of his subjects.

Simeon watched this mighty procession in awe from an elevated ledge in the rock. "I wouldn't want to be Aristobulus, standing on those walls in Yerushalayim," he said to Baruch. "Who is the man in robes riding beside Antipater, near the king?"

"That is Phalion, brother of Antipater," Baruch said. "He is a mastermind."

"How strange to have two brothers vying for one throne," Simeon said. "I wonder which one will prevail."

"I wouldn't want to be either brother right now. They're not from the line of David and can't have Ha'Shem's blessing for the throne. They're not from the line of Aaron either and can't have the blessing for that role either. Two men fighting for power they can't hold onto…"

On the edge of the crowd watching the departing soldiers, a young woman stood next to the governor. She was bedazzled with rubies around her neck and wildflowers in her hair. Even more surprising, she dared to walk publicly like a man, without a head covering.

Simeon scratched an itch on the palm of his hand. There seemed no obvious reason for this woman's display. "Who is the brazen girl?" he asked.

Baruch stepped forward and fixated his gaze on the girl. "It's Antipater's niece, Trophina. I last saw her as a child. She's become a woman. Does she please you?"

Simeon released a snort. "Me? I don't even know her. Besides, she's an Idumean. How would an orphaned peasant like myself even come close to someone like her?" He turned his back. "The last thing I need is to be tied down to a woman of privilege."

The two men retreated from the ledge and returned to the lecture hall as if nothing in the world had changed. Simeon unrolled his scroll, squinted his eyes, and traced the ancient revelation letter by letter.

It was four weeks later when a messenger returned to share news of the battle. Simeon was walking through the Petra market when the man stood on the back of a cart and shouted.

"We beat the forces of Aristobulus without any serious trouble!" he announced. "Many of the enemy gave up and joined us. Now we have the city surrounded and have laid siege."

"What of the king?" someone yelled.

"If you mean Aristobulus, he's locked inside the walls like a bird in a cage," the messenger replied. "Hyrcanus, the true king, is with the troops. I have to tell the governor."

He jumped down and headed off to convey his update.

Simeon selected an orange, tossed a coin to the vendor, squeezed it thoroughly, and then opened up a hole in the peel so he could suck out the juice. Life was good.

Midafternoon, two months later, another messenger rode into camp on a camel. He waved a white cloth above his head for attention.

"Trouble is on the way," the man called out. "Aristobulus has bribed the Roman general Scaurus with four hundred talents of silver and his legions are marching from Syria to join against us in battle."

Simeon set aside his sketch, released a lungful of air, and sighed. It was good that he'd chosen to stay behind.

Two weeks later, a third messenger charged into camp on a stallion that looked ready to drop.

"Aretas is abandoning the quest," said this latest courier. "He and his soldiers are coming home. The Romans have demanded his withdrawal and are too many. Antipater and Phalion will now be forced to lead the remaining forces of Hyrcanus against the enemy."

Simeon walked away from the game of knucklebones he'd been watching. Baruch strolled in his direction. It was a gift from God that he'd refused to go with the troops.

Baruch grimaced when he got close. "Hyrcanus cannot win against the Romans," he said to Simeon. "You might as well start looking for a bride among our people here. It looks like we're destined to make our home among the Nabateans."

"My only desire is to see the Messiah," Simeon said. "A wife may be a distraction. These are uncertain days and may not be the best time to raise children. Many others are better suited to settling and nurturing a family."

"There are no good times to raise children," Baruch assured him. "Yet it is the command of Ha'Shem that we multiply and steward all creation. The next generation must be raised by the righteous or they will be left to the influence of the wicked. Walk with me and we will see who the Almighty has provided for this time and place."

The first woman they encountered around the next corner was Trophina, granddaughter of the governor. She stood patiently by her grandfather's side, listening to the messenger.

For no apparent reason, Trophina pivoted and looked toward Simeon. When their eyes locked, she smiled and looked away for a moment. But then she looked back. His mouth hung open and he forced himself to close it.

The itch in his hand was back.

* * *

The rumble in Hannah's stomach was a steady part of her day. Fewer pilgrims meant fewer sandals and fewer coins. Tension sat like a morning fog over the Temple Mount and the nearby capital. Aristobulus, in his high priestly garb, frequently paced the courtyard in front of Solomon's portico, standing on the raised platform to survey the hills.

"Where are they now?" he shouted to his advisors on the wall.

"The Romans are pressing south to Jericho," one yelled in return. "Aretas has abandoned the battle and Hyrcanus is falling back to the north. He will soon be isolated from his supply lines. Then we'll have him. It is time now to take your place as our leader."

Aristobulus scurried down the stairs from the platform, doffed the outer robe identifying him as the high priest, and accepted the scarlet robe of the monarch.

"Bring my scepter," he called. "It's time for me to finish this imposter and take my place—before the Romans arrive. Assemble the cavalry. Let's deal with this vagrant once and for all."

Through the gates, Hannah could see the cavalry and militia gather. Weeks before, the men had been shoring up the city's defences. A wall of silence and a cloud of fear had hovered over the sacred space. Now the soldiers spoke loudly and moved confidently into formation.

She climbed up onto the platform where Aristobulus had observed the Nabatean mercenaries. The king's forces were flowing like a giant river of humanity toward a distant battlefield.

Somewhere in that direction was the last place she'd seen Simeon, near Jezreel. She remembered his smiling face and weary eyes after he'd dug a deep enough grave for the murdered villagers. His blistered hands had oozed as he'd trusted her to apply healing salve.

"Shalom. Looks like I came at a bad time," a man's voice called up to her. "Can you see Ha'Shem from up there or is it he who only sees you?"

It was Caiaphas, standing at the bottom of the stairs. His eyes sparkled and his beard spread generously across his chest.

"Shalom," she answered. "The tides have turned. Why these brothers have to fight is beyond me. Why can't we all get along in peace and rebuild this nation while we can?"

"So many things to trouble a pretty mind," Caiaphas said. "I assume you have not yet had the chance to wash the feet of the righteous One."

"No, the Messiah has not appeared." She descended the stairs slowly, keeping her eyes on him. Could she trust another man? "Why have you come now, when the city is in peril? Surely you have discernment to know you are not safe here."

He stepped away from the stairs to allow her room. "I couldn't get your face out of my mind. I thought I would take you away from here. You could serve in my home. I have plenty of space and enough work to occupy you with dignity."

Her gut twisted. After years of intricate, and sometimes intimate, conversation, all he wanted was a live-in servant girl?

"Where do you live?" she asked.

"Gibeah. It's less than a day's journey south by horse. I can arrange a carriage. You can come as soon as the battle is finished."

She hung her head. "I cannot leave this place. It's a sanctuary, for someone has put a price on my head. Even now, his men watch for me to step away from safety. Your offer may be meant in kindness, but leaving the city would be to forfeit my life."

Caiaphas stepped toward her. "We can disguise you. They'll never know who you are. Antipater will never find out where you've gone."

Hearing that name felt like getting whacked in the head with a tree branch.

"Antipater? How did you know it was Antipater who put the price on my head? Who are you working for?"

"You must have brought up his name before," Caiaphas said. "We've talked so many times. Somehow I knew."

"He sent you to trap me, didn't he? Guards!" she called. "There's an enemy spy among us. He works for the Nabateans. Help!"

A pair of Temple guards marched over with their javelins extended.

"Wait a moment!" Caiaphas said. "I'm a priest who was offering a job to a destitute woman. I'm not a spy. I will leave her alone, but she's a woman—you can't trust anything she says."

As the guards escorted Caiaphas out of the plaza, Hannah sank to her knees. She had felt something for this man, something she'd never had the chance to feel for Jeroboam. But now there was only emptiness. If Caiaphas truly was a priest of Ha'Shem, another divine tragedy had been dumped on her.

She looked toward the Holy of Holies.

"Do you truly see me?" she asked. "Do you see me and withhold your laughter at my gullibility? Who am I to kneel in the dust for your pilgrims? Now my last coins have been snatched from my hand."

As she rose, one of the guards returned and held out his palm. In it was a gold shekel.

"The priest said that this belongs to you," the man said. "He claims he meant no harm. He will trouble you no more."

The emptiness transformed within her. A deep inner darkness now snaked its way up her legs, into her gut, curled around her heart, and settled finally in her mind. Loneliness covered her like a shroud of ice. Where was Simeon at a time like this?

\* \* \*

Aretas had entered Petra the day before, surrounded by bodyguards. Hundreds of dead mercenaries had been piled into donkey carts and brought home for burial.

"They unleashed the fury of Hades on us as we peaceably withdrew," a general was reporting. "The fires of immolation will not cease for days to come. Many mothers and children will mourn the loss of the mighty."

Simeon and Baruch assisted a group of other Pharisees in caring for the survivors' physical needs. They tended wounds, wrapping what they could and amputating what they had to. They made meals and offered prayers.

Among the survivors was a mercenary of high standing who had been responsible for a large cohort of soldiers on the battlefield.

"We should have had you Pharisees with us," the mercenary said. "We kept a pious saint named Onias as a token of favor with the divine. Hyrcanus urged him to pray for the demise of our enemies, but he refused. So the king's bodyguards stoned him. This made the priests of the Temple furious with us." The man shifted uncomfortably so Simeon could stitch up another slash in his thigh. "During the siege, some of our suppliers offered to sell cattle for the Passover sacrifices. They sold them for a thousand drachma, way higher than the usual price. But when the time of sacrifice came, they refused to turn over the cattle to the priests inside the city." He groaned as Simeon sealed the wound with stitches. "Whatever hope we had of securing the people's support disappeared after that. The Temple priests may not care who their high priest is, but they sure care about their sacrifices."

After tending to the man, Simeon yanked his hand back. The itch on the back of his palm was unbearable. He held it up to the sunlight but saw no sign of rash or blistering. Why did this keep happening?

Antipater and Hyrcanus rode side by side into Petra as the sun set in the sky. Simeon, carrying a clay lamp from the lecture hall, paused to let them pass. Bloodstains soaked their once pristine royal robes. A corner of the deposed king's robe had been sheared off and a jagged red gash ran the length of Antipater's arm.

With the arrival of the vanquished, Antipas, the governor of Petra, strode out from a group of nobles and met the pair.

"What is the news?" Antipas asked.

Antipater dismounted and kissed his father before kneeling in the red dust. "We lost six thousand warriors. They surrounded us and only the gods spared us this time. Your son Phalion fell fighting at the head of his squadron."

Antipas clutched Antipater and let out a cry of grief that echoed off the walls of the city. "What has become of my son? How can I live another day?"

"I am with you, my father," Antipater said. "When Aretas betrayed us and turned his back, we didn't stand a chance, not against General Scaurus and the might of Rome. Hyrcanus, the true king, fought bravely. We must now consider what else we can do."

"There is nothing to do now," the governor said. "Wash yourself and I will have a meal prepared in your honor. We live to dream of another day."

Hyrcanus stepped forward and gripped the governor's wrist in greeting. "Shalom, my lord. Our only hope now is to petition Rome, to reach out to General Pompey and trust that he is able to deliver us. The general is away fighting in Armenia, but when he is done he will march this way and we shall implore him to intercede to the Roman Senate on our behalf."

"Why would this Roman general choose us over your brother?" Antipas asked. "Rome has spoken. They're willing to share power with whoever is willing to buy it."

"Pompey is the fist of the Republic and has brought order to all the lands east of us," Hyrcanus persisted. "He created the province of Syria, showing his intent to maintain order in the region. He is coming this way, and even gold will not sway his hand. He is incorruptible."

"No one is incorruptible," Antipas said. "Come! Wash! Eat!"

Simeon turned away and almost tripped over a form kneeling in the dirt, crying. A girl.

He knelt beside her and placed his hand gently on her back. The strange itch on his palm had returned. "What is the matter? How can I help?"

The girl continued to sob but then slowed to a whimper. "My abba is dead… my abba is dead and no one can help that."

Footsteps approached and Simeon looked up. It was Antipas.

"I call on you to take your hand off my granddaughter," the governor intoned.

A gust of wind whistled through the pillars of rock and snuffed out the clay lamp in Simeon's hand.

"I hope that isn't a portent of things to come," Baruch said from behind him.

# CHAPTER SIX

# POMPEY ARRIVES

*57 years until Messiah (63 BC)*

For a full month after Aristobulus's triumph, Yerushalayim buzzed with activity. Merchants and vendors proliferated on the streets and plazas. Worshippers returned to the Temple and the coins slowly rolled in again for Hannah.

She knew the sandals and feet of the regulars and listened hard to their conversation. A young Temple guard proved especially talkative and one morning Hannah discretely placed herself next to a pillar near his post. He and the partner assigned to him paid little attention to the rabble wandering around the colonnades, but they shared their own thoughts on life.

"Aristobulus has returned from Damascus," the young guard said. "He and Hyrcanus both petitioned General Pompey, but there seems to be no decision—yet. The Roman said he would decide when he arrived here. Now the king is doing all he can to ensure the city's ready."

"If the Romans are coming, why did Aristobulus lock himself away in the fortress of Alexandrium?" the other asked. "Is he afraid the decision will go against him? I thought he had bribed the Romans well enough."

"You would think so," the first affirmed. "He took a solid gold vine of the finest craftsmanship, worth five hundred talents, and offered it to the general, kneeling before him as if he was a slave. The general hardly even took notice." He tapped the end of his javelin on the pavement. "Aristobulus didn't trust the general and was furious to learn the decision might go against him. I don't know why he thinks he can hide in that windblown place at the end of the world."

An image of the reclusive fort high on Mount Sartaba, where she had spent so many days with Jeroboam, surfaced in Hannah's mind. Her arms twitched as she recalled the memory of holding her newborn son. The son who had been offered to Molech as a bribe for fertility and abundance. A sacrifice.

The fury in her own belly still burned, hotter than the fire in the idol. Maybe the Romans would get rid of both kings and settle this dispute once and for all. How else could there be peace?

Days later, she once again overheard the two guards in conversation.

"I guess you heard," said the first guard. "Aristobulus was surrounded at Alexandrium by Pompey. The hammer of Rome has come down. The general demanded that all our fortresses and walled cities be turned over to Roman control. Aristobulus agreed, but since then he's come to Yerushalayim to hide."

"Is that why the stonemasons have been called on?" the other asked. "My brother's a stonemason and says they're being asked to shore up the city's defences. We had better prepare for another siege. And this time we'll have no one to help us."

Hannah returned to her post, arranging sandals near the foot-washing station. Dozens of high-ranking soldiers and guards were pressing together to enter the Temple courts. Something was definitely happening, but she couldn't tell what.

"The king is arranging to surrender the city," one of the men said. "We can only hope that the fury of Pompey stays under control. With both our kings running off to seek outside help, it's clear we have lost our way. It's time to get rid of the monarchy and put ourselves under the control of Ha'Shem's anointed ones."

"We are the eternal city where the Almighty has set his name," replied his companion. "Surely he wouldn't let us go through another Passover under the foot of a foreign oppressor. The Hasmoneans have given us back our pride and dignity. We're a fortress on a hill and our people are ready to fight."

"The spies in Joshua's day prophesied it well," the first man said. "We are grasshoppers in their eyes."

One day later, a pair of familiar sandals stopped in front of her. Hannah waited for the feet to step out of them, but they stayed in place.

"You know what's coming, don't you?" asked the voice of Caiaphas.

Realizing that he was speaking to her, she reached to adjust another pair of sandals that had been left askew. "I understood that you wouldn't be back this way."

"Circumstances have changed."

Hannah nodded appreciation for the coin Caiaphas dropped on the ground beside her.

She sat back on her haunches and dared to look up into his eyes. "I still can't go with you."

"Understood." Caiaphas stepped out of his sandals and began washing his feet. "But General Pompey is here now. He's decided that Hyrcanus would be easier for Rome to manipulate than Aristobulus. The city will soon be turned over to the older brother and his handler Antipater. Anyway, many here have been advocating to abolish the monarchy since the Hasmoneans aren't from the line of David. The coming change may be one our people never recover from."

"Are you a prophet or the son of a prophet?" she asked. "What can you know how today will affect tomorrow? I thought you priests believed only Ha'Shem can know the future. Isn't that why you spend your days in endless sacrifice and prayer?"

"That is one reason we spend time in sacrifice and prayer. We also believe Ha'Shem controls what's happening right now and we express our gratitude for his goodness and guidance." Caiaphas motioned toward the stairs and began walking barefoot, gesturing for her to follow. "Pompey has the power of the Republic in his hand. No one across the entire world has been able to stop him. I believe he is thinking to crush us under the heel of the Roman eagle."

Hannah nodded as she walked after him. "Aristobulus is a proud and arrogant ruler. He's also a humble and effective high priest. He takes his position seriously and works hard to guard the Temple and the priesthood."

Caiaphas ran his hands through his generous beard and itched his chin. "Aristobulus will be broken one way or another. Even if he gives in, his followers have barricaded themselves in the plaza by the palace and sealed the gates."

"I have seen the increase in worshippers coming to pray," she said. "Are you telling me that this may be the last time we speak? I'm not yet ready to die. Isn't the Messiah supposed to step in and save us at a time like this?"

"Perhaps the Messiah will come and perhaps he'll wait until we've humbled ourselves under an oppressor. I know I can take shelter in the inner courts of the Temple. But you? If you're able, find yourself a place of safety to hide."

Hannah twirled in a circle, indicating the Temple with her arms outstretched. "These courts are my home. I'll rest here until the end comes. Be safe in your Temple and guard yourself from the enemy within. Remember what your mother has whispered in your ear from birth."

"And what is that?" he asked.

"Shmah, Yesrael, Adonai, Elohainu. Hear, O Israel. The Lord your God, the Lord is One."

He bowed. "May that be the last prayer I pray,"

After rewashing his feet, Caiaphas moved into the Temple without a backward glance.

\* \* \*

Simeon and Baruch had joined a dozen other Pharisees on the journey toward Yerushalayim. They slogged up the Jericho Road in the hot sun, stopping frequently to cool off at creeks along the way. The dry shrubs evidenced the lack of rain on the land.

"We are feeling the curse of the Almighty," Baruch grumbled.

"Like the curse I felt when the governor caught me trying to comfort his granddaughter," Simeon said.

"You're fortunate that it wasn't her father or her uncles, Herod or Joseph. I think Antipater has been training them to be as cut-throated as he is."

"How did a man with no scruples gain so much influence around here?" Simeon asked.

"Antipater married smart," Baruch answered. "He married a Nabatean noblewoman who had great wealth and position. The people loved him for that. Antipater trusts the king of Petra so much that he left his three children with him when he and Hyrcanus went to war."

Suddenly, a messenger on a donkey rode toward them. "Shalom, pilgrims," he called. "You would be wise to turn back. General Pompey has captured Aristobulus and has laid siege to the city. Thousands have barricaded themselves in the Temple, vowing to die rather than yield the sacred heart of our faith."

"It will be a just end for Aristobulus and his hunger for power," Baruch declared. "He is not from the line of David and his Sadducee followers are not people of the book."

The messenger sighed, not seeming to care for these matters of internal politics. "You people can resolve your differences. I have a family who needs me in Jericho." He pointed ahead. "When you top the rise at Bethany, you will see an endless camp of Romans. I would turn back now."

Simeon nodded his appreciation and watched as the man urged his donkey onward.

"Well, nothing has changed. I have come to see the Messiah," Simeon said to Baruch. "If not now, then when?"

When they crested the Mount of Olives, the pair looked down at the city stretched before them. Just as the messenger had reported, an endless stream of carts, camels, and donkeys were spread out through the valley. Leather tents dotted the landscape. Simeon couldn't even count the number of Roman battalions.

"They're staying just out of range of the city's archers," Baruch observed. "Once they've prepared their siege ramps, the Romans will target the gates."

As if on cue, they watched two battalions raise shields over their heads and begin marching on the main gate of Yerushalayim. Smaller cohorts of soldiers had been dispatched to test the other gates. Each was met with a barrage of arrows and catapulted boulders.

When they'd absorbed enough casualties, the Roman attackers withdrew and reestablished their previous formation under the protection of interlocked shields.

"Do you think we're safe?" Simeon asked.

"I think the Romans are focused on the siege," Baruch said. "As long as we stay out of the way, we should be okay."

Ten rows of Roman archers were lining up now, and within about a minute the first row unleashed a fusillade of projectiles. After releasing the arrows, the men ducked back to make room for the next line to step forward. The men at the back drove donkey carts packed with arrows to keep the supplies flowing. Wheeled platforms launched javelins, rocks, and beams toward the top of the walls, intending to destroy any hiding place where the defenders could seek refuge.

"Those things look like giant crossbows," Simeon remarked. "Look at that cart filled with round stones! They're using stones from our own rivers to knock through the walls—"

"Those crossbows can pick off our men one at a time," another Pharisee said. "They can pierce armor."

"We won't last long," Simeon said. "Should we pray for those within?"

The Pharisee shook his head. "Not if they're Sadducees. They're reaping the consequences of their delusion."

"But we should pray for the peace of the city," Baruch said.

As they knelt in prayer, hands extended toward the city, a great shout sounded near the Temple.

An hour later, dozens of men raced up the hill toward the Pharisees.

"Help us!" the lead man pleaded. "Water... we need water..."

The Pharisees shared their gourds of wine and water as the men gasped around them.

"What happened?" Simeon asked.

"Hyrcanus has many followers near the northwestern part of the wall. Some of them opened the gate for the Romans, thinking to spare the city. Now the enemy is pouring through the breach and destroying everything in sight. They have the upper city and the palace. Everything is lost. Our only hope now is to run for our lives and warn others."

"Perhaps we should move elsewhere to pray," Baruch urged. "It seems the Messiah may not choose to come today."

* * *

Hannah had chosen a perch high on a ledge above the Temple courtyard. Shielded by a pillar and crouching in shadow, it was hard to see exactly what was happening below, but the sound of battle rattled her teeth. She couldn't see outside the city walls, but she could get a sense of its impact by the boulders and beams of wood hurtling into the defenders. Men were running one moment, then lying crushed the next. Arrows flew overhead in continuous arches, landing amidst those seeking refuge. Dozens of men had fallen prone, writhing in pain.

She couldn't estimate how many people had sought sanctuary in the Temple grounds, but she figured it was twenty thousand or more. They were working together to erect defences, distribute food, and pray. Boys as young as ten were learning to handle spears and swords under the watchful eye of their fathers and grandfathers.

Three long days crept by before a huge roar alerted her to a change in circumstances. A rush of Romans sped through a gap in the upper city wall, plunging inward like a river through the breach in a dam. She knew Aristobulus's loyalists had barricaded themselves in the eastern section of the capital. The Temple Mount remained under their control. But now they were under threat and defenders were hurrying to break down the Tyropoeon bridge which connected the upper city to the Temple, preventing the attackers from entering.

Hannah watched a regal warrior on horseback move forward toward the edge of the broken bridge.

"Hear you this, O foolish children," the man said. "I am General Pompey, hand of the Roman Republic and terror of all who defy us. Lay down your weapons and bow on your faces and you shall not die this day. You and your children will serve the might of Rome to extend our dominion until there is peace on earth and goodwill to all men in our realm."

These declarations echoed in a great silence atop the hill. Then, as Hannah listened, she discerned the distant sound of chopping. She strained to see over the gate and glimpsed only bare land beyond, the trees stripped bare as though left in the wake of a swarm of devouring locusts.

Pompey was smiling. "When my ram's head hits your gate the first time, it will be the end of mercy! Your blood will be on your own head. There is nothing more I can do to stop the sword from your necks and the javelins from your hearts."

The general waited a few moments, then turned his mount to face his troops. He raised his hand and brought it down again in a gesture of finality.

Instead of a massive charge, the Roman soldiers began to withdraw. In their place, a parade of donkey carts proceeded forward, filled with wooden beams. Hannah watched as a horde of laborers began to dig ditches outside the Temple wall. Others constructed barricades that rose twice the height of a man.

For two days, Hannah watched. It didn't take long to realize that the Romans were building a wall of their own. Once complete, it would mean that no one sheltering on the Temple Mount would be able to get out. There would be no relief for them.

The following day, Hannah lowered a ladder and descended from her perch to search for food. She encountered dozens of women working hard over cook-fires. They roasted lamb, prepared bread, and boiled tea. Others chopped vegetables. Hannah herself was put to work immediately at a table, placing slices of lamb between loaves of flatbread. The line of hungry men filing by seemed endless.

By evening, she had collected her share of food and climbed back into her shelter, and this time she was joined by two other women.

Over the course of the next week, they took turns each day descending to wash, collect food, and help where they could. And each time they retreated to their hiding place, they hoisted the ladder away to maintain their privacy.

"We have to protect this space," Hannah said. "There will be no Messiah, no warrior, to help us now. We're on our own. We must work together to survive."

"How long will this go on?" one of Hannah's companions asked. "I was supposed to be married right after the feast of Tabernacles..."

Outside the Temple, the Romans kept busy. They had figured out that they could build their fortifications with impunity on the Sabbath, when no one inside the Temple would dare attack. Thousands of slaves were set to work under the whip of their harsh masters. They dug trenches where the soil permitted and redirected water into them. Giant towers had sprouted up like palm trees in a desert oasis, and from them archers trained their bows down at anyone who might venture to cross these makeshift moats.

To make matters worse, the Romans had buried sharp spikes in the ground near the trenches. These fortifications would be impossible to cross, even if the Romans weren't encamped directly to the southeast. Meanwhile, General Pompey had made a point of pitching his tent just north of the Temple.

Two full moons came and went before the Romans hit the gate for the first time with their ram's head. Hundreds of defenders had already fallen by this time under the endless barrage; their bodies were stored in a large reservoir which had been drained of water and covered over by wood. The stench of decaying flesh could not be ignored. Small fires had been set with pitch to disguise the odor.

Women, children, and many men knelt in terror, crying out to Ha'shem. There seemed to be no point, however. Hannah had given up on prayers long ago. She watched in horrific fascination as the righteous collapsed into desperate, numb stupors of their former selves.

When the ram's head struck, thousands of Roman slaves and legionnaires joined to fill the ditch along the northern wall of the Temple. They scurried like ants, supplied by an endless train of donkey carts loaded with stones, dirt, and debris. The Romans had also constructed two ramparts, one next to the city's citadel and the other further to the west.

Hannah watched, mesmerized by these latest developments.

Before she knew what was happening, though, she was startled by the sound of one of her companions suddenly thrashing in her sleep, as though from a nightmare. Instead of rousing, the woman inadvertently plunged straight over the edge of the wall, crashing onto the pavement below. Apart from her brief scream of surprise, the Romans' movements muffled her quick death.

In the morning, the two surviving women added their companion to the reservoir of corpses.

Once safe on their ledge again, it became clear to Hannah that the siege was entering a new phase. The Roman archers began a concentrated attack against a particular length of the Temple wall, driving back all defenders.

"They're coming, aren't they?" Hannah's companion stuttered. "What are we going to do?"

"It will be over soon."

When the end came, it was quick and bloody. Two streams of armored Roman legionnaires poured into the midst of humanity weakened by hunger, worn out from terror, and disillusioned by the lack of answered prayer.

Hannah and her companion cringed, pushing themselves ever deeper into the shadows, hardly daring to peek at the carnage below. They covered their ears and curled into fetal positions waiting to meet their deaths. The smell of pitch filtered up to them and soon flames were engulfing sections of the Temple. A great roar went up from the conquerors.

No, Hannah decided. There was nothing left to pray for.

CHAPTER SEVEN

# REUNION

*54 years before Messiah (60 BC)*

The callouses on Simeon's hands spoke of much hard work over the past few years. But the smile on his face spoke of something even greater.

In the aftermath of the slaughter at the Temple, the Romans had scoured the countryside for survivors to clean up bodies and debris. The Romans had surrounded the site for weeks before allowing outsiders in. Hundreds of men had been assigned to the task of churning up the hillside for graves while hundreds of others prepared and hauled bodies to impromptu burials. Baruch had estimated there must have been at least twelve thousand dead, drawing innumerable jackals, hyenas, and wild dogs—not to mention thousands of vultures and crows—to feast on the carcasses.

Simeon and Baruch, along with the dozen Pharisees accompanying them, had been swept up in their net and put to work. Simeon's first task had been digging graves outside Yerushalayim. Being elderly, Baruch had been given the task of cataloguing the dead and overseeing burials.

Within weeks, Simeon's hands had blistered and calloused. The work brought back memories of dealing with the aftermath of the village slaughter involving his family many years earlier. Familiar faces faded in and out of his dreams.

Hyrcanus had been reinstalled as high priest over what remained of the Temple. Aristobulus had been taken to Rome in chains, walking in humility before the golden chariot of the conquering hero, Pompey. Meanwhile, survivors of the purge had been put to work dismantling the Roman fortifications, cleaning debris, filling ditches, and removing siegeworks.

Around a fire one night, Baruch placed a hand on Simeon's back. "Just think, my friend. If you had stayed in Petra to be with Trophina, you may never have had to face all this."

"Yes, and I'd likely be in a grave," Simeon said. "Sometimes I see the eyes of a woman in my dreams. I reach out for her, but she's like a reflection in water, disappearing before I can touch her…"

What he knew but didn't say was the face belonged to Hannah, not Trophina.

It was three weeks after Simeon dug his first grave that he saw her, stumbling out of the city, grimy, blood-stained, bleary-eyed, and numb. He recognized Hannah's eyes as she feebly swung a broom at the carrion crows attempting to feast on the unburied dead. Indeed, he would know those eyes anywhere… her nose, her cheekbones… the way she held her lips as she focused… the way she slipped her foot out of her sandal and rubbed it against the back of her ankle…

His throat was parched under the blistering sun, so when he attempted to call only a hoarse rasp whispered out of his throat. Unable to hear, Hannah knelt by a grave as two men lowered a body into it. When the deed was done, she rose without hesitation and retreated through the mounds of rubble before he could catch her.

At the end of the day, Simeon wandered into the Temple grounds, but Hannah was nowhere to be seen.

He looked for her daily, to no avail.

Five weeks later, he finally came upon her standing over a spit of lamb where the food was being prepared. He approached slowly, captivated by the royal blue scarf hanging around her neck. He couldn't imagine how his changed appearance might impact her.

"Hannah!" he called.

She turned and stared. "The line is over by those tables," she said, pointing. "The fire is perfect… I must keep slicing the meat to keep everyone fed. I hope you've washed yourself."

"Hannah, it's me!"

"You have no decency to greet me with a shalom. You don't tell me your name. And yet you expect me to know you?"

"Shalom!" he said, bowing. "It's Simeon. Simeon from our village."

She dropped the knife and let it bounce toward the fire. Her hands flew to her mouth and her eyes grew large.

"No!" She ran the dozen steps toward him and flung herself into his arms. Then pulling away, embarrassed at her impetuousness, she stared into his warm eyes. "You've grown taller… and you didn't have a beard the last time I saw you. You look so strong."

He held out his hands and revealed his calluses. "I'm still digging graves, it seems. I was outside the city when the Romans arrived."

"Some things change. Some things don't," she said. "I was in the Temple when the Romans came. It seems I too am always on the edge of death. I've lived in the Temple so long that it's like a home to me."

"I joined the Pharisees in Petra and spent my days in study and charity," Simeon said. "But now that Hyrcanus is restored to high priest and Antipater is governor, it looks like we'll be able to move back into Yerushalayim." He choked back tears. "When you were taken, I was certain you were lost to me forever."

She hung her head, then crouched to retrieve the knife. "One day I will share my journey, but it is filled with darkness and sorrow. But the workers are lined up for food and I must do my duty."

His grin spread from ear to ear. "Now that I know you're here, I will seek you any time I am close. I praise Ha'Shem because of his goodness to you."

"Don't praise him too quickly," she said. "He may have forgotten to pass on whatever goodness you're thinking of. Now get in line before the others think I'm favoring you."

\* \* \*

Seeing Simeon, large as life right in front of her, took Hannah's breath away. Despite his scraggly beard, earth-stained tunic, gawking stare, and lack of manners, he had found her and looked, to her eyes, every part a prince. Every impulse in her had called out to take his hands, to cover them with salve, and cater to his every want and need. As youth they'd only bonded a short time, over the graves of their families, but he was the only one from the village who still lived.

"Hannah! We need more meat," someone yelled. "What's got you dreaming?"

Of course she'd been dreaming of Simeon.

In the coming months, she saw him weekly. He had joined the workmen repairing and rebuilding the city. He spent his evenings huddled around candles with other Pharisees, studying the scrolls.

"Everything I read tells me the Messiah is near," Simeon said to her one day during their regular visits. "Would that Ha'Shem let me see his face. That would be peace for me."

"For my part, I feel he missed his chance," she responded. "We needed him and he was nowhere to be seen."

Simeon's eyes held a deep sadness for her. He tried to disguise it, but she recognized the emotion. The truth was that she had nothing more to give and no longer had any desire to open her hands or heart. Every time she had done that, only pain and death answered.

Simeon turned back, clutching his scroll, his passion and zeal sucked away like morning dew under the summer sun. With twelve thousand dead and most habitable dwellings damaged or destroyed, accommodations had to be constructed. There was no end of responsibilities calling on his time and attention.

Still, it was almost enough to have him close again.

For a time, Hannah searched for the kindly Caiaphas, but then she found his name on the list of those who had perished. She built her own fortress around her heart and determined not to let anyone close again. It was clear that Ha'Shem had designed a life of solitude for her—that was, if he had any designs for her at all.

One day Hyrcanus called dozens of workers into the refurbished Temple courtyard. His high priestly robes shone in the sun and the jewels of the ephod glistened.

He stood on a temporary dais. "Shalom to the righteous who do Ha'Shem's work," he said. "You have persevered despite the struggle between my brother and I. Many of you connected with the Pharisees felt that only a descendant of King David had a right to the throne and implored the Roman Senate to end my family's reign. For generations, we have fought for you and secured the identity and traditions of our nation." He rubbed his jaw and paused, looking out at the sea of faces before him. "We stood up for you. We established a system of governors and judges to see that you received justice."

Hyrcanus beckoned to an assistant, who brought forward a scroll. The high priest rolled it out on a podium and took a deep breath.

"The Pontifex Maximus of Rome, Caesar himself, has decided not to side with my brother or me when it comes to the sovereignty of our nation," Hyrcanus continued. "Instead the Romans will rule us and determine all matters of legal justice for us through their governors and surrogates."

A white-bearded elder near the front raised his fist. "No! We want Jewish kings for Jewish subjects."

A few other voices joined him, but they quieted when Hyrcanus raised his hand.

"The decision is final," he said. "I will remain as your high priest. Your desire for a Davidic ruler, a Messiah, and a prince from the tribe of Judah means that you will have no ruler at all."

His speech continued for some time. He spoke of the changes to be instituted by their new overseers, but all Hannah could wonder about was what this would mean for the Temple. And what of Antipater's old threat against her?

A group of passionate young extremists stood up in the middle of the assembly and began to shout.

"Away with Caesar! Bring us the Messiah! Away with Caesar! Bring us the Messiah!"

Temple guards rushed in and pulled several protestors away. Many more men felt emboldened to stand with them. The guards were forced to pull swords and daggers to silence the outcry. These efforts only encouraged extremists.

Hyrcanus held up his hands to no avail and soon his bodyguards were ushering him off the platform.

As more and more men stood to raise their fists, a white-bearded elder took his place at the front and called for unity and sovereignty. It was all in vain and before long the Temple guards withdrew to the cheers of the assembly.

"There's going to be trouble," Hannah said to the woman beside her.

"We've seen enough trouble in this place," the woman answered. "We need to find shelter."

The two women backed away from the mob.

For a few moments, all was orderly as the most passionate men joined together in chanting for the life of their nation.

Then a terrifying drumbeat and pounding echoed through the plaza, growing louder and louder. Once the chanting had stopped, a cohort of fully armed legionnaires marched through the gate of the Temple. Some of the chanters knelt and bared their necks. Others fled in panic.

The Roman militia didn't hesitate to use their might.

More graves would need to be dug. More blood would have to be washed from the pavement of the Holy Place.

\* \* \*

Simeon had been running an errand for Baruch in the upper city when the legionnaires intervened at the Temple. The thudding of studded sandals on pavement, accompanied by the pounding of swords on shields, echoed in his mind long after the dreaded Roman forces had finished their march of terror.

Where was Baruch? Where was Hannah? He sprinted through the streets.

He encountered a line of bloodied Roman warriors standing shoulder to shoulder in front of the gates. There was no way in and no way out.

Not again!

Simeon backed away slowly as a golden carriage pulled up, drawn by six black horses. Sheltering behind a vendor's stall, he slipped around a drooping canopy to observe. A noble figure dressed in the garb of royalty stepped out of the golden box and surveyed the scene.

It was Antipater, wearing a fur-lined cape over his blue robe.

What was he doing standing with the Romans?

Simeon quickly understood. He must have been appointed governor, meaning it was his task to protect the people and bring peace to the land. But he was clearly a traitor.

Antipater nodded frequently as he interacted with the centurion overseeing the Roman fighting force.

Before Simeon's eyes, a jeweled sandal extended from the curtained carriage. A woman, elegant as a swan, stepped up behind Antipater and draped her hand on his arm.

Simeon looked harder. A mistress?

The young woman stood with her back straight, confident in the face of the warriors all around. As if drawn by magnetic force, she suddenly turned.

Simeon gasped. It was Trophina, and she had recognized him. She held his eyes and smiled.

He slipped away and ran back toward the upper city, itching his hand all the way.

A merchant he had recently done business with welcomed him into his home.

"Antipater is with the Romans," Simeon confided.

The merchant nodded. "That Idumean has been with the Romans from the time he represented Hyrcanus before General Pompey. He's fascinated with Roman wealth and might. As the new governor of Idumea and Judea, he has all the position and influence he has ever sought."

"What can be gained by courting the Romans?"

"He seeks still more power. He will have the right to tax us all, increasing his wealth more than we can imagine. He will set the rules by which we are forced to live. What Hyrcanus can no longer do politically, Antipater will do."

Simeon was aghast. "Will he become king?"

"No! He will have to submit to Rome." The merchant handed over a tray of bread and cheese, then beckoned for his servant to fill mugs with wine. "He is training his sons to take up his legacy, and they are learning well. With Antipater courting Rome, I don't hold much hope for this land."

"Surely, we can do more than provide bodies for their graves and crosses," Simeon said. Suddenly, he remembered Trophina. "What do you know about his niece?"

The merchant raised his eyebrows. "The one who acts like she's already a queen? Many men will be smitten with her. Guard your eyes and your heart. That is not a family you want to be part of." He stood. "Now come. I have a friend who travelled with Antipater on his latest trip. He can tell you anything that might be happening in the world."

Two streets away, in a palatial home surrounded by armed sentries, the pair was welcomed by an Ethiopian servant who ushered them into a triclinium. In the elegant dining room, a fountain featured two carved dolphins spewing water from their mouths. Persian carpets lined the walls and marble benches surrounded them. Intricate mosaics featured hunting centaurs, flighty nymphs, and glaring goddesses.

An Egyptian youth bowed and served them a tray of dates, figs, cheeses, and flatbreads, along with wine.

"The master will be here shortly," the youth said.

Simeon had to look twice at the giant of a man who soon ducked under an overhang and settled onto the bench opposite him.

"Shalom to the ones who breathe despite the suffocating presence of Rome," this giant said. "What do you dare ask about at such a time? The troops have emptied my wine cellars and demanded that I turn over my herds for their consumption. Their gold will do little to help me replenish my supplies."

The merchant chuckled. "Petronius, you would declare poverty no matter what supplies you had hidden away." He gestured to Simeon. "My friend has seen Antipater standing with the Roman legions outside the Temple. What can you tell him?"

Petronius pressed a knuckled fist under the trimmed beard on his chin. "General Pompey has proved himself. He is about to be welcomed into a triumvirate with the great Julius Caesar and Marcus Crassus. Antipater has a nose for what's about to happen and has worked hard to make himself known to Pompey. Pompey has brought an end to the great Seleucid Empire and there is now a vacuum of power… a vacuum ready for just such a man of opportunity as Antipater."

"So the Romans have laid waste to the Greeks," Simeon said. "What of the Arabs?"

"You are fortunate you are no longer in Petra," Petronius answered. "Another Roman general, Scaurus, has sought the aid of your high priest Hyrcanus to lay siege to Aretas. I hear that Hyrcanus will soon dispatch Antipater to Petra to barter for peace, and no doubt the price in silver will go to Scaurus as a bribe to withdraw his forces." The man rubbed a rag over his bald head. "Antipater finds himself the voice of reason at every exchange and he will soon be granted more power than he can dream of. With that power, he will make significant enemies."

"Are you a prophet then?" Simeon asked.

The big man shrugged. "I say what I know. Antipater makes himself useful to the Romans and gains a little power with each transaction."

"So our leaders are no more than vassals of Rome." Simeon hung his head. "As are we?"

Petronius nodded. "In our time, a monarch can ride his golden chariot in victory one moment, only to be buried under a pile of dust the next. He who thirsts for power will die by the vengeance of others who want that same power. It's best to be a man of peace and avoid the knives."

"Perhaps this isn't the best time for the Messiah to come after all," Simeon said.

Petronius stood and placed his hands flat against the ceiling. "The Messiah will come when the Messiah comes. Neither Antipater nor Rome will stop him."

## CHAPTER EIGHT
# SEPARATION

*53 years before Messiah (59 BC)*

The hundred and fifteen bodies from this latest purge weren't nearly as many as the twelve thousand who'd died in the siege the year before. The Romans were determined to eliminate all significant protests before they gained traction.

Hannah retched as she recognized the corpse of the mentor Simeon had venerated. Baruch's neck was mostly severed and his tunic stained a deep crimson. A rat had been chewing on the man's toe when she brought the broom down hard on it.

She had already looked for Simeon and was relieved not to have found him. Four of the men she had helped in the kitchen were among the fatalities, too. Only one woman appeared to have died.

The legionnaires permitted a single cart into the grounds, meaning that only two bodies could be ferried to the gate at a time. There, they were carefully laid out.

Although several of the women had prepared food for the survivors, few could bring themselves to eat. Chasing off carrion crows and rats added to the distraction.

She watched as two men gently laid Baruch's body in a cart, but not before Hyrcanus spoke a prayer over the dead man.

Hannah had exchanged her role of guarding the sandals of the righteous to sweeping the dust where those feet should have walked. There were no longer any pilgrims, and certainly no sacrifices.

Hyrcanus, the former king, sat on the stairs by Solomon's portico, staring blankly at the carnage around him. And when Hannah brought him a tray of flatbread and fruit, he glared unseeing as she put it down.

"What hope do we have left in this world?" she asked.

Hyrcanus startled and looked at her. "We are a people without hope." He reached for a date and chewed it, all the while continuing to look out over the Kidron Valley toward the graves dotting the slope of the Mount of Olives.

Hannah left him alone and strolled back down. She once again approached the cart by the gate; it was in the process of removing the last of the bodies from the plaza.

"Where will they bury the bodies this time?" she asked. "Who will dig the graves?"

The Syrian slave pushing the cart stopped to stare at her. "They aren't going to bury these ones. We've been ordered to burn them as a lesson to any others who might want to rebel."

"But burial is essential to our faith and practice."

"I guess these men should have thought of that before they decided to resist the Romans."

"One of them is a friend I have to honor," she said. "Let me have that one body to bury. I must show proper respect."

The slave shrugged. "Most of the bodies have already been removed. There's no place to bury someone under all this pavement. I thought you people believed this was a sacred place to your god. Why would you want to desecrate it with the dead?"

Hannah looked around at the devastation. "Look at this place. There's nothing sacred about the top of this hill. If some god wanted to have the place, the least he could do is take care of his people. Why should I respect his space when things like this happen?"

The Syrian shrugged and pushed the cart toward the exit. "I guess he let you live for some reason."

His comment squeezed at her heart so strongly that she pressed on her chest and fought for breath. Why was she alive after all this devastation when so many others hadn't survived?

She rushed after the cart and looked at the pile of bodies near the gate. Two sentries with javelins and swords stood tall to prohibit the living from getting too close. They crossed their javelins to bar the gate as she neared.

"Where is the old man with the beard?" Hannah called to a man piling bodies on another cart just outside the gate.

He ignored her and pushed his load away.

"I need to bury my friend," she said to a different sentry. He ignored her. "My friend is one of the righteous. I need to bury him!"

She stood by the gate, refusing to be intimidated, until the last of the bodies had been taken away. When the gate closed, she fell to her knees and sobbed.

* * *

Simeon waited in his hovel for Baruch until the end of the third day. When his mentor still hadn't shown up, he put on his best robe, a robe he'd purchased in Petra from a noble, and dared to wander toward the Temple. Baruch wouldn't have fought or created any trouble for himself. He was a man of peace.

As he approached, he saw that the Roman presence was still strong. Apart from soldiers and slaves bringing out the bodies, no one appeared to be leaving or entering the Temple complex.

He noticed a vendor selling figs and dates from a cart about a stone's throw from the gate. Simeon gave him a silver shekel.

"Have you seen anyone going in or coming out of the Temple grounds?" Simeon asked. "I'm looking for an old man and young woman, not necessarily together."

The vendor shook his head. "It doesn't matter who you're looking for. They aren't coming out. I still don't know if anyone survived." He dropped the shekel into a leather pouch which he tucked into his robe. "I'm here because the Romans need food like everyone else and there isn't a lot of competition. It would be better if you didn't ask too many questions. There are spies walking these streets looking for people who might get a visit from the Romans at night."

Simeon walked the perimeter of the Temple wall, then stood on a large rock and took note of the activity in the valley below. Apart from a few extra checkpoints, all seemed peaceful. A blind man sat on the side of the road near the gate to the lower city. Three other men stood alongside a camel. As a regiment of soldiers investigated them, two other young men skirted the checkpoint.

A dozen legionnaires were blocking the way into the city. As people approached, they were forced to walk through a phalanx of ill-humored killers. It looked like few people were willing to take that risk. A number of tradesmen and vendors had therefore relocated outside the walls and set up an impromptu market there.

Simeon put up with the intense questioning of these hostile soldiers and made his way out of the city and walked toward the garden of Gethsemane, where he rested among the olive trees. From here, the city looked tranquil and strong. He stopped by a small stream and cupped his hand, slurping up the cool drink.

Rejuvenated, he stepped amongst the mounds of fresh graves. Ten men were working here, just west of where he himself had dug graves not so long ago.

Two of the men recognized him.

"If it isn't the book learner," one said in acknowledgement. "Shalom. Have you come to help us? If so, you're too late. We're almost done."

"I came to see if you remember any of the faces you put in the ground," Simeon said. "My mentor is missing and I don't know where he may be."

"We don't see faces, as you should know. The rabbi wraps the bodies up tight. Besides, if you're looking for the ones just killed in the Temple, the Romans burned them as a warning to the rest of us."

"But that's sacrilege. The righteous must be buried!"

The gravedigger nodded. "Perhaps those who were killed weren't righteous."

"There was no man more righteous than my mentor," Simeon declared.

"Perhaps he's still locked up in there." The man pointed up toward the Temple. "For your sake, I wouldn't try too hard to find out. People are starving. When passersby try throwing food over the walls, the Romans intervene. In fact, they're killing anyone who tries to help."

Simeon was watching the carts, caravans, and carriages go by when he noticed the golden carriage with six black horses.

Antipater.

His heart skipped and his gut twisted. Was *she* here as well?

As the carriage neared, the curtain moved a fraction and there Trophina was, smiling. And once again she seemed to have spotted him, against all odds. Her hand snaked through the cloth and imparted the smallest of waves before disappearing back inside. He immediately started to scratch.

If only he could get to her and convince her to make her uncle release those inside the Temple.

* * *

Two days of hard rain filled the Temple pools enough to allow the survivors inside a few sips each day. Hyrcanus thanked Hannah for having scrubbed those pools upon seeing even the smallest of clouds on the horizon from her perch.

"We are at the mercy of Ha'Shem and people like you," the high priest mumbled.

Guards needed to be posted around the two main pools, one reserved for drinking water and the other for cooking, while four smaller ones permitted the survivors to clean their feet and soak rags to place around their necks and foreheads. Vessels were set out during the rain and afterward stored in the kitchen to serve as emergency rations; guards stood around these as well.

There wasn't enough water to scrub the Temple clean, but using old rags and brooms they were able to keep busy removing as much dust and grit as possible. Still, the stench of unwashed flesh percolated through the premises as a curse. The only scent stronger was the smoke from burning flesh outside the walls.

Hyrcanus kept incense lit and urged everyone to place oil lamps strategically around the plaza.

"I would give my child for a chance to wash my face and hair," a woman said to Hannah on the tenth day. "Even the rats have abandoned this cursed place. How can you press on when you look like the worst beggar in the garbage heap?"

Hannah smiled. "I press on because I know I'm not the worst beggar in the garbage heap. I press on because I don't hope for more than I have."

Three dozen of the survivors tasked themselves with prayer and perched on benches, bobbing up and down while chanting. Everyone else found other ways to distract themselves. There was no telling whether the Romans meant to starve them completely, but in the meantime the pace of life inside was slow and measured. Every bit of their precious energy had to be conserved.

A young man was the first to notice that the sentries had gone from the gate. Hannah watched him as he clambered up onto a section of wall to look down over the barrier to see no guards, but rather a lone vendor arriving to set up his cart. Curious, she hauled her own ladder to the wall and climbed it to the top.

The youth shimmied down from his perch and strolled to the gate. He pushed on it, found it barred, and then formed a bridge for himself with discarded timbers to climb back atop the wall, this time directly in front of the gate.

"Vendor," he called. "Open the gate!"

The vendor glanced back and forth along the length of the wall. "Where are the Romans?"

"Perhaps they forgot to show up this morning," the youth called.

Hannah lowered the ladder and descended from her perch.

"Where are you going?" her companion asked.

"The Romans are gone. Perhaps today is the day we wash our hair." Hannah stumbled across the plaza with one focus. "The Romans are gone…"

As she murmured the good news, several others around stirred from their slumber.

When the gate was open, the enterprising young man raced back through the Temple enclosure yelling: "The Romans are gone! The Romans are gone!"

The place stirred to life and a long line of survivors began to stumble out of their entrapment, the vendor out front staring at them wide-eyed.

Hannah didn't slow down as she passed through the gate. She fell twice on her way down the hill but finally reached the stream running through the Kidron Valley. She lapped up the water from her cupped hands, then dunked her head into the cool flowing source of life.

She could breathe again! It was like being reborn.

Her companion had waded into the water and Hannah joined her, allowing her tunic to float up so she could scrub her skin underneath.

A crowd of onlookers formed alongside the bank of the stream as the survivors washed away their grit. One woman, loaded with laundry, frowned at the unruly behavior. Some of the men had stripped down to loincloths. Hyrcanus himself had doffed his high priestly robes to soak his feet.

"They're muddying the water," the laundry woman complained.

"Go upstream if you want drinking water or washing," Hyrcanus told her. "I will not be the one to deprive these children of joy."

Hannah smiled at the high priest. "Thank you for staying with us until the end."

"I didn't have much choice," he said. "Will you be back to help us set things right again?"

"I have no family and no home. I still fear that Antipater will find a way to trap me when I'm away from the Temple. I need a place to stay."

"I have just the place," Hyrcanus said. "As long as the Temple is open, you will always have a place."

* * *

Simeon followed the golden carriage as it rattled along through the maze of homes in the wealthier section of the upper city. After a while it disappeared from view and didn't reappear, suggesting that it had stopped somewhere.

Perhaps Petronius would know. Simeon jogged in the direction of the giant man's home.

As he rounded a corner on the way, he saw Petronius's Ethiopian servant running by him with several baskets of fruit in hand, no doubt fresh from the market.

"Wait!" Simeon called. The man hesitated a moment but kept backpedaling. "I was with you earlier in my visit last year. Please, tell me whether you've seen a golden carriage in your area of the city."

"It's at our house," the servant confirmed. "I have to hurry now. We're providing dinner for the governor and his niece."

"I need to see her."

"You'll have to find your own way in."

Simeon kept pace with the servant until he reached the home. The front door was guarded by two Roman sentries. Petronius's servant was permitted to enter, but Simeon didn't even try to bluff his way in. His noble robe from Petra might fool the sentries, but not Antipater—or Trophina.

The house next door was slightly elevated up the slope, and it had no sentries in place. This gave him the start of an idea.

Simeon wandered the streets until he found a vendor selling dates and pomegranates. He bought the whole basket with his last two silver shekels. Basket in hand, he then marched into the yard of Petronius's neighbor. He went boldly to the door and shouted his greeting.

"Shalom, neighbor! A delivery for your household."

A generously proportioned house slave answered the door. "No one here ordered anything," she said. "You must have the wrong house. Try next door. They are having a celebration of some kind."

"Pardon my mistake." Simeon set the basket on the ground. "I don't want to disturb the guards at the entrance, nor do I wish to bother the master of the feast. Is there another way into the property from here?"

The woman waddled to the corner of the house and pointed toward three palm trees leaning over a hedge into Petronius's yard. "I've seen the young worker next door climb up that palm and hop over the hedge. You look young enough to do it without breaking your leg. Watch that fruit, though, or you'll spill it."

"Thank you."

Simeon moved to the trees, conscious of the house slave's eyes watching him the whole way. When he leaped up and landed on the other side, she smiled, waved, and waddled back inside.

He navigated around a fountain, past a shoulder-high hedge, and then stepped out into the open. The first person he saw was Trophina herself, standing on a balcony overlooking the city.

She noticed him immediately and smiled. "Are they no longer letting people in through the front gate?"

He pressed fingers over his lips in an attempt to silence her, but she laughed instead.

She held up her mug as if in invitation. "I need to talk to you."

A servant girl slipped up beside her and Trophina pointed at Simeon. The girl shook her head and went back inside. Soon a male servant appeared.

"If that basket is meant for this house, you need to come through the front gate," this servant said.

Simeon set the basket down. "I went next door and they told me to come this way."

The servant left and returned with the Ethiopian servant, who nodded at Simeon in recognition. He waved Simeon forward. "My friend, what brings you so late?"

Trophina spun on her heels, gave Simeon a cheeky grin over her shoulder, and wandered back inside. He would have to risk the wrath of Antipater if he got close to her in public. Why did women have to be so frustrating?

"Bring the basket," the Ethiopian said. "You can come through the servant's entrance and take your chances." He smiled at him. "The woman you set your eyes on will only be happy if she is a queen someday. If you cannot fulfil her desire, turn your heart elsewhere before you're destroyed."

"How can you know the heart of a woman you don't even know?"

"Ask yourself that question when you're lying with a dagger in your belly. I've seen the way her uncle watches the other men who pay attention to her. He stares with the dagger of his eyes even while his hand reaches for the one behind his back."

"Perhaps I can write a message to be placed among her belongings," Simeon suggested.

"Write your message and I'll see that she finds it," the Ethiopian said. "By then, you should be far away."

# CHAPTER NINE
# LOST GOLD

*46 years until Messiah (52 BC)*

Several of Hannah's companions had warned her that Simeon had his heart set on the governor's niece, Trophina. Although he seemed to have given up that quest, it didn't mean his heart wouldn't sway in her direction again. Once, when a golden chariot rolled by, he jumped to his feet and stared after it.

"Someone you know?" Hannah asked.

He hung his head. "Maybe someone I would like to know. I left a note for her five years ago and she slipped away from her guards for a moment to meet me. We stood looking into each other's eyes without a word... and then her uncle found her and took her away. I keep trying to send messages, but I never hear back."

"Someone like the governor's niece is probably well-guarded."

He chuckled. "So you know. I figured that being locked up inside the Temple walls might mean you never hear anything of the world outside."

She smiled. "I still have friends who know about our kinship. With my life at risk, nothing is easy."

He met Hannah frequently at the market near the garden of Gethsemane. She was always on edge when she emerged from the protection of the Temple grounds. They often spread a blanket and shared picnics and discussed what life may have been like if their time together had started differently. Simeon even probed her about the possibility of establishing a more formal relationship.

She declined.

"We're the only ones left of our people," he said. "It's been twenty-six years and neither of us is young anymore."

"You don't know my story. When the bandits kidnapped me, the leader took advantage of me. I gave birth to his child. I would never be worthy of someone like you."

"All I need is a companion."

Her head drooped and a tear trickled from her eye. "His name was Jeroboam. We lived in the fortress at Alexandrium until Antipater came one day to set a trap. They sacrificed my son to Molech and then burned my husband as well for allowing it to happen. I cannot tell you about all the horrors I have experienced."

"We can forget the past and look to the future," Simeon insisted. "The Messiah will surely come soon."

She turned away. "You are a man who follows Ha'Shem and all he says in his law. I have been too defiled to believe anymore. I live as a fraud in his sacred house, daring to collect the sandals of the righteous and clean the floors in hopes of earning enough coin to survive."

However, Simeon persisted in their picnics, even though they grew further apart. Sometimes it was the weather keeping them apart, other times his duties, his studies, and his travels. She stopped looking for the invitations.

Hyrcanus found her a spacious room in the Temple. She slept well and the coin from her work was more than sufficient to provide for her needs. She had no one to care for and no one to care for her, so her extra coins went to beggars and the occasional rabbi who appeared in need. And of course there was the ever-present offering boxes, whose proceeds were set aside for the repair and restoration of the Temple.

More religious nobles seemed to come through the Temple than ever. One morning, when a large group of flowing white robes strutted by, Hannah called to Hyrcanus as he stood watching the parade of important men.

"Who are these men and why are they here so often?" she asked.

Hyrcanus continued to gaze after the retinue. "They are the Sanhedrin. Aulus Gabinius, former proconsul of Syria, split his kingdom into five districts of legal and religious councils: Galilee, Jericho, Perea, Gadara, and Yerushalay-im." He cinched his robe tighter. "You and I may not be able to meet so openly in the future. The Sanhedrin has been tightening the rules of contact between men and women. They follow the law of Moses to the letter and add many extra unwritten rules as well."

"But we are friends!" Hannah said. "We're doing nothing wrong."

"Nonetheless, if I walk by one day without acknowledging you, it will be nothing personal."

"It must be difficult for you. As king, you made the rules. As the high priest, others tell you what you must do."

A ruckus at the gate drew Hyrcanus's attention. Hannah followed him as he stepped quickly to see what situation his guards were dealing with.

A man waved frantically toward Hyrcanus. "They're coming here, I tell you!"

"Who is coming here?" Hyrcanus asked.

"The Romans!" the man explained. "I rode all night to tell you. Antipater failed to send the necessary tribute and General Crassus is coming to claim it from the Temple."

Hyrcanus stopped in his tracks. "No! Even Pompey didn't touch the gold here. This place is sacred. Surely you are mistaken."

"I sat at their fire in Syria less than a fortnight ago. They have been marching hard and have passed through Jericho already."

Hyrcanus knuckled his chin and grabbed hold of his own beard. "Crassus already has more than enough gold. His defeat of Spartacus has given him lands and wealth greater than most could dream. Why hasn't Antipater raised the tribute to satisfy him? Why am I in the path of Rome once again?"

Hannah watched as the high priest turned toward an approaching group of the white-robed Sanhedrin.

"The richest man in Rome is coming here!" Hyrcanus shouted. "Why? Because he doesn't yet have enough. He displayed six thousand slaves on crosses outside Rome until they rotted off their spikes. Surely he wouldn't do that here."

"Perhaps he is coming to see the governor," one of the Sanhedrin replied.

Before Hyrcanus could reply, Hannah's attention was drawn to the street outside the Temple. Was that the sound of swords beating on shields? Of hobnailed sandals on pavement?

"Crassus has been appointed governor of Syria and wants wealth to pay for his war against the Parthians," the Sanhedrin spokesperson continued. "He craves the glory of Caesar and Pompey and will not be satisfied until he has it. I would offer gold to preserve the peace."

Only minutes later, Hannah stepped towards the safety of shadows as an imposing Roman general entered the Temple grounds. He paraded toward the middle of the plaza surrounded by dozens of centurions and bodyguards. His broad forehead and large square chin gave him an air of confidence. His piercing eyes appeared to see and know all. His crimson cape and gold-encrusted helmet marked him apart from the lesser officers around him.

"Take me to your Temple!" Crassus shouted.

Hyrcanus stepped forward and attempted to nod in deference. Two bodyguards grabbed him and forced him to his knees.

Crassus had no patience for him. "To the Temple!"

The guards turned Hyrcanus and forced him toward the Temple doors.

"I can only enter once a year for atonement," Hyrcanus said.

"Pompey told me about all the gold you've stored inside," the general barked. "Today, I need that gold. My men will relieve you of everything you don't need and take everything I do need. Tell your people to stand aside or I shall crucify every man, woman, and child in this city."

Hannah watched helplessly as the army of Romans used spears, daggers, and swords to tear off every gold item attached to the building and complex. The silver was snatched as well and loaded onto carts. It pained her to see these sacred items tossed upon the growing pile like discarded trash.

When it was done, Crassus marched again to the center of the plaza. "Take me to your god! Pompey failed to find him, but I will succeed where he came up short. Where have you hidden him?"

Hyrcanus bowed before him. "Our god has no form and cannot be seen by mortals. He is a spirit."

Crassus stepped toward Hyrcanus with his sword raised but stopped at the signal of a warrior near him. The general turned, conferred with a few advisors, then signaled the men to move the carts out.

In moments, the ravishing of the Holy Place was complete.

Hannah curled up on her reed mat like an infant, trembling. The rape of the Temple unleashed dark feelings inside her gut. No one held her down, but her limbs felt tied and unable to move. Once again she'd been helpless to resist.

She felt a strange sisterly bond to this place, connecting her in some fashion to the God of Israel. This unseen host knew her pain and loss. She stretched out her hand, touched the wall nearest, and felt a sudden tremor. Her eyes widened in surprise at the unmistakable sensation.

"I will stay here until I die," she whispered into the gloom.

* * *

The view from the top of the Mount of Olives soothed Simeon's spirit as the sun unleashed its healing rays. He'd never been so alone, yet he felt right at home. For forty years he had embraced life. Nonetheless, his hands were empty. Baruch was gone, Trophina had proven an empty pursuit, and Hannah seemed well beyond his reach.

Twice he had penetrated the security around Trophina's home to catch her eye. Her smile drew him like nothing else.

He passed a note to her a second time as well, only to have her uncle snatch it from her hands and tear it to pieces. The guards had chased after him that day, but he slipped away.

The itch in his hand had been replaced by a deep ache in his heart. Love was not his to have.

He'd hunkered down among a group of scholars translating Hebrew scrolls into the language of the Hellenists. Two hundred years ago, the seventy-two rabbis in Alexandria had made these holy words accessible to the common people; their miraculous effort to bring the Torah to contemporary life had been done in seventy days.

Simeon had been working on the Isaiah scroll, painstakingly copying it letter by letter. As he worked by candlelight in an underground cave near the Temple, it felt like it would take seventy years.

His passion for the Messiah only grew as the words flowed under his pen. Isaiah's Messiah seemed to be different than the one projected by his fellow scholars. Truths began to rise up from the text. The Messiah would be born of a virgin and bring light to the northern tribes of Zebulun and Naphtali. He would be a son entitled as the Almighty God. He would come from Judah, through Jesse and David.

A messenger interrupted his ponderings by handing him a piece of vellum. "A message from the high priest."

Simeon unrolled the small scroll and scanned it. The news was bad: Hannah was ill and wanted to see him.

He laid aside his special robes and donned a tunic he could run in. Scrambling up the hill toward the Temple left him winded, but he soon staggered to the gate and showed the sentry the velum note to gain entrance.

"Take me to the woman who begs for my prayer," he said.

A priest in training took him to a set of rooms at the side of the Temple plaza. "She is feverish and calls for you. The high priest has tried to minister to her, but she wants you."

A woman knelt beside the bed with a cool cloth on Hannah's face. She looked frail and withered, as wrinkled as a prune.

"Take her into the sunlight."

Two young men dragged her mat out to the porch where the rays of light still reached.

"More cool water," Simeon said to the woman.

As she left, he knelt and placed a hand on Hannah's forehead. It was hot, yet she shivered. Her teeth chattered and she reached a hand toward him.

"Pray for me," she said.

He knelt, hands raised toward the heavens. "O King of the universe," he began. "O Sovereign of your people. O Lord of this Temple and those who worship here. Your daughter is sick unto death with no other hope but you." He laid a hand on her head. "Ha'Shem, Isaiah saw your glory in this place. We believe the Messiah will once again reveal your glory here. Now, for your glory, and the good of this daughter of yours, spare her life, heal her fever, raise her up to health and strength. Show yourself mighty again."

Several of the attending priests echoed their amens, but nothing happened. Hannah groaned as the woman caring for her placed a cool cloth on her head again.

Simeon put his forehead to the ground. "Raise her up! Raise her up!"

He remained in that position interceding in ways he had never done before, refusing to give up. And as he prayed, a gentle hand stroked the back of his head. He kept praying.

A voice whispered in his ear: "Your prayers have been heard."

He pulled back on his haunches and stared into the face of Hannah. She knelt before him, smiling with her hands held out.

"He is here," she said, tears flowing down her face. "He is here, and he hears your prayers."

Ignoring Temple protocol, Simeon crawled forward and hugged her hard, rocking back and forth. "Thank you, thank you, thank you…"

When Hyrcanus arrived on the scene, he called for assistance. "Bring food. Bring wine! Today we celebrate a miracle in the house of Ha'Shem."

Later that night, Simeon stumbled into his own room feeling overwhelmed with the goodness and grace of the Almighty. Overcome with joy at being reunited with his friend, he chanted psalm after psalm until the darkness faded to morning and the scroll of Isaiah called him back again.

The very first section of the book proclaimed how the Messiah would cause the deaf to hear and the blind to see. Surely the age of the Messiah was near!

He promised himself that he would visit Hannah each afternoon and share the things he had learned. She would yet come to believe and embrace the faith of the Messiah.

\* \* \*

Hannah continued to chop vegetables in the Temple kitchen as Simeon rattled on and on about what he had discovered in his studies. He was like a child unleashing secrets held inside for so long. She smiled as he spoke of his confusion as to whether the Messiah would be a glorious king or humble servant, or whether there were two Messiahs. One seemed to be a compassionate healer who demonstrated the glory of Ha'Shem while the other seemed destined to be beaten and even tortured and killed.

On one of Simeon's rants, Hyrcanus stopped to listen, nodding at each point.

The high priest finally held up his hand. "You speak of confusion, my son. Your problem is that you don't realize the idea of a suffering Messiah is the picture of our nation under the hand of the Almighty. Have we not suffered and shown this picture to be true in us?" He turned toward the Temple itself. "The hope of a conquering Messiah who will rescue us has disappeared like the gold from our Temple. It is the one teaching that made us shine with hope and reflected our former glory. Now we are decimated and left to struggle under the hand of those who care nothing for what this sacred place stands for."

Each evening, as the weather permitted, Hannah sat with her back against the wall in the courtyard. She looked up at the stars, the same stars she remembered watching as a child with her father.

"Ha'Shem," she dared to pray one night. "Ha'Shem, I desire only to live in your house, to be all you want me to be. Satisfy my desire for love with yourself."

A strange shiver curled its way up her spine and settled in her shoulders. She shook and a feeling of intense warmth, like a hug from a father, enveloped her. It was enough. She looked one last time to the stars, watched a meteor race above the hills, and settled in for the best sleep she'd had in years.

Her work in the Temple changed. Adjusting the shoes of the righteous was a delight most days. Sweeping the dust of the plaza was an exercise in peace and opportunity for praise. A young priest took her on as a student and taught her psalms to sing. Meanwhile, Simeon continued to engage her with his thoughts of the Messiah from the Isaiah scroll he was translating. On occasion, he even dialogued with her about which word might catch the best nuance of what the author was saying.

One day she noticed a pair of turtledoves nesting on the ledge where she had once hidden from the Romans. When they laid eggs, she set her ladder and hovered over them like a mother hen. When the hatchlings emerged, another priest engaged her in a dialogue about the squeakers—or squabs, as they were called.

Sometimes a little excitement disturbed the oasis. There was the day when a demoniac snuffed around on his hands and knees barking like a dog, chewing on the sandals Hannah had carefully arranged. His strength had been incredible and it took a dozen men to wrestle him back out of the gates. For hours he had hurled large boulders over the walls; one of them had nearly crushed Hannah.

Vendors began to set up shop alongside the perimeter of the Temple plaza, selling pigeons or sheep for offerings, exchanging money for Jews from other lands, and trading in icons or carvings to make a living. The commerce made it easier for worshippers to get what they wanted without the rabble of uncircumcised vendors hawking food, clothing, and artifacts outside.

The house of Ha'Shem had been stripped of its gold and silver, but it now felt like a haven of comfort and luxury. Hannah had found her family, and her Creator had found her.

CHAPTER TEN

# THE PROCURATOR

*39 years before Messiah (45 BC)*

Phineas, the Pharisees' new head rabbi, hovered over Simeon as the last letters of the Isaiah scroll dried. It was the third scroll Simeon had written out, yet each copy of the prophet's words left him with a sense of new revelation.

Lingering clouds of frankincense lay thick in the enclosed cave complex. The strategically placed smoking pots countered the sweat of unwashed humanity. Workmen involved in the Temple reconstruction continued to wrestle stones into shape above them and pilgrims from all over the known world stopped by to express their curiosity at the den of scholars hunched over their quills.

"Do you see this part?" Simeon said to Phineas, using a wooden pointer. "It's as if the prophet thinks the Messiah will be crucified. Do you see the detail of suffering he includes? How can he know of such things so many years before men died this way?" He stared hard at the words. "And how can the Messiah save us all if he is to die? It almost appears that the prophet says he will see the light of life again. Can such things be? Can a man die and live again before the day of resurrection at the end of time?"

"You ask good questions, ones that are worthy of our council debate," Phineas said. "We will consider it tonight, right after we consider the promotion of Antipater to become procurator of Judea. Julius Caesar has been named the sole dictator of Rome and some are hailing him as a god. The battle for power in Rome seems to be over and we're about to find our fate in the hands of a new warlord."

"Antipater is to be procurator? What has he done to manipulate someone like Caesar to receive such an honor?" Simeon asked. "Antipater will bleed us dry to satisfy his thirst. But how can he pry more shekels out of our empty pockets?"

"Antipater fought to save Caesar and he makes a great show of his scars from that battle. The Romans fawn over him as if he's on the way to becoming a god himself." Phineas sighed. "But the news gets worse. Antipater has promoted his own sons to serve as governors. Phaesel is governor over Yerushalayim and Herod is governor over the Galil. Those two neck-breakers are the very ones tasked with taking every shekel you dare to earn."

Simeon chuckled. "It's a good thing then that you have so few shekels to pass on to us in our work. I'm sure the nobility, not to mention the Sadducees, will have to carry us until Rome's hunger is satiated. Perhaps you can raise our pay so we don't make it so hard on these poor rich folk." He lowered his head. "May Ha'Shem guard your back from the Roman whip. May he guard your hands from the claws of Antipater and his sons."

"You asked how Antipater won his position," Phineas said. "He did it strategically. You and I both know that Antipater promised his undying loyalty to Pompey when he came through here." Phineas picked up an orange from a counter and held it high. "But when Antipater saw that Caesar would defeat the great Pompey, he shifted his allegiance." He moved the orange to the other hand. "While Caesar was trapped in Alexandria, Antipater pursued alliances to gather thirteen thousand men and rescue him. For his valor, Caesar gave him Roman citizenship, freed him from taxes for life, and declared his eternal friendship and support. Antipater also gained the prize he had maneuvered to possess: our land."

"So we've gone from the Hasmoneans, who aren't from the line of David, to Idumeans, who definitely aren't from the line of David," Simeon mused. "Will he dare to make himself a king?"

"Of course! Why else would a slithering rodent like him climb to the top of the garbage heap? Keep your eyes and ears open. I've already heard rebels make plans for what might happen next."

Simeon let out a long sigh. "Perhaps the Messiah will usher in a new era."

Phineas gripped Simeon's shoulder and gave him a pat on the back. "Ha'Shem raises men up and takes them down at his own good pleasure. If we focus on preserving his word for future generations, they too will one day see his goodness and glory." He leaned closer to the scroll. "This copy looks dry. Roll it up and take it to the rabbi at the synagogue. He will ensure that it gets to a learning center where it is needed most."

Simeon rolled up the scroll. "I can't tell you how blessed I've been to focus on this scroll. It keeps my mind off other things."

"Trouble with women?" Phineas asked.

"One for sure. I had my eye on a young girl who's way above my class or status. My heart led me where the rest of me couldn't go."

"Can I help you with anything?"

"Do you know of any widows who might be looking for companionship?" Simeon asked. "To be honest, I'm lonely."

"What came of your quest for the governor's niece?" Phineas asked.

Simeon smiled. "That's the one girl I was talking about. You know she was raised to be a queen. Look at me. What would I do if I had to share a meal with Antipater at the governor's table, all dressed in the finery of the wealthy? I love my rags."

"What about that woman in the Temple who came from your village?"

"She has set her mind on serving Ha'Shem alone," Simeon answered. "She has found her home and will remain as a friend… well, she's more like a sister to me."

"I know of someone," Phineas said. "A priest's daughter named Deborah. Her husband perished in the last skirmish, the one when your mentor Baruch died. She's still of the age to bear children and her husband had no brothers to act as her kinsmen-redeemer. Perhaps you can play that role for her and be her companion as well."

"I will trust your judgment," Simeon said. "Only do not wait too long."

\* \* \*

Among the wonders of life in the Temple was the diversity of worshippers who found their way onto the grounds. Hannah soon became familiar with a particular newcomer from Gaul. From the very first moment he doffed his sandals and allowed her to straighten them as he washed his feet, this young man was chatty.

"My gracious woman," he said. "What penance are you offering to perform the task of a slave when you are clearly a woman of noble blood?"

Hannah sat back on her haunches and adjusted her head covering. "Shalom to you, my good sir," she said. "My name is Hannah and I serve willingly, under no compulsion or penance."

He was tall, lean, and weatherworn. His sandals spoke of some familiarity with wealth.

"I am Pharos," he said. "I have come from accompanying Julius Caesar to the ends of the earth, where we invaded a place called Britannia. I even rode in one of the barbarian's war chariots with horses that galloped faster than lightning. We took five legions, two thousand cavalry, and eight hundred ships."

Hannah adjusted a few more sandals. "This place is a house of peace. There's no need to bring your conquering attitude into our presence. Ha'Shem raises up leaders and takes them down as he pleases. Why have you come?"

Pharos sat on the ledge of the pool and soaked his feet. "I'm not sure. I encountered a worshipper of the unseen god who was a slave assigned to row. He bowed in prayer and served without complaint. I inquired of his faith and he told me many stories about this land, this people, and this Temple. I came expecting to find something magnificent, but it has no special majesty of its own."

"General Crassus stripped it bare to pay for his war with the Parthians," Hannah informed him. "It is not the gold which determines the grandeur of the almighty One who brought his people to this land."

"Perhaps Crassus invited the wrath of your deity. Besides, he has been killed in his war with the Parthians, just as Pompey was killed in his opposition to Caesar. I will tread carefully while I'm here."

"Tell me about the place you discovered with Caesar," Hannah said. "There are few who speak to me of life beyond these walls."

Pharos nodded. "When we landed on the island of Britannia, it was the middle of the night. We marched inland until we encountered enemy forces at a river crossing. About forty of our ships had been damaged badly in a storm. We repaired the fleet and built a fortified camp only to hear the news that Caesar's own daughter had died." He pulled his feet out of the water but continued to sit on the ledge. "Caesar mourned her loss but finally led us into the battle at the river. Our cavalry beat back the forces opposing us, but they used their four thousand chariots and knowledge of the land to slow us down. We used a war elephant to circumvent their defences and they ran."

"What are the people like?"

"Near the coast, they are barbarians, much like the Gauls," Pharos said. "Inland I saw people covered in blue and dressed in animal skins, living off milk and meat. They have long hair with every part of their body shaved except their heads and upper lip. They share their women and raise their children as a village. They are a strange people." He pointed to a scar on his arm. "I got this wound on our last day there. These warriors drove around in chariots, keeping no order and attacking from all directions, screaming and driving into our ranks. When they penetrated our formation, they jumped off their mounts and fought us hand to hand."

"It must be frightening to encounter such strange peoples," Hannah said.

"I seek to understand all peoples. After this, I shall go to the Persians and even Indians to record their beliefs. If you can take me to your high priest, I will record the beliefs of the Jews. We Romans seek to understand all those we conquer."

A strong urging to explore outside these walls pulled at Hannah's heart. "Will you return to this Britannia? It seems dangerous."

Pharos stood, stretched, and waited for Hannah to join him as she pointed toward the residence of Hyrcanus.

"If you are searching for knowledge of what we believe," she said, "you need to talk with the high priest."

"Rome searches the world for wealth of all kinds," he replied. "Britannia has people, and we will take them as slaves. Knowledge gives us power over them. They have cattle and iron and tin. They use brass rings for wealth and bartering." He retrieved a small ring from his pocket and handed it to her. "Give that to your money traders and see what they think it's worth. You may keep it in appreciation of our conversation."

She slipped the small ring onto a silver chain someone else had left for her. What a strange world she lived in! Perhaps one day even the barbarians would worship the Creator who cared for the righteous.

\* \* \*

The first time the governor's daughter stepped out of the golden carriage, Simeon was smitten. Salome was twenty years old with golden hair that fell in waves around her shoulders. Her headscarf lay loosely on her bare shoulders and her linen stola snugged tightly to her form. The palla, meant to be worn over her shoulders, was folded neatly over her arm. A string of rubies circled her bronzed neck. She carried herself with the confidence of one who knew she was pleasing to the eye.

Simeon was fifty, but his eye was keen and his step strong from walking up and down the hills around Yerushalayim.

Phineas elbowed him. "Look to the ground, my friend. That's the daughter of Antipater and Cypros. She is here to visit her brother, no doubt to cause more trouble."

"What trouble could such a woman cause for us?"

"She has no morals," Phineas said. "You're old enough to be her father, so don't attract his wrath by looking too long. Men follow her every movement to their own demise."

"I can see why," Simeon said, turning away. "She looks a lot like Trophina when I first met her. I guess I still appreciate beauty when I see it."

As he turned, a messenger raced by holding up a leather scroll.

"Caesar is dead!" he yelled. "Caesar is dead!"

Phineas and Simeon hurried after the messenger as he mounted the podium in the market square. A local official stood beside him and raised his hand for silence.

Once sure that he had the crowd's attention, the messenger delivered his news.

"Caesar is dead. The Roman senators have conspired to eliminate the last of the triumvirate," he shouted for all to hear. "The great conqueror of Gaul has fallen under the dagger of his friends, those determined to protect the Republic. All citizens should remain at peace and go about their business. Caesar is no more!"

"What does this mean for Antipater?" Simeon asked. "He was appointed by Caesar. Without the protection of the Republic, what might happen?"

"If even Caesar can fall under the daggers of his friends, no man is safe," Phineas said. "It's best that we go about our business and avoid the treachery of those who seek to use this time of instability to carry out their plans. Our synagogues and study halls must not be threatened. The Torah must continue to be copied and distributed and studied. While everyone and everything else around us might fall, we must persevere."

"The Parthians may be emboldened to strike in this area again," Simeon said. "They crushed Crassus and his army. Pompey, a formidable force, is gone. And Caesar has been assassinated by his own people. The Parthians will see no one to oppose them."

"Yerushalayim is too valuable to be left to the whims of the Parthians. Don't worry about what you can't change. Focus instead on what you can."

As Simeon turned away from the square, the governor's golden chariot raced by. No doubt Antipater and his beautiful daughter understood their vulnerability in a world without a strong leader. They might not worship the same sovereign as the Jews, but they understood humanity's fickle nature and thirst for power.

"Now aren't you glad you didn't fall under the allure of that temptress, or the one before her?" Phineas said. "Let me take you now to meet the woman I told you would be good for you. She's up the hill at Bethany."

Within an hour, the two men paused at the crest of the Mount of Olives. They looked back over the city. The once green hillside had been covered in countless tombstones.

Phineas pointed toward a section of market stalls. "She'll be among those vendors. You probably won't guess which one she is."

As they neared a canopied booth filled with candles and pottery, a woman stepped from behind the counter and bowed toward Phineas.

"Shalom, my friend," she said.

Deborah was in her late twenties with sturdy shoulders, strong hands, and generous hips, but she knew how to laugh and put a man at ease. She had a habit of brushing her long dark hair away from her face, which only drew attention to her sparkling eyes and flashy smile.

"Phineas, you didn't tell me your friend was such a handsome man," she said as they approached. "I expected a balding greybeard as heavy as a horse."

Phineas laughed and stood to the side as Simeon stepped forward to greet the woman.

"Shalom, Deborah," Simeon said. "I have been called many things, but never a horse. I assure you that my intentions are honorable and respectable. I place myself under Phineas's assessment as to how we will move forward with any relationship you might desire."

Deborah smiled. "Oh, Phineas has sold me on your character, commitment, and competence. I only desire to be protected and provided for, since I have no one else to meet my needs. I can assure you that I know how to care for a man. I don't expect you to raise up my former husband's children. But if you do, I will value your sacrifice."

"This sounds so formal," Phineas said. "Come! Let us share a meal together and get to know each other. Love is more than business."

\* \* \*

Masking the tearing in one's heart can be hard. On the afternoon that Simeon revealed his betrothal and upcoming wedding to Deborah, Hannah watched him walk away. Well, she'd had her turn at a relationship and it was only right that he now have his. He was like a brother, although at times her dreams betrayed that perhaps she might have wished for more.

"Someone you know?" a voice asked from behind her.

It was Pharos—again.

She pivoted slowly. "A childhood friend from my village. He told me about his upcoming betrothal and wedding." She knelt to receive the man's sandals. "I thought you were going on to Persia and India."

Pharos sat on the ledge of the pool and kept his sandals on. "I have been talking with the high priest about your faceless god who is everywhere at once. I can understand why a man like him, who is paid to perform rituals and sacrifices, continues in his craft. What I don't understand is why a woman like you would continue to serve." He pointed at the iron ring still hanging from the chain around her neck. "I gave you something of value which you could turn into a small portion of wealth… and you refuse to use it. Instead you crawl around in the dirt of other men and express a piety I have seen in few other places. What makes you humiliate yourself in this way?"

"Is that what you consider my act of service?" she asked. "Humiliation?"

"What else would you call it? You could leave this all and travel the world. You could start a relationship and experience the love of someone who cares for you. You could dress in finery and know the respect of kings and queens."

"You mock me," she said. "Who would want to build this relationship, to take me traveling, to dress me up in finery, and to parade me before kings and queens?"

Pharos knelt before her. "I would. Come! I will take you to Persia and India. You will see exotic beasts and taste foods you can't even imagine." He reached for her hand. "We will confirm our relationship here and now in your sacred space, and then we can go. Say you wish this to happen."

His eyes pleaded sincerely. His hand trembled only slightly.

A few of the priests and Temple workers had stopped to gaze at the sight of a foreigner kneeling before a lowly servant.

"I cannot," she said quickly. "Our faith doesn't permit us to marry foreigners. I have committed myself to serve in this place. I am needed here."

"I understand what I must do to become ready for you," Pharos said. "I am willing. I have talked to the high priest about converting. Don't give me your answer now. Wait for me to return from my journey and prepare yourself."

He rose and surveyed the gathering group around him.

"Isn't she beautiful? Look after her until I return." Pharos looked deep into her soul and smiled. "Yes, you are beautiful and I shall be yours. First your god shall have me… and then you shall have me."

Hannah was too stunned to say anything. Her fingers brushed self-consciously at her hair. She pulled her head covering tighter and then sank to her knees as Pharos backpedaled through the main gate. Never had she imagined a man might seek to woo her in this fashion.

# CHAPTER ELEVEN
# THE SONS

*34 years until Messiah (40 BC)*

Governor Phasael rearranged the large train of his robe and took his place on the dais before the people of Yerushalayim.

"People of the Temple and those who have chosen to make this great city your home, there are messengers of fear circulating among you. But I call you not to listen to them. When the great Julius Caesar was assassinated by his own friends, some of you feared for what would happen to my father, Antipater." He paced back and forth across the platform. "These daily riots in our streets must stop. We are a city of peace. Return to your Temple and pray for the peace of our nation."

Simeon leaned over to Phineas. "He seems worried."

"Listen!"

Phasael stepped forward and continued his proclamation. "My father failed to see that his heroic actions as a leader might set him up as a target for the usurpers closest to him. He died of poisoning! My brother and I inherited his responsibility to rule this nation. Now you are hearing that Antigonus, the nephew of your own high priest, has offered the Parthians a bribe to help him recapture his family's former kingdom from the Romans."

An assistant bowed before Phasael and held out a scroll. The governor took time to read it. His face blanched.

"What do you think it says?" Simeon asked Phineas.

Before Phineas could reply, the governor began to speak again. "The Parthians have arrived! But don't be worried. Everything is under control. Please return to your place of service and I will sort this out."

"Wasn't Aristobulus and his son Antigonus imprisoned in Rome by General Pompey?" Simeon whispered. "How could they be working with the Parthians to re-establish their kingdom now?"

Phineas pulled Simeon away from the crowd. "That was seventeen years ago. I've heard they hid in Judea somewhere. The Romans think the family is weak and without influence anymore. Aristobulus already tried and failed to regain his rights." He looked around and then pulled Simeon further from the Temple plaza. "He tried again with the help of his brother-in-law but met with no success. Under Antipater and his sons, things have gotten worse for us. I think the people are ready for a return to Hasmonean rule. Antigonus has been rallying the Pharisee leaders to his cause."

"I agree. They're the ones fueling the recent riots. I haven't been able to see Hannah or hear how she's faring in the middle of all this craziness."

"You need to go home and care for your wife," Phineas said. "I'll let you know if you're needed for anything here. Isn't Deborah with child?"

"Yes. She's due any day now." Simeon smiled. "I need to pick up a scroll from the stadium before I go home. I can't believe I'll be a father after all these years. I've never been sure it was a good time to bring children into the world."

"With the Parthians arriving, I hope things don't get worse."

"Why bring the Parthians into this?" Simeon asked. "Rome and Parthia have been fighting for centuries. It won't end well for us Pharisees to be implicated in a failed coup."

"The Parthians are confident after wiping out Crassus and his forty thousand soldiers. They took Syria a month ago. News is that Antigonus has promised them large sums of gold plus five hundred female slaves, one for each of the first five hundred troops to enter Yerushalayim."

The two men stepped out of the hot midday sun into the coolness of the stadium.

"I hope Phasael has hidden his sister," Simeon said. "You have to know those men will be wanting Salome as part of their tribute."

"Don't worry about her," Phineas said. "She fled with her brother Herod some time ago."

Simeon proceeded to roll up his scroll, set aside his writing instruments, and change his garments.

Just then, a Nubian slave arrived and motioned for the men's attention.

"Speak up!" Phineas said.

The slave looked concerned. "Simeon, your wife is struggling in childbirth and calls for your presence."

By the time Simeon walked through the door of his home a few minutes later, two midwives were huddled together in the center of the front room. They looked his way… and then averted their eyes.

"Shalom!" he said. "What's happening?"

"We tried our best," one of the midwives answered.

The sun was high overhead as Simeon rushed to their side. He looked down and discovered a tiny body lying still on the ground. The second midwife was pressing on the baby's chest while the other wiped it clean.

"It refuses to take a breath," the first midwife said. "The others are working with your wife. She has lost a lot of blood in her delivery."

"She'll be okay, won't she?" Simeon asked.

"If you know how to pray, this is a good time. It might be best if you went outside and walked in the garden. There's nothing you can do in here."

He turned toward the garden, but for the first time in his life he couldn't find words for his prayer. Was this how Hannah felt?

The sun had hardly moved when the first wailing began. Every muscle tensed as Simeon sank onto a bench. Was it the baby? Was it Deborah?

He walked to the door, head down as he waited to learn what had happened. A midwife emerged, tears running down her cheeks.

"Deborah is gone," she said. "She asked that we thank you for trying to restore her honor. The little one never did take a breath. We will prepare them both for burial in the tomb of her first husband."

The rabbi arrived shortly thereafter, laid a hand on Simeon's shoulder, and chanted a prayer for the departed.

"The women will wash the bodies and then we will offer our prayers," the rabbi said. "Take something to eat while you wait."

Two bodies encased in shrouds lay in the home, one as small as a melon. Pallbearers soon arrived with a stretcher and placed the two together. The sun had not yet set and the rabbi rushed to complete the rituals.

The walk to the graveside at the Mount of Olives was slow. Simeon walked alongside the donkey cart ferrying the bodies. Below him, Yerushalayim continued to bustle as though nothing had changed.

The service was brief and heart-rending. They each placed rocks as memorials before sharing their final thoughts and offering prayers.

"You would have made a great father," Phineas said as he and Simeon stood by the grave. "Perhaps you will find another to share your love."

"My only desire is for the scrolls and for the Messiah," Simeon said. "Do not tempt me with another."

\* \* \*

Hannah stood in front of the gate leading out of the Temple plaza, blocking the way of the high priest. A dozen members of the white-robed Sanhedrin stood nearby, wringing their hands.

"Don't go, Hyrcanus," she pleaded. "If you go, I know you won't be back."

"Move aside. I'm the high priest and the uncle to Antigonus," Hyrcanus replied. "The Parthians are on his side. They won't harm me. I'm the only one who can resolve this family dispute."

With that, one of the Temple guards took her gently by the elbow and pulled her out of the way.

"This is more than a family dispute," Hannah insisted. "The future of our nation is at risk."

"I'm going to meet with Governor Phasael and the Parthians to explain our cause," Hyrcanus said. "I will encourage them to return home. We have enough trouble without foreigners trying to invade the Temple. If our people are caught between the Romans and the Parthians, none of us will survive."

Before Hyrcanus could depart, however, a messenger stepped through the gate.

"The Parthian general, Barzapharnes, and the Parthian prince Pacorus await you," he announced to Hyrcanus. "News is that Herod has fled to his fort in Masada and left his brother to deal with this conflict. Antigonus Mattathias will also attend you."

"We are in the hands of Ha'Shem," a member of the Sanhedrin moaned.

Hyrcanus joined the messenger and left through the gate as Hannah watched in despair.

Once three nights had come and gone without any word, Hannah knew that the worst had happened.

In the afternoon, she encountered a familiar priest at the gate. He wore the simple tunic of a workman and his head was covered.

As she approached, he knelt to the ground and wept.

"Shalom," said the priest on his knees. "The high priest and I will not be back to serve the people. The Parthians cut off his ears and left him mutilated. Indeed, Hyrcanus has been taken captive to Parthia. They sent me as a witness that Antigonus has been anointed by the Parthians to serve as the new high priest. He will be here once he is purified."

Hannah watched as a member of the Sanhedrin came closer, having overheard the priest's grim tidings.

"And what of Phasael?" the member of the Sanhedrin asked.

The priest shook his head. "I overheard one soldier tell another that Governor Phasael bashed his own head open on the stone wall of the prison cell where they kept him. I don't know if this is so, but I don't think he will be returning to take his place in the city."

After this, the river of worshippers slowed to a trickle. Hannah adjusted her schedule in the coming days to work with a few loyal priests to remove the belongings of Hyrcanus. New furnishings arrived and she helped arrange them in the rooms set aside for Antigonus.

"He will take on the roles of king and high priest again," an elderly priest mused. "The Hasmoneans will restore the glory of our land and purify us from the scourge of the Romans. They may not be of the line of David, but they know how to lead our people."

Hannah continued to arrange a vase of flowers in the corner of the room. "I hear Herod will appeal to the Roman Senate," she said. "The Romans will be only too pleased to find in him a proxy to push the Parthians away from Yerushalayim. With the loss of Crassus, Pompey, and Caesar, they will be looking to renew their glory any way they can."

"You heed the news too much," the priest responded. "Ha'Shem knows how to raise up warriors. He has done it all along and will do it again. This is his Holy Place and he will fight for it."

"I would ignore the news of the day, but it seems I cannot be deaf to those worshippers who whisper prayers about the curse on our land. The famine. The death of children. The restoration of shrines long gone."

"All that will be eliminated soon," the priest said. "Peace will cover this land like an ocean."

"I have a friend who says we will know no true peace until the Messiah comes. He has reviewed the law, the prophets, and the writings... and he is convinced that the time is soon. But it is not now."

"If you're alluding to Simeon, he knows nothing more than to set his pen to copying old manuscripts. We are in a new age, a golden age for our people. We will rule and people from all over the earth will stream to this place for worship."

Hannah leaned back against a counter and smiled. "You speak as if we're still in the days of Solomon. The Temple is little more than a rundown shrine to a forgotten god, and we are little more than housekeepers cleaning up dust. My fear is that Antigonus will only serve to raise the ire of Rome. Soon we may be reduced to nothing but a pile of rubble for the world to pity."

"Speak your blasphemy somewhere else," the priest said. "Antigonus has tried for seventeen years to wrest the throne away from the Idumeans. He has finally succeeded in securing the support of nobles and the Pharisees. We do well to bow with respect when he walks through our gates. He is not only our high priest, but our king as well."

Hannah pointed behind her. "When he enters those gates, I will sweep up his dust in the same way I sweep up the dust of the lowest beggar. All men are alike to me."

"All men except Pharos, you mean. It's been almost five years since that charlatan conned you with his promises of glory. Where is he? Perhaps he found an Indian princess or Persian queen on whom to spend his flirtations."

"Save your cruelty for those who deserve it," Hannah said. "I have suffered enough at the hands of men and don't need another to add to my misery. Why do you think I turn my hopes toward the Messiah? If Simeon is right, the Messiah is the only man someone like me can count on."

* * *

Phineas motioned for quiet in the scriptorium where a dozen scribes were busy penning new copies of the sacred texts.

"My brothers in the faith," he called out, "word has come that the Roman Senate has crowned Herod king of Judea. It won't be long until the Romans are back to recover this land. We need to prepare our people for more bloodshed. Antigonus and the Parthians will not go quietly."

"How long do we have?" Simeon asked from his place near the front of the room. "Will we be able to complete these scrolls and hide the worn-out ones? I'm only halfway through my latest Isaiah scroll."

"It will take Herod and the Romans some time to raise an army," Phineas said. "They will travel here and lay siege. We will be fortunate if the city isn't reduced to rubble again. Finish the scrolls you're working on and then take them to where they're most needed."

Once out in the sunshine again, Simeon turned his eyes to the slopes of the Mount of Olives where Deborah and the stillborn child had been laid to rest. At the end of his time on earth, when it was his turn to take a last breath, there would be no one to mourn him, no one to remember him.

He sighed and turned his steps toward Bethlehem. The synagogue there needed a new scroll.

One of the shorter scrolls he had copied held a prophecy that Bethlehem would be the birthplace of the Messiah. For that reason alone, he had volunteered for the task of delivering this latest scroll. It was such a small and insignificant place. Clearly no place fit for a king.

Nothing made sense anymore. If Antigonus remained king and raised his offspring to succeed him, then the king would be Hasmonean, not Davidic. If Herod rallied the wrath of Rome and regained the throne of Judea, then the king would be Idumean, not Davidic. What hope did his people have to throw off the might of either Parthia or Rome? And why would either king choose to have their son born in Bethlehem?

The dust kicked up in little puffs as he made his way over the last hill and looked down on the town below. Shepherds strolled along the side of the road, pushing their flocks toward Yerushalayim. Passover would soon be here again and the new high priest would need lambs to slaughter, in order for Ha'Shem to overlook the sins of the people.

A young woman nursing a child at the side of the road smiled kindly as he passed. Could this little one be the Messiah?

Images unfolded like a scroll before him. A virgin. A child who was called Almighty Father. A suffering servant. A king. A healer. A prince of peace.

Oh, how he needed peace.

The rabbi at the synagogue in Bethlehem rose from his seat on a boulder to greet Simeon as he entered.

"Shalom, teacher," the rabbi said. "Have you brought us the scroll we requested?"

"Shalom, rabbi. I copied it myself," Simeon said. "We heard that Herod and Antigonus may clash for the throne soon and didn't want your people to do without."

"We are waiting for the birth of Messiah. Most of the scholars who used to visit us have given up on the prophecy. They no longer envision us playing an important role in our people's history. The lands of David still await an heir to claim them."

"I see that the fields are rich again with wheat and barley," Simeon said, pulling the scroll out of the bag he carried. "The recent famine reminded me of the times of Naomi and Ruth, when they suffered so much. Perhaps a new Boaz will arise to restore Bethlehem to the place of our nation's breadbasket."

The old rabbi chuckled. "It would take a miracle of Ha'Shem to bring people back to this place. All the young leave as soon as they find work elsewhere. The allure of Yerushalayim is too strong. Few of us are left to dream of what might have been if the Messiah had come as prophesied."

Simeon handed over the scroll and waited as the rabbi unrolled it.

"You have captured the words of the Holy One with the hand of a master," the man said. "Come inside! We will share tea and bread before you journey home again."

CHAPTER TWELVE

# HEROD

*29 years until Messiah (35 BC)*

By the time the five-month siege ended, the supporters of Antigonus had battled hard. The Romans had pressed them into the inner courtyard of the Temple where Antigonus eventually stood amongst the dead and dying, flashing his sword, determined to hold the glory of his dynasty.

In the end, his efforts were no match for the might of seasoned legionnaires thirsty for blood. The wrath of Herod was savage against the people he sought to rule.

Hannah, hiding on her ledge, saw it all. She would never forget the words of Herod ringing in her ears as he surged through the gate to finish it: "Bring me that reprobate Antigonus! Take him to Antioch and sever that rebellious head from his shoulders. Then crucify what's left of him. This is the last Hasmonean monarch, the end of a dynasty of pitiful fools."

The smell of blood singed the air as Romans took liberties to throw the bodies of priests onto the altars where sheep and cattle were usually sacrificed. The old priest who had demonstrated confidence in Antigonus and mocked Hannah about Pharos had been among them. She had covered her ears as they dragged him screaming from his hiding place behind the pillars of the portico.

"No Idumean will sit on the throne of David," the old priest shouted. "Ha'Shem sends a curse on you! Unleash me, you ungodly filth!"

When the shouting, screaming, clashing of swords, and smoking altars had finally ceased, Hannah raised her head, numbed her heart, lowered her ladder, and refreshed her efforts at scrubbing the red from the marble tiles. Others had already removed the bodies, but the death masks of previous calamities rose up to haunt her in her attempts at sleep—especially the face of Baruch, Simeon's mentor.

Three younger women joined her, scrubbing away the stains and remnants of battle. Men carted off weapons, broken furniture, and the huge stones that had been hurled against the Temple. The glory of the limestone house of worship had gone up with the last smoke.

"Why are men so intent on violence?" one of the three women asked. "What is this evil lust for power? Surely the Messiah will not leave us soaked in blood like this."

Simeon's overseer, Phineas, stopped by with food for the workers and sat on the portico stairs with Hannah as she ate.

"Simeon sent me to see that you are alive," he said. "It must be hard for you to see this place of purity and peace desecrated over and over by foreigners. How you've lived through so many conflicts in this place, I can't fathom." He handed her a gourd of diluted wine. "From the outside, we could see that this end was inevitable. The Parthians were struggling to hold so much territory so far from home. It seems the nation with the most gold attracts the most mercenaries, and in turn the most territory."

He sighed and rested his head on the knuckles of his hands.

Hannah handed the gourd back to Phineas. "The last I heard, Herod was besieged in Masada, Hyrcanus had been killed by the Parthians, and Phasael had killed himself in prison."

"And I heard Herod escaped to Petra," Phineas said, drinking deeply. "The Nabateans wouldn't help him, so he went to visit his ally Cleopatra in Egypt. When she tired of him, he pressed on to Rome, where Marc Antony convinced the senate to announce Herod as king of the Jews. To Antony, Herod is no more than another pawn."

But Hannah was barely listening. "Look at this Temple," she lamented. "Who would want to be king of this? What worshipper will ever come this way again?"

"Come with me!" Phineas urged. "Simeon has agreed to help you find lodging, and he'll care for your needs. You've served in this place longer than anyone could ask. It's time to find yourself a home."

Hannah shook her head. "I have served here almost forty years. I've seen the Temple's glory stripped away, just as my own was stripped from me. I've seen the violence and savagery of men who care so little for that service." She surveyed the ruins around her. "Someone has to stay and preserve what glory remains. I feel a kinship with this place, so I'll sweep the dust of the righteous until there are no more righteous."

Reaching for her broom, she smiled.

"Thank Simeon," she added. "Tell him that my memories of him have carried me through many dark days. I only hope his dream of the Messiah comes true while I'm still here."

\* \* \*

On his way from meeting with Hannah, Phineas dropped by Simeon's home in Bethany.

"Shalom, my friend," Phineas said, huffing and bending over to catch his breath. "That climb up the Mount of Olives is getting harder every year." He collapsed onto a padded chair. "I've just come from the Temple. Hannah passes along her greetings."

He relayed the details of their conversation to Simeon. Afterward the two men shared their admiration for such a woman as Hannah, who never wavered under the terrors around her.

When Phineas had regained his strength, he rose and paced back and forth across the small sitting room. "I have another reason for coming. I've made contact with a new group of freedom fighters called the zealots. One of their leaders is coming from the Galil to inform us of what Herod has been doing up there. It might prepare us for what that scoundrel might do down here."

While they ate, a newcomer joined them. The man appeared to slip in like a phantom and stood with his back to the door. He wore a cap down over his eyes and a scarf that filled in the space between his bushy red beard and his eyes. His broad shoulders and large hands gave the impression that he could wrestle a bull to the ground.

"Shalom, Japheth," said Phineas. "How was your trip from the Galil?"

"By the mercy of Ha'Shem, I am here," Japheth replied. "The Roman presence is heavy along the way. There are many checkpoints! But at least the bandits are few."

Phineas arranged a tray of dates, nuts, figs, cheese, and flatbread. He laid the food down in front of Simeon and Japheth, then poured cups of tea.

"I'm glad you are safe," Phineas said. "It's good to take the role of a servant. We must humble ourselves and release any temptation for power, wealth, or prominence. Such idols are worse for us than the shrines of the godless who have surrounded our city for generations past."

Japheth nodded solemnly. "I recently heard the news that a Roman general, Publius Bassus, drove the head of the Roman spear into the gut of the Parthian forces in Syria. The Parthians may have crowned their king here in Yerushalayim, but they never had the desire or resources to provide for him. Besides, the infighting among the Parthians left them unfocused and vulnerable. They found themselves overextended and lost battle after battle to Antony. They tried to mount a defence, but with their Prince Pacorus killed and their leadership in tatters they wisely retreated from Judea. As a result, Herod was able to ride into the city on a white steed. He looked like a conquering hero even though the Romans were the ones to do the hard work."

"Herod did some of his own work," Phineas allowed. "He landed at Ptolemais and made war in Galilee. He took Jaffa and then rescued his family at Masada. Rumor has it that the family would have died of thirst in that siege if a rainstorm hadn't come…"

"Are you saying the Almighty worked a miracle to preserve the family of this Idumean imposter?" Japheth asked.

"Guard your tongue." Phineas glanced around the room and moved his bench closer. "We are under new leadership now. Spies are everywhere, rooting out rebellion. The freedom we thought was small is even smaller now."

Silence reigned for a few uncomfortable moments.

"So many things went against Herod. He was ambushed by Antigonus's trained assassins. Then the Roman troops rebelled against being commanded by an Idumean. How did he turn all that around?"

"He united the soldiers by focusing them on an easier target," Phineas said. "They were given the task of eliminating all the bandits of Galilee, Samaria, and Judea. And they could keep all the wealth they captured." He refilled Simeon's cup of tea and helped himself to a fig. "I think Antigonus felt overconfident. He thought that he was holding Herod at bay, but by venturing out to fight the Romans in Jericho and Samaria he made himself vulnerable. His defeats discouraged his supporters…" He trailed off, sounding contemplative. "Last winter was hard for us, waiting for Herod to attack. So many chose to leave Yerushalayim in order to save their families. Antigonus didn't keep any of us here against our will. I think he expected Ha'Shem to provide another miracle to save us."

Simeon stood and looked out a window at the remains of the city. "I guess we both know that miracle never came."

"Upon his arrival outside Yerushalayim, Herod had thirty thousand men under his command," Phineas continued as if uninterrupted. "He pitched his tent in the exact same spot as General Pompey twenty-six years ago, north of the Temple. As he waited, more Roman legions arrived to support him." He frowned, as though lost in memory. "Those Roman engineers are so efficient.

They built that wall of circumvallation… cutting us off from support… cutting us off from escape. They stripped the countryside of trees and set up those ghastly siege towers and terrible machines …"

Simeon nodded. "Herod knew it was our sabbatical year and that we had no extra crops to rely upon. He starved us into weakness. I watched as our men ambushed those soldiers who tried to scale the walls, or even those miners who tried tunnelling under them. It took them forty days to breach our outer wall and another fifteen days to get through the inner wall. Not long after, the Temple fell."

"We are fortunate to be alive," Phineas said. "Antigonus always said that Herod is a common Idumean who doesn't understand the proper rites and rituals of the Temple. Well, that fox had a plan. Herod ignored those who hid in the citadel, inner court, and upper city. Instead he marched straight to the Temple, bringing sheep and bulls for the sacrifices as a way to boost his popularity. Once he'd done that, he released the troops to slaughter the populace without mercy."

"He is a cunning one," Japheth agreed. "You're fortunate to have escaped. And I hear you're expanding the tunnel network under the Temple."

"That's a secret we tell no one," Phineas said. "With Herod taking control of the land, it's more important than ever that the work continues. Some of us are using quills and others are using spades."

Simon turned to Phineas. "But I'm glad you knew about the tunnels. We were able to save hundreds of people down there." Through the window, he turned his gaze toward the Temple. "I still don't know how Hannah managed to survive again. It's as if Ha'Shem covers her with his hand, just as he did with Moses in the cleft of the rock."

Phineas washed his hands, shook them vigorously, and then dried them on his robe. "She may need more miracles still. I'm told that Herod is publicly executing anyone connected to the Hasmonean dynasty, whether they be descendants or sympathizers. Hannah has been serving them in the Temple for forty years!"

"I'll take your report back to the Galil," Japheth said as he got ready to depart. "Besides, the hand of Herod seems to be too strong to stop at this point."

* * *

It wasn't long before Herod, the new king of the Jews, arrived in a golden carriage to inspect what remained of the Temple. This was the very man whose father had pronounced Hannah's death sentence so long ago. He walked through the rubble and destruction his troops had caused.

"What glory is there in such ruins?" Herod asked aloud to anyone who would listen. "I will rebuild it so the world will know there is a king in Judea."

Hannah knelt with her nose to the marble floor, cracked and misshapen from the heavy bombardment. The king passed her by without a word.

"Yes, I will rebuild the walls," Herod pronounced. "I'll create a plaza for millions to gather and raise up a Temple worthy of the greatest of gods!"

In the coming weeks, it became clear what Herod's priorities would be. His engineers destroyed what was left of the citadel built by the Hasmoneans. He seemed determined to eliminate all traces of his predecessors.

"We will build the Antonia fortress to house Roman troops in honor of my benefactor, Antony," he announced on another visit to the Temple. "Those who remain alive will pay their fair share of taxes so our nation can be strong and proud again. We will not be ruled by weaklings who have no will to overcome the challenges in our world."

Some days later, Hannah witnessed an Egyptian engineer fall from the scaffolding while overseeing the construction of a new tower. Severely injured, he found himself under her compassionate care. He lay stretched out on a reed mat on the small section of the portico that remained intact.

"Tell me what you're building," Hannah said to him as she handed over a platter of food and a cup of tea.

"We're building a tower to the greatest man who ever lived," the engineer replied. "To Mark Antony."

He shoveled the food into his mouth as if he hadn't eaten for a week.

"Do you know this man personally?" Hannah asked.

The Egyptian shook his head and spoke through his full mouth. "Antony rules Rome with Octavian and has taken our Queen Cleopatra as his lover. They have three children. They've even deified themselves! Antony has claimed the role of Osiris and Cleopatra has claimed the role of Isis." He smiled at a memory. "You should see them parading their three children as if they were little gods. They also paraded Caesarion, Cleopatra's son by Julius Caesar. These gods and goddesses have me so confused, though. It's hard to keep track of who is who!"

"That's why it's nice to have one God," Hannah told him. "We know exactly who he is and what he expects of us."

"I've walked through your god's house. No one's here! If he is, then he is faceless and powerless against the might of Rome."

"You must admit the same is true of your gods in Egypt. If you know your nation's history, our people once served yours. For four hundred years, in fact.

Then it was one of our sons, adopted by your Queen Hatshepsut, who became a great leader and confronted your gods with miracles that nearly destroyed your country." She refilled his tea and set it before him. "One day a leader seems invincible and the next day he is dead. You must know this from watching the Romans. Only a God beyond the limits of time and space can continue unchanged and unchallenged."

"How does a woman who sweeps floors know so much about the world of the gods?" the engineer asked.

"I have a friend who has taught me to read the scrolls of our God," she said. "I only know what I see written. Ha'Shem also speaks to me in ways I do not understand."

"You are a prophetess then? How much do you know?"

Hannah sighed. "If only I knew more. At one time, I tried to stop believing. So many things in life had gone wrong. Somehow I ended up here in the Temple with no choice but to face those who still believed despite everything falling down around them."

She took away the empty tray and mug and set it on a counter. But before long, she returned to perching on a stool.

"Someone once told me there are millions of gods in the world and we have stopped believing in most of them," she continued. "When you realize that you already disbelieve in most gods, it's not hard to stop believing in the rest. My problem is the one God who won't let me stop believing. He keeps showing up in my life."

"Which is easier? To stop believing in the gods you do see or to start believing in the one you don't?" The engineer sighed. "At least the gods I do see give gifts I can appreciate. Did you know that our Queen Cleopatra begged Julius Caesar for the right to rule your country? He refused her. Now Antony has given the city of Jericho to Cleopatra as a gift. She wanted to control the plantations of persimmons. She says the perfume drives men wild."

Hannah stood and moved her stool out of the direct sunlight. "I spoke with a trader from Jericho who said that Cleopatra was going to lease the land back to Herod for two hundred talents. For Herod, it was the groves of balsam trees he loved…"

She returned to his ministrations.

"You rest here and I'll be back to feed you," Hannah said as she stood to leave. "I have some sweeping to do. It looks like the worshippers are beginning to return."

\* \* \*

With Herod in the city, the network of hidden shafts under the city took on new urgency. Men had been digging into the heart of the Temple Mount for the better part of a decade for such a time as this.

"None of us can trust that dark heart of his," Phineas said to Simeon as they watched from inside one of the tunnels. He watched the secret door, hidden behind a movable bookshelf, that led into the scriptorium. Men with spades were sliding in and sealing it again behind them.

They moved slowly through the tunnels, picking their way through the dark until they reached a junction located beneath the house of Phineas.

Four dozen Pharisees soon joined them, the blackness of the tunnel wrapped around them all like a cold shroud. There was not a shred of light or noise.

Leading up to this secret meeting, each of them had been drifting through the city in disguise, listening to the talk of people in the markets, in gathering places, and along the outskirts of the Temple.

One by one they had accessed the shafts today and found their way to this junction. The men sat shoulder to shoulder in this cramped space, concealed behind the older man's living room. A single table loaded with a pile of wooden trays, and two chairs in the center, were the only furniture.

"What's Herod up to?" Phineas asked.

"I think he's trying to destroy the last of the Hasmoneans so no one can contest the throne," Simeon replied. "Word is that he killed off one of his wives, Mariamne, as well as her two sons, her grandfather, and her mother. I've heard the tyrant has had eight wives and fourteen children, so I hope the rest are okay. Herod is paranoid."

"And once he's done erasing the Hasmoneans, do you think we might be able to breathe easier and get back to the markets and synagogues?" one of the Pharisees asked.

Phineas bolted the door leading to his living room. He grasped the shoulder of a young man he'd brought with him. "Tomorrow we'll send Hosea to the market for supplies. He used to be a house slave and knows the vendors. He'll buy what we need and find out what we need to concern ourselves with."

After dismissing Hosea to bring food for the men, Phineas hobbled to the table and distributed the stack of wooden platters.

Simeon sat down at the table. "What's wrong with your leg? I haven't noticed you limping so much before."

"Age is an unkind master," Phineas said, grimacing. "I was knocked down some stairs this morning by a mob panicking when the king's soldiers charged up the street toward us. A trader threw me into his cart and helped me get away. I've had worse bumps and bruises."

"I wish I knew where Herod stood about us," Simeon said. "With the Hasmoneans, we knew our place. If Herod restores the Sanhedrin, we should be okay. I think he's furious that he can have the kingship but not the high priesthood."

# CHAPTER THIRTEEN
# OCTAVIAN

*24 years until Messiah—(30 BC)*

Joshua ben Fabus stood barefoot in the middle of the Temple plaza, surveying all he could see. Herod had appointed him the new high priest, replacing Ananelus. His generous girth, jovial spirit, and hopeful demeanor marked him as a natural representative to oversee the Temple sacrifices and rituals.

Hannah had liked him instantly and set her heart to serve.

This week, she had drawn laundry duty. For some reason, the garments unique to the high priest could only be handled by a Levite assigned to the task.

She laid out the sacred garments for him. It was amazing how special cloth could transform a man and impact the deference of those who encountered him. The new priestly tunic covering the big man's body resembled a small tent. Its embroidery and the priestly sash were intricately sewn in blue, purple and scarlet. The majestic high turban, with its broad, flat top, had taken weeks of winding and unwinding and rewinding for her to learn its proper shape. Overtop of the tunic was the sleeveless blue robe, its lower hem fringed with golden bells and pomegranate-shaped tassels. The ephod was a richly embroidered vest with two onyx gemstones on the shoulders and the engraved names of the twelve tribes. A breastplate with twelve fixed gemstones, each engraved with a different tribal name, had a pouch where the urim and thummim nestled. On the front of the turban, a golden plate was etched with the words "Holiness to YHWH."

Fabus's predecessor, although a priest, had not been a member of the Hasmonean lineage. Indeed, Babylonian blood had run deep in Ananelus's veins. He'd served only one year.

Ananelus himself had been the replacement for a Hasmonean who had eventually proved to be too popular with the people. Herod had ordered this Hasmonean drowned in the ritual pools at a time of day when he'd thought there to be no witnesses.

Of course, Hannah knew that a few had seen the act—and a few had talked. The incident had only added to her mistrust of Herod.

Anaelus's last act had been to prepare and sacrifice seven red heifers in a Mosaic ritual which had continued unbroken from the time of Ezra. This ritual of cleansing demanded a perfect heifer that had never been yoked. It involved the collecting of ashes, a ritual bath, the washing of robes, and the passing of time. People defiled by contact with a dead body had to be purified by applying these ashes, which were added to the water of cleansing. A stream of soldiers, vendors, and traders made regular use of the ceremonial cleansing.

"Why do you go through so much to serve?" Hannah asked one of the assistant priests who helped clean the altars.

The young man adjusted his head covering and tugged on his short beard. "We priests see the world differently, I guess. We believe we have to maintain the sacrifices and rituals in the Temple to ensure God's blessing and protection of this land. It's our duty to ensure everything is done right so we'll have abundance and security. The prayers and practices of an impure priest would count for nothing. The whole land would suffer."

Hannah set her broom aside and sat on a bench. "Don't you think Ha'Shem knows the hearts of the righteous? Surely he hears even the prayers of those who aren't priests."

The young man tugged on his beard again. "Priests are trained to make decisions around law, tradition, health, literature, and justice. We are proud to be who we are, descendants of Aaron, the brother of Moses. Perhaps you should talk to some of the Levites to find out why they serve." He waved at two youths who stood near the Temple gate. "Those descendants of Levi clean the Temple like you. They slaughter animals for us and perform the worship music in our services. We work closely as a team because we understand our roles."

"If the sacred writings clearly declare that an offspring of Aaron must bear the office of high priest, how can Herod or others appoint unqualified men?" Hannah asked. "For example, if a priest must be at least twenty years of age and of Aaronic descent, how did Aristobulus, a Hasmonean, take on the role when he was seventeen?"

The young man swiveled his neck quickly. "I need to return to my duties. It may not be a good idea to ask too many questions around here. The high priest is going to be anointed and I have the oil. Be careful of what you speak…"

After he had hurried away, Hannah heard a man's voice speak to her from behind.

"He is right, you know," the voice said. She turned and realized it was Phineas. "Soon only the Sanhedrin will be able to appoint the high priest. The high priest is expected to be superior to all others in wisdom, dignity, wealth, and body. He will no longer be able to mingle with the common people and must never be seen unrobed by simple folks like us."

Phineas stepped in front of the bench and sat beside her.

"From this day on, he will not be able to assist in the burying of his own family members," he continued. "While he is mourning, he may not leave this place. He cannot cut his hair or leave it unkempt. He will work hard to spend his time in the sanctuary and may even serve here more than you from now on."

"Where is Fabus's wife?" Hannah asked. "I can show her the quarters and let her know how the routines work around here."

"Herod has promised to build new quarters for the high priest when he refurbishes the Temple," Phineas said. "Perhaps he will be merciful and build a decent space for all those who have dedicated their lives to service. But once this king starts the reconstruction, I'm not sure where people like you will stay. If you change your mind about leaving the Temple, Simeon and I have extra rooms in our home. He's moved in with me now that my wife has passed. He sets aside his own home for special business."

Hannah chuckled. "Yes, I can see it now. All you two men want is your own private housekeeper, cooking your meals, cleaning your feet and clothes, making it seem like there's someone waiting for you at the end of the day."

"Simeon would really enjoy the companionship," Phineas remarked. "I'm afraid he works far too many hours on those scrolls. He talks more and more about the coming of the Messiah. I don't think he'll find peace until then."

"With an Idumean on the throne killing everyone he considers a threat, how can we ever welcome a Messiah?" Hannah asked. "Isn't the Messiah a priest and king who saves us all?"

"You should talk with Simeon about that," Phineas said. "He's thought about that question more than all of us."

\* \* \*

Japheth sat cross-legged on the cushion in Simeon's main room with his back against the wall. He'd gained considerable weight since his last trip from Galilee, but on this day he seemed flexible enough to remain comfortable. Before him, a tray overflowed with a lamb shank, a stack of flatbread, cubes of cheese, a few dates, and chopped cucumbers, figs, and various vegetables, betraying why the man had grown so large.

"Do you have any goat's milk left?" he called to Simeon.

Simeon looked up from the scroll he was bent over. "I think you finished all we had. You may have to walk to the market to see if they still have some at this time of day."

"I couldn't move another stride," Japheth said. "I've ridden twelve hours from Joppa, stopping only to change horses and get water. I overheard a sailor sharing news you needed to know."

"You should share it with Phineas." Simeon refocused on the letter his pen formed. "We're a long way from Joppa and it's not likely anyone followed you."

"One of Herod's spies from Galilee would recognize me, and you know it. It's a crazy world out there. Octavian eliminated Lepidus from the triumvirate and then went after Antony and Cleopatra." He shoved another handful of bread into his mouth and talked around it. "Antony divorced Octavian's sister and enraged him. Then Octavian went after Cleopatra, who was Antony's lover, to seek revenge."

"Antony and Cleopatra," Simeon mused. "Why would those two join forces?"

"Simple. Cleopatra thought Antony could help her regain all the land from the Ptolemaic kingdom, including Judea. And Antony needed Egypt's resources to help him in his battles against the Parthians."

"Didn't I hear that Antony pronounced her Queen of Kings and her son as King of Kings?" Simeon asked.

Japheth nodded. "Yes. That was Julius Caesar's son. And meanwhile Octavian thought Antony had sold out the Roman Empire and was giving territory over to the Greeks."

"I hope they don't bring their war here," Simeon mumbled.

"I don't think it's possible," Japheth said. "Antony and Cleopatra committed suicide."

Simeon sat up, fully alert, and spun on his stool. "How did that happen?"

"Octavian landed in Alexandria after beating Antony and Cleopatra in a naval battle. Finding themselves cornered, Antony fell on his sword and Cleopatra let an asp bite her."

"That means Herod will be going after Jericho," Simeon said. "He'll want to reclaim the city from Cleopatra. We've got to warn the Pharisees there that trouble is coming."

"Don't look at me," Japheth said. "I fought these occupiers all I could. I've seen too many of my friends hang on crosses. All you have to do is to look at my condition to see that I can't make the journey."

Simeon rushed out the door into the street. Where was Phineas? He would know what to do.

He began to search for the man, making his way down the Mount of Olives toward the Temple and the weaver's shop where his mentor often travelled. The weaver assured Simeon that he'd seen Phineas only an hour earlier.

Simeon almost missed the old man lying comfortably in the back of a donkey cart near the market.

"Phineas! We've got trouble," he said. "How's that leg of yours?"

The old man sat up. "Shalom to you, too." He pulled up the edge of his tunic to reveal purple splotches just above his sandal. "I was favoring my knee and ended up twisting my ankle... what seems to be the trouble?"

"That looks painful." But Simeon was forced to change the subject. "Japheth has arrived from Galilee with news that Antony and Cleopatra have committed suicide and Herod will soon be waging war on Jericho to reclaim it. We need to warn the synagogue there."

"As you can see from the swelling of my leg, it looks like you're on your own," Phineas said. "There's a horse at the stable, owned by the baker. He uses it for quick runs down to Jericho. Although the Romans patrol that road at this time of day."

"If not during the day, when? You expect me to ride alone through a dark canyon filled with bandits who would lop my head off for a shekel?"

"It seems that you're the one determined to warn everyone," Phineas said. "You could send a vellum message with the next caravan or trader heading that way."

"It may be too late by then." Simeon paced back and forth beside the cart, stopping to look toward the stable. "Do you think the baker would mind if I borrowed his horse one time?"

"He owes me a few favors," Phineas said. "Tell the stableboy you're taking the horse on an errand for Phineas. That should ease your trouble."

Phineas's name worked like an amulet at a pagan shrine.

In no time, Simeon was on the horse and hanging on for dear life as they charged out of Yerushalayim. Twice he bit his tongue when he left his mouth open too long.

A Roman soldier on the road raised his sword in warning—but his gladius was still in the air when Simeon raced by, and none of the soldier's shouts did anything to slow him down.

The cobblestones were soon behind him and the dusty dirt paths ahead.

* * *

Hannah shouldered her way through the crowd of priests and worshippers standing on the portico overlooking the valley. An endless stream of men was marching up the road. Even more were digging their way through the fields around the city.

"Is it a siege?" someone asked.

"No! Herod has decided to rebuild the whole Temple Mount," a workman answered. "I heard he's bringing in ten thousand men to double the size of the gathering space. I'm one of the engineers, but most of the architects are from Greece, Rome, and Egypt."

"Does he expect all seven million Jews here at once? Where are they going to get the stone?"

The engineer turned and pointed up the hill. "Chiseled into blocks from the top of the Mount and hauled down with oxen. We'll have to build some retaining walls first."

This explanation caught one priest's attention. "You're going to chisel out a Temple from the mountain, like in Petra?"

"No. This mountain was chosen by Ha'Shem for a reason. It has horizontal layers of limestone perfect for shaping and severing. We have the best minds in the world figuring out how to get this done."

A member of the Sanhedrin stepped forward. "Only priests are permitted to work on this holy site," he said. "None of those foreigners will be permitted inside... on penalty of death."

The engineer raised his hand in a calming motion. "Shalom, my friend. Of course only priests will work on this site. The rest will prepare the limestone so the priests have something to work with. Priests have their skill and we have ours. Together we'll fashion this into one of the wonders of the world."

"We won't stop our sacrifices for any building project, certainly not on account of the king's ego," the Sanhedrin member said. "If Herod expects us to interrupt our traditions and rituals, he can build his Temple on another hill."

"Don't worry. You won't have to stop a thing. Your own priests will lay the stones and can figure out the best time to get things done." The engineer cleared his throat. "Now, I should get my hammer and chisel before I miss my shift."

Hannah stepped forward. "Will those of us who occupy the residential quarters have to move out?"

"Not at all. We'll try to stay out of your way."

"'We'll try to stay out of your way,'" mimicked the Sanhedrin member as the engineer headed for the gate. "I say we hire some sentries to make sure they keep out of our way. This Idumean king can't qualify himself to be high priest, so he draws attention to himself by building a Temple even he can't enter? What sense is that?"

"Imagine the taxes we'll have to pay," a worshipper said. "My grandchildren's grandchildren will be paying taxes for it... if we're all still alive by then."

* * *

Simeon and Phineas stood to the side of the worksite upon the Temple Mount. Thousands of stonecutters were chiseling out channels in the blocks of limestone with pickaxes. Some used chisels to square off blocks while others hammered dried blocks of wood into grooves. Still others poured water over the wood.

As Simeon watched, he couldn't help but reflect on his recent return from Jericho. Thanks to his warning, the Pharisees there had relocated three weeks before Herod's soldiers locked the city down. The purge of Cleopatra's supporters had passed like an angel of death over the synagogue.

Simeon had been relieved to get back to the relative safety of the scriptorium in Yerushalayim. Somehow they would live under the new tyrant.

"What are they trying to do?" Simeon asked as he watched the workmen.

Phineas lifted his cane and pointed toward a large stone being pulled off its foundation by a team of eight oxen. "The water they pour onto that wood in channels swells the wood so the force of the expansion severs the stone from its foundation. The large blocks of limestone produced are a thousand times the weight of a man, true, yet between the strength of those oxen and the gravity of rolling them along logs, they move downhill with little trouble."

"Why are they leaving those nodules on the side of each block?" Simeon asked. "Won't that make them hard to fit together later?"

"They'll remove those projections," Phineas said. "Watch the wooden cranes with winches... right there, by the cart. The workmen fasten ropes around the projections, the cranes pick up the stone, and then they load it onto the cart for transport. The two cranes move larger stones onto the log rollers... and the oxen? Well, they number at least a thousand." He hobbled around a team of oxen being hitched behind a large block. "They have to keep some oxen hitched to help restrain the momentum. Can you imagine if one of these boulders got loose on this downhill slope?"

"I sure wouldn't want to get in the way of that," Simeon said. "Remember the earthquake last year? It felt like chunks of limestone were raining down on us." He shivered at the memory. "I notice that the walls are about five strides thick. I don't think any army or earthquake could ever break through that."

"It looks like Herod intends to build retaining walls thick enough to hold all the fill for the platform he's going to raise," Phineas said. "The platform will be about five hundred strides wide and thirty strides long. Look at that monstrous stone! Fifteen strides long and four strides thick… and more than twice my height…"

Simeon let out a low whistle. "It's almost enough to make you feel like this place will be an impenetrable fortress. I wonder if Ha'Shem is happy with such extravagance?"

"Herod is building this monument so people will notice him."

"You'll have to give a talk to our group about how Ha'Shem has plans for us just like these architects have plans for the Temple."

"I think the prophet Jeremiah already covered that," Phineas said. "Anyway, it's time for you to share your own insights. You're a teacher who knows the Scriptures. You've learned enough about life to apply it."

As the two men crossed in front of a large block about to be moved, a workman shouted a warning. Phineas planted his cane and swiveled slowly in place. Just then, the ground rumbled.

Simeon watched in horror as the stone fell toward them, picking up speed. Four oxen harnessed to the limestone were crushed, yet still it descended. He backpedaled out of the way, but Phineas tripped over his cane and fell into the path of the rock.

The mountain erupted in chaos. Workmen and oxen further upslope dug in, doing everything they could to slow the stone's momentum, but it wasn't enough.

Half of Phineas's elderly body was crushed before the rock finally came to a stop.

Simeon rushed to his mentor's side, along with several of the workmen. The old man's eyes were wide and his mouth open.

"Hear, O Israel, the Lord your God, the Lord is One," Phineas gasped, his eyes bulging toward Simeon. "You must finish the work…"

Blood spurted from his mouth and then he went limp.

"Move the stone!" Simeon shouted. "Move the stone!"

A workman pulled him away from his mentor's body. "It's too late," the man murmured in regret. "It's too late…"

# CHAPTER FOURTEEN

# THE TEMPLE

*19 years until Messiah (25 BC)*

The priests, adorned in linen robes and tubular hats, scurried over the Temple site like ants at a picnic. Curiosity seekers from across the Roman Empire gawked at the massive walls forming a foundation under the new plaza. Thousands of vendors hawked their wares, sold souvenirs and curios, exchanged money, and showed off the animals they had for sacrifices. Young men offered themselves as guides to the complex.

In all this, Hannah found it harder and harder to guard her privacy. With her return to faith, she had slowly instituted the practices she learned from the new priests. One of the latest involved ritual washings for purification. After each monthly cycle, women had to immerse themselves unclothed in a pool to demonstrate their cleansing. The new mikveh pool in the Temple residential complex was tiled and ready for use.

She had been about to use the mikveh in the residential quarters when a group of sightseers barged in through the door. Fortunately, she was still holding onto her towel. She covered herself and backed into a changing room amidst the raucous calls of a few men. Next time she would post a guard at the entrance.

Similar complaints had arisen from other women tasked with cleaning the purification pools. Without modesty, men had been plunging into these bodies of water to fulfill their cleansing rites. The only logical solution would involve having two separate pools.

When a priest marched out with a ram's horn and blew the shofar, Hannah jumped. She'd forgotten it was Rosh Hashanah. By the time the priests had completed the full 101 shrill blasts of the shofar, she was so used to the sound that she hardly turned to glance toward them.

As she watched, two young priests then stopped in the middle of the plaza and began to debate each other on when it was proper to blow the horn.

"The blast should be blown during the first standing prayer," one argued.

"No longer," the other said. "That hasn't been true since those worshippers were killed for blowing the ram's horn and people thought was a war cry. Now we are to give the shofar one long blast, three short blasts, and then another long blast three times a day during Rosh Hashanah."

The first one seemed to consider that. "I've been asked to blow the shofar next year. I have this year to learn it. Thirty blasts to obey Ha'Shem's commandment right after Torah readings; this is our mikveh, our good deed. Then I am supposed to recite two blessings, followed by three blasts of three. Then we blow thirty more blasts during the silent prayer, while standing, and ten more blasts after each of the three main blessings. I think we finish with ten or eleven blasts. It's a very complicated part of our worship, requiring great dedication."

"And don't forget to blow your blasts with a single breath," the other priest said. "Rosh Hashanah is a day for blowing the horn and we must all excel at it. Some of the blasts are meant to sound like moaning, others like whimpering."

Hannah stepped forward, catching their attention.

"Why do you blow a hundred blasts?" she asked. "It seems like one or two should be loud enough to get our attention."

The older of the two initiates turned to her and spoke as though a teacher to a student. "We blow a hundred blasts to correspond with the number of tears shed by Sisera's mother when her son was killed in battle. Each shofar blast nullifies one of her tears of hatred toward us. Sometimes we leave one tear uncovered to recognize the pain she suffered in her loss."

After offering this instruction, the man stood as if waiting for praise.

"It's also a wake-up call to remind our nation of our need to repent and turn back to Ha'Shem," the other added. "Sometimes the blasts of mourning impact our minds, causing us to relive the grief of what happens when we go our own way. Sometimes they impact our heart and allow us to feel the losses of others in our common bond before the Almighty."

"You are proving to be worthy students," Hannah said. "The worshippers will be well served."

The two lifted their chins higher and proudly strolled back toward the lecture hall for more learning.

On another morning, immediately following a Sabbath, Hannah took up her post to arrange the sandals of the righteous. A young man released his sandals but remained standing in front of her. She sat back and waited, but he didn't move.

Looking up, she saw the man's beaming smile erupt from a black face.

"Shalom! You are doubtless the one," the man said.

"Shalom," she said. "I am only the one who serves."

"Are you the one who captured the heart of my master, Pharos?" he asked. "Yes, I can see it. You are the one."

Hannah hung her head. "He captured my heart and took it away with him. Do not plague me with news of him."

"My name is Melchior," he said. "Pharos was captured by pirates and imprisoned. He has leprosy now but longs to return to you with a crown and jewels. He is alone, disfigured, and ashamed of his lot."

Hannah gazed at the man's face. "I have no words."

Melchior pulled out a leather pouch. "There is no crown, but he sends you rubies and sapphires from his treasury. He asks that you restore your comfort and find the peace and rest you need. Take this as his offering and demonstration of love."

Tears streamed down Hannah's cheeks. She bent over and sobbed, her shoulders shaking. Deep moans escaped from within as she collapsed on her side and curled into the fetal position.

Melchior crouched beside her and uttered soothing whispers. "Shalom, my lady. Shalom."

Others began to gather around.

"What have you done to her?" a priest shouted. "Leave her alone."

"I have done nothing but share news of a friend," Melchior said.

"What have you got in your hand?" the priest continued.

"They are her jewels. A gift from a friend."

"Let me see that…"

A scuffle ensued during which the priest accused Melchior of being a thief. Hannah uncurled and stood in time to witness a dozen men holding the foreign visitor down, pummeling him.

"Stop!" she shouted. "This man is no thief. He is a friend who came to comfort me."

Slowly, the men stepped away from Melchior. His nose was smashed and bled. His lip was swelling along with one eye.

"Shame on you," Hannah continued. "Leave him alone. Where are his jewels?"

The men stood around with open hands, shaking their heads.

"There are no jewels," the first priest said. "Perhaps he is a thief and a liar."

Hannah escorted Melchior back to the residential area and attended to his wounds. "I am so grieved that you experienced violence in our Holy Place," she said.

She placed a cool cloth over his swollen eye.

Melchior smiled feebly. "It is not the first time I have faced misunderstanding and trouble. Pharos truly did send those jewels for you. I have nothing else left to give. Perhaps your guardians can track down whoever stole them by finding the one who would seek to sell such luxuries."

"Ha'Shem knows," Hannah said. "I was going to tell you to give the jewels to the orphans and widows you know. I have everything I need here and the worshippers often drop coins I can use for my food."

"You are a noble woman," Melchior said. "Pharos is right to speak so highly of you. I will return and share your heart with him. My master will be happy to hear of you before he dies."

Hannah stood up and stepped in front of a window through which she could look out over the city below. "Throughout my life I have known loss after loss, yet I am full because Ha'Shem sees me and knows me. One day he will send his Messiah to overcome all injustice and oppression. Do not lose faith because of the deeds of a few greedy men."

Melchior wiped at his swollen lip. "When I'm tempted to lose faith, I'll think of you," he said. "I will return to my country and share the news of this house where you serve."

Hannah turned toward him. "Don't speak of the house or the servant of the house. Speak of the one who lives to demonstrate grace and compassion to his people."

Melchior rose and stood at the doorway. "I hope you recover some of those jewels," he said. "I must go. May peace find you when you need it most."

* * *

The period of mourning for Phineas had ended too quickly for Simeon. His world had darkened, his desires for life withered, his hope for the Messiah dwindled. For five years he had hidden away in a darkened tunnel without picking up a pen to write out a manuscript. He'd spared no dream for the Messiah or thought of the outside world. After a short time, most of the Pharisees had refocused on their tasks in the scriptorium and synagogues. Only one young man, Nicodemus, committed to staying by Simeon's side to make sure he was fed, washed, and cared for.

One morning, a giant of a man stepped through Simeon's door and knelt beside his reed mat.

"Shalom, my foul-smelling friend," the giant said. "It's Petronius, or has your mind forgotten how I wined and dined you in my home?"

Simeon groaned. "Shalom."

"I heard about the loss of your friend," Petronius said. "When I asked about you, no one had heard anything. I was sure you must have perished. And look at you... you are nothing but skin and bones." The big man slid his arms under Simeon and scooped him up. "There's a pool and fresh tunic with your name on it. It's time that you and the sun got reacquainted."

"Leave me alone," Simeon said, feebly pushing against the giant's arm.

Around the corner from the scriptorium stood a fresh pool, built to welcome newcomers to the city. Without hesitation, Petronius waded in and gently dunked Simeon under the refreshing water. Simeon came up sputtering and hanging on tight.

Twice more the giant dunked the Pharisee until Simeon found enough resiliency to struggle to his feet. Petronius looked around, saw no women of significance, and stripped off Simeon's tunic before he could be stopped.

Simeon's young attendant, who had followed them, held out a fresh tunic. Simeon stumbled to the edge of the pool and slipped it on.

"Sit in the sun and dry yourself," Petronius said. "Your young friend, Nicodemus, happens to be friends with my sister. She insisted I come and find you. I was in Alexandria earning a great profit, but the thought of your sorrow touched me." He nudged Simeon with his elbow and almost knocked the Pharisee back into the water. "I came through Joppa, spent three days negotiating my way to this city on a Phoenician caravan, then started looking for you. While at the Temple, an old woman looking after the sandals told me where to find you. She seemed quite worried that you hadn't seen her in so long."

Nicodemus stepped up and dropped a pair of new sandals alongside Simeon. "This is a gift from the woman at the Temple," said the young man. "She is a prophetess for sure, because she knew you were in distress without me telling. She says that she'll not stop her prayers until she sees your feet in these. I almost persuaded her to leave the Temple to see you in person."

"Your beard looks like a dozen rats have claimed it for a nest." Petronius gently tugged on the side of Simeon's jawline. "At least let my servant give you a massage, clean up that face, and fatten you with something worth eating. I've exchanged all my Greek and Roman coin for your shekels. I've sacrificed a lamb and am ready for a chance to see how this city has changed under your new king."

"What is happening in the world?" Simeon muttered. "I'm too weak to walk anywhere."

Petronius signaled to a nearby carriage. "I'll walk you home and give you an update along the way. Five years is a lot of time to cover.."

Nicodemus helped Simeon into the carriage and Petronius walked alongside as they moved.

"You may not know that Octavian has restored power to the Senate. They now call him Augustus, the first Roman emperor. He's instituted the first imperial census and says there are over four million citizens. I may have inflated the number by constantly moving from one place to another."

"What about what's happening here?" Simeon asked, chewing on a date he'd been given. "What's that old fox Herod up to?"

"First of all, he rebuilt Samaria and named it Sebastia. He's building a new palace not too far from here. He calls it the Herodium."

"And of course he's building the Temple," Simeon prompted.

"Yes, there is that." Petronius halted the carriage outside his home and paid the horseman. "Let's get you cared for. Then we can talk about how you can retake your place in the world. Hannah and my sister will both be glad to know you're much improved."

He helped Simeon dismount and supported his arm as the Pharisee wobbled toward the stairway.

"It looks like we also need to get you to the Temple," Petronius said. " Who knows how many unconfessed sins you have lingering all around you?"

Simeon chuckled. "More than I'd like to admit. Wouldn't it be great if the Messiah could find a way to do away with our sins once and for all? I wonder if that would make a difference in the way we lived…"

"I'm sure a few cows and sheep would be glad for that. Maybe we wouldn't be so poor! The Temple seems to charge more each year for those pure animals. Did you know they've changed the entrances?" He turned and looked back toward the building project. "Now we have to go in through the south side, check our animals, visit a mikveh, then retrieve our animals and proceed up three staircases to get to the main court. I got tired trying to carry that sheep! No wonder so many people are choosing to sacrifice pigeons."

"I see you can still find things to complain about," Simeon said. "What are you going to do when they move the animals closer so you don't have to walk so far?"

"I'll probably complain that the animals make too much noise for me to pray."

"No doubt you'll be among the first ones to set up a market stall to profit off pilgrims." Simeon sighed heavily. "Bring me to that masseuse of yours. I think I'm ready to live again. Besides, I've missed my talks with Hannah."

"For now you have me," Petronius said. "More news. You may have heard that Herod's lust for his beautiful wife Mariamne got him so jealous that he had her executed." The big man pulled out a bench and retrieved a brass chalice of wine for Simeon. "They had five children. He also drowned Mariamne's brother in his pool in Jericho. Their mother Alexandra couldn't forgive that."

"I should have stayed in my room in the dark," Simeon muttered. "Every time I hear this king's name, it's because of a new murder. How did things get so bad?"

"It gets worse. Years ago, when Herod visited Rome, his wife and sister were in such conflict that the king had to separate them. The sister went up to Masada and the wife went to Alexandrium. Herod ordered that his sister should be made queen in the event of his death, and his wife should be murdered."

"I guess that didn't go over well."

Petronius shook his head. "But that's enough for now. You need some rest to further recover…"

* * *

Melchior's news sustained Hannah for weeks, long after he had disappeared from sight. It meant something that Pharos hadn't forgotten her. He still cared. She grieved for his condition and how it separated them. But she had made a vow to Ha'Shem to never leave his house; that vow couldn't be broken.

Opportunities to leave came regularly. When Nicodemus had approached her with news that Simeon was near death in mourning of Phineas, she almost broke down and stepped out of the Temple. Ha'Shem would surely understand such a mission of mercy.

"Just come to share one prayer," Nicodemus had pleaded. "We know you're a prophetess whose words travel straight from your lips to Ha'Shem's ears."

His words hadn't persuaded her.

Some days she hardly had time to sort sandals. One visitor after another asked for prayer, and it wasn't only women who sought her out. They came for prayers—that they might bear children, that their husbands might cease their violence or drunkenness, that their fields would bear fruit, that their children would be healed. Each time they left coins in appreciation which she passed on to those who begged her for food or help of another kind.

The men were few at first, preferring to seek out a priest, but there came a day when the priests were all busy and a trembling man fell on his knees before her, begging for a blessing.

"I have no children and my wife bears the scorn of our village," he said. "Pray for us that we may conceive. I weep from the shame I bring to the one I love."

Her prayer was simple: "May Ha'Shem give you the desires of your heart."

Within three months, the man was back, dancing around the Temple plaza.

"Praise the almighty King of the universe who has granted my desires through the prayers of this prophetess!" he shouted in glee.

Others stopped him to discern the source of his joy. He just pointed at her, attributing the blessing to her prayer.

After that, the number of male seekers almost outnumbered the women.

When Simeon shuffled in one day, with a giant of a man supporting him, Hannah hardly recognized him. His lengthy gray beard was peppered with dark specks and his gait and bony figure belonged on a figure preparing for the grave.

Nicodemus trailed the two men. If he hadn't mouthed the name *Simeon*, she never would have guessed who stood before her.

"Shalom," she said. "It appears you have decided not to walk all the way into that tomb with Phineas. Were you afraid Ha'Shem might not take you, or did you miss our little talks? Perhaps you realized how many sins you needed to confess."

The big man sat Simeon on the edge of the foot-washing pool and helped remove his sandals.

"Thank you, Petronius," Simeon gasped.

"He needs you to pray for his strength before we go for the sacrifices." The man named Petronius turned to her. "It's been years since he's eaten properly."

Hannah sat back on her haunches and addressed her old friend. "Remember the day you met me in the village, Simeon? Everyone we knew had been slaughtered like sheep." She awaited his solemn nod. "You were my strength each night. You pressed on when my mind and heart were shattered. Death did not defeat you then and it won't defeat you now."

Simeon reached out a bony arm and rested it on her shoulder. "You have been my strength each night."

A tear came to her eye and she blinked it away.

"Nicodemus tells me of what you're doing for our people through prayer," Simeon continued. "Many days I have questioned Ha'Shem's wisdom and then thought of what he has brought you through... what he has made you to be. It pulls me back to remember how our nation has been delivered from Egypt, from Babylon, and perhaps one day from Rome." He dropped his hand, breathing heavily. "You know my one desire has always been to see the Messiah. I gave up that dream. But then a vision came to me. I saw your smiling face, remembering those times when I opened the scrolls with you. Yes, Hannah, you and I shared the words of the prophet and I longed for us to do so again. I had to come hear your prayer for me."

"Rest a moment and then finish your sacrifices," Hannah said. "I'll be here every morning and evening until Ha'Shem takes me away. Bring your scrolls and bring your students. We'll have a time of teaching in the Temple courts so everyone will know this dream of our Messiah."

She picked up his sandals and arranged them neatly beside others in their row.

"I'll continue my prayers so you may help us all grow wise in our understanding of what Ha'Shem is doing during this period of pain and suffering."

# CHAPTER FIFTEEN

# COΠSTRUCTIOΠ

*13 years until Messiah (19 BC)*

Forty-three eager students sat erect listening as Simeon unrolled the scroll in the Temple courtyard. Hannah sat on a stool like a proud grandmother watching over her grandchildren. The transformation in the complex around them was stunning compared to how it had looked only a few years ago, especially the Temple building itself.

The last few years had been busy. One thousand priests had been employed as masons and carpenters to work on Herod's masterpiece. Eighteen thousand other workers had buzzed like bees around the hill, chipping out massive blocks of limestone and moving them into place. The monument emerged like a flower out of the rubble and soon towered above gawking pilgrims navigating their way toward the place of sacrifice.

"Impressive, isn't it?" a priest intoned to Hannah, nodding with his chin toward the Temple. "This king wants his legacy to last forever. You should see what he's done near Bethlehem with that place he calls the Herodium. The walls there are twenty times the height of a man." He stopped for a moment to listen to Simeon. But soon he continued. "His fortress at Masada is a master-piece, too, and imagine what he's doing at Caesarea! The Romans have got to be impressed."

"What goes up can come down," Hannah said. "I hear he's also creating Roman baths, a Roman theatre, and all manner of other temples. He hands out honeycomb with one hand while bringing down a whip with the other. Everything he does is for his own glory. It cannot last."

"We'll enjoy it while we can. I've seen the plans drawn by that Egyptian architect, and I think they'll be building here for a hundred years or more. All this building boosts our economy and unites the people. Visitors will soon be streaming here from all over the world."

Hannah sighed. "He's blinded by ambition. One of these days he'll overstep his bounds and there'll be bloodshed again."

"That may be," the priest said, "but I worked as a craftsman on the inner sanctum and it's covered completely in gold. The walls and columns are made of white marble from Greece. The floors are of carrara marble. It almost looks like you're walking on water."

"You're clearly very proud of the work you've been able to do," Hannah said. "I admire your skill and effort. I only hope worshippers will be humble when they come to this place. I trust that when they see this building, they won't focus on its temporal builder but on the one who calls us to meet him here."

The priest nodded. "Well said, my friend. If you stood atop the Mount of Olives right now and looked this way, the sunlight would shine off the gold plates of this building. All the white marble makes the Temple look like a mountain of snow, with the fiery bush of Moses flaming from its heart. It is an impressive sight."

"May it never outshine the Shekina glory of the Almighty," Hannah said. "My name is Hannah and I am a servant of Ha'Shem in this place."

"Shalom, Hannah," the priest said. "I am Zechariah."

Hannah smiled beatifically. "And what does it mean for you to be among the thousand chosen to build this Temple for Herod?"

"It means that I need to get back to work."

As Zechariah turned away, a cacophony of shouts erupted from the gate. The group that had gathered around Simeon to hear his teaching rose as one and moved toward the fracas. Hannah followed along behind, taking the time to find higher ground atop a limestone block not yet fitted into place.

The cause of the disturbance soon became apparent. A cohort of Roman legionnaires formed a phalanx at the entrance of the Temple, pushing members of the Sanhedrin and a group of priests out of their way. Before them, sprawled upon a cart, lay a giant golden eagle of Rome. The procession had halted when the white-robed members of the Sanhedrin had joined arms to establish a blockade.

A centurion arrived on his horse and rode it through the gates. "King Herod has ordered the eagle to be mounted on the Temple. All who delay this project will be killed where they stand."

Promptly the mass of protestors knelt in place, arms interlocked.

The soldiers went to work, prying men from the end of each line and dragging them away.

A few minutes later, someone scaled the outside of the inner wall and yelled to the city below. "They're killing all the protestors! They're killing the protestors!"

Panic spread through the protestors, several of whom broke off in an attempt to run away, as the legionnaires pressed on in their grim duty.

Hannah counted forty-six members of the Sanhedrin who were dragged away and presumably killed. Several priests and a few worshippers also sacrificed themselves.

"Ha'Shem, have mercy on your children," she prayed.

A great wail rose like a pillar of pain from the Temple, reaching toward the heavens. There was no response. No storm clouds. No lightning. No thunder. Instead workmen, worshippers, soldiers, and priests alike looked on as the eagle was mounted.

The sun set and the workmen and soldiers withdrew from the site. Many of the students who had sat quietly in front of Simeon now rallied under the offensive image of the eagle, their passion burning with tangible energy. Within moments they produced a ladder and used it to scale the side of the Temple. They drew up bags of hammers and chisels and began to hack at the golden bird.

When the bird fell and smashed against the marble, the cheer was deafening. The students scrambled down and disappeared into the evening shadows.

By the time the Romans returned, they found their symbol shattered into pieces. Much of it had been hurled over the walls into the valley below.

Hannah sank to her knees and wept.

\* \* \*

Simeon hung his head as the flames surged around his students. The smell of singed flesh mixed with choking smoke and ash. The chains around his wrists and ankles strained as he tried to turn away from the sight and sounds of his friends being burned alive.

Herod had sent his spies out into the population to hunt down those students of the Torah who had smashed the golden eagle. They'd been located hiding in the city of Palms near the remains of the crumbled walls from the days of Joshua. Their trials outside the king's palace in Jericho had been swift and ruthless. Simeon had been discovered hiding, shackled in a cart, and taken down to attend the trial.

"So you strive to be a Torah teacher for the next generation?" Herod had said mockingly to Simeon as he was paraded before the king. "I should have you burned with the rest of the rebels. Instead I'm going to let you watch what happens to those who dare get in my way. If you ever decide to teach again, forget this nonsense of a Messiah. As long as I am king, there will be no Messiah."

No atrocity like this had been seen in Judea before. Forced to watch the fiery crucible, Simeon found his faith withering. Why didn't Ha'Shem show up like he had for the three friends of Daniel when they'd endured the fiery furnace? Had the almighty King of the universe shut his ears to the cries of his children? Had he shut his eyes to their suffering?

Simeon hung in place for a day and a half as the charred bodies smoldered before him. Crowds passed, spitting on him, and on the remains crumpled at each blackened post.

"May your name and the name of your children be wiped from the records of our people," people hissed. "May those who know you forget the day of your birth and curse the day of your death."

Some ruffians took liberties to punch him while the soldiers laughed. He lost four teeth that day from unmerciful knuckles. A few others pulled out handfuls from his beard.

At the end of the ordeal, Herod stood face to face with Simeon and added his own spit to the old man's face.

"You self-righteous hypocrites disgust me," Herod said. "You speak of Ha'Shem as if you own him. As if there is no other god for the nations to bow before. Your small minds focus on scrolls and rules and rituals of the past while the world outside builds toward a future that will move on without you." The king stepped toward a pile of charred remains and spit on that body as well. "Good riddance to those of you who are food for worms and dogs."

The soldiers lay Simeon in the back of a donkey cart headed for Yerushalay-im and released him as the sun set. Stars twinkled above, then receded before the light of the full moon bathed the landscape in silver tones.

Somewhere in the luminous night, the donkey stopped and waited as the chilly darkness surrounded Simeon like a shroud. A group of riders thundering by slowed and approached.

"Shalom. What are you doing here, old man?" One of the riders dismounted and came closer. "It looks like someone has tried to kill you. What happened?"

Simeon rasped out a response. "Herod burned my boys."

"Alive?"

"Yes. For tearing down his eagle at the Temple."

"Then they are heroes," the man said. "Where are you going? A few of us can take you to the capital if you have someplace to stay. I'm sure the Romans will appreciate taking a night off from our ambushes."

The riders moved slowly toward Yerushalayim. It was almost noon when they arrived at the top of the hill overlooking the Temple. By this time the sun had sucked the life from Simeon. His bloody lips had dried, the ache over his eye throbbed, and a searing dagger of pain pulsated in his head.

Pilgrims, vendors, and traders surged by them singing and chanting. But it turned out that coming home was no source of joy.

"Old man, we need to be cautious," the lead rider told him. "The Romans will be looking for us. We'll find a willing pilgrim to take you the rest of the way. May Ha'Shem have mercy on your soul. May he grant power to our hands to avenge your loss."

It wasn't long before just such a pilgrim was located—a young carpenter who agreed to take Simeon the rest of the way.

The carpenter spoke to him like a son. "The Temple is especially bright today, Father. The sun shimmers off the shields of a thousand soldiers standing on the ramparts. Priests stand with trumpets ready to welcome us to prayers. The golden litters of nobles glisten as they parade toward the Temple gates. Priests strain alongside the workers to unload giant ashlars for the next concourse on the retaining wall. The plaza sparkles with marble, enough to blind the eye."

The young man urged his donkey forward. In a spare moment, he reached over and patted Simeon on the shoulder.

"I will take you through the gates as my father and you will guide me to the home where you can be cared for," he said. "It looks like you've been trampled by the chariots in Herod's hippodrome. I love the thrill of the races, but I'm not sure why the unleashing of blood and violence must take a central role in it."

When the donkey cart stopped, Simeon found himself peering up into the face of a Roman legionnaire.

"By the gods, what happened to this man?" the soldier inquired. "It looks like someone prepared him for crucifixion."

"He displeased someone powerful," the carpenter said. "I need to get him home so he can die in peace. We're going to the home of Petronius."

"Proceed! Two shekels for your cart and one shekel for your father."

"I don't know how you sleep at night," the young man murmured. "That's twice the price I paid last time I came through this gate. Where were you born?"

"I'm from Germanica, and I don't set the rates. Someone has to pay for your Temple. Two more years in this stinking place and I can go back to my wife and family."

The carpenter chuckled. "At least you have someone waiting for you. Take an extra shekel so you can buy them something special when you arrive home."

"Thank you, my good man. May whatever gods there be add a blessing to your head. Let me walk in front of you and clear the way."

When the cart turned off the crowded street into a side alley, the carpenter thanked the soldier and completed the journey into the upper city toward Petronius's home.

"My father, we are here," the carpenter said at last.

Simeon sat up and saw the Ethiopian servant he remembered well.

"Who did this to him?" the Ethiopian asked.

"The king!" the carpenter answered.

The Ethiopian shook his head. "I think we better hide him away then. In case anyone asks, forget that you brought him here."

* * *

There were too many sandals to keep up with. Two girls joined Hannah on their knees, helping to maintain order for the faithful. They added to her joy as they sang and chanted Temple songs, chattering away about the young men their eyes had considered that day. In fact these girls were sisters, almond-eyed, raven-haired, and finely figured, orphaned after the recent purge of Simeon's students.

Hannah's withered limbs and aching joints limited her movement, meaning fewer coins were tossed her way. On good days, the two sisters gave her a few extra shekels.

"Thank you, Phoebe. Thank you, Fiona," Hannah said. "May the King of the universe multiply your blessings a thousandfold."

Everything going on at the Temple was an adventure for these girls.

"Auntie Ana," Fiona called to her one morning. "Did you know they're opening up the Hall of Columns tomorrow? Can you imagine so much white marble in one place? One hundred sixty-two towers of beauty in four rows!"

"My name is Hannah," she reminded them.

Fiona seemed confused. "But all the priests call you Ana the prophetess."

"Auntie Hannah," Phoebe said, vying for her attention. "Have you seen the marketplace and synagogue? With all the money we earn, we want to open a stall and sell some of those date cakes you make. Maybe one day we'll be the richest women in Yerushalayim and take a litter all the way to the Great Sea."

"You'll be the most fortunate girls in the world if you find four men able to carry you that far," Hannah said. "Even I haven't been to the Great Sea."

As they finished speaking, a Phoenician man, broad-chested, firm-shouldered, and bronzed by the sun, stopped nearby.

"I heard your dream," the man said. "King Herod is building a harbor which will be one of the wonders of the world. The harbor there can hold three hundred ships! And the theatre can hold three thousand five hundred. The palace and its pool are like nothing you've ever seen. It's built on a projection of land out into the waters and has a gigantic statue in the middle of it all." He glanced around at the hall of pillars. "These are worth seeing as well. They would make a great base for the new aqueduct that runs ten miles from Mount Carmel to the sea."

"A friend of mine once told me about a place called Straton's Tower, somewhere along the coast," Hannah said. "Is this palace close to that?"

The Phoenician rubbed his bald head and furrowed his eyebrows. "I think it's the same place. One of your Hasmonean kings captured it about seventy years ago and used it to expand his shipbuilding. Herod renamed it Caesarea to honor Caesar Augustus. We hold gladiator games and theatre productions every five years. This will be my year to prove myself."

"Why are you here if you have to prove yourself there?" Hannah asked.

"I am Hiram, the dagger of doom," he said. "I'm performing sacrifices at all the temples in the land. I must raise my fortunes with whatever gods might be favorable at this time. It seemed wise to come to this new Temple, but the priests won't let me in. I'm looking for an advocate who will perform the sacrifice for me. These Jews seem very focused on their own sins, and very uninterested in anyone else's."

"Shalom, Hiram," Hannah said. "Why don't you sit with me a while and I can tell you about this one who has chosen this place for himself. The girls can take care of the sandals."

The girls went about their work as Hannah and the Phoenician settled on a bench.

"It seems to me that much of what I see Herod do is a competition with what Cleopatra did in Alexandria," Hiram said. "I heard that he tried to assassinate her once. He seems determined to make a name for himself and ensure no one else interferes with his legacy."

"Ha'Shem is like that with his people," Hannah said. "He is known as the gracious and compassionate One. He gave us laws which reflect his character and he sends us teachers who show us the way to him. This place was chosen by him to provide peace and reconciliation."

"Why does that inner wall say that all foreigners who trespass the barrier will be responsible for their own death?"

"We look forward to a day when a great king will free us from all these barriers and unite us as one people again," Hannah said. "We call him the Messiah, the anointed One."

"Haven't some of your people believed this idea for a long time?"

"I have a friend named Simeon who studies the scrolls of our prophets. He believes we will see this One soon."

"Perhaps when he comes, I can get him to make the sacrifice for me," Hiram said. "It seems a shame to build such a magnificent structure and keep most of the world out of it."

"Go in peace, Hiram. If you survive the games, please take the time to return and I'll tell you when he arrives. I'm sure we will all know when the time comes."

"If you can say a prayer over me, I know I will perform well," Hiram said. "You are a prophetess who speaks words even the Messiah would love to know."

CHAPTER SIXTEEN

# FORTRESSES

*6 years until Messiah (12 BC)*

The trip to Bethlehem refreshed Simeon. He sat by the village well, pondering the distant silhouette of the new palace Herod was building on the plains to the southeast. The Herodium was to be the Idumean's memorial of triumph for his victory over the last Hasmonean king, Antigonus—a reminder to anyone who dared look that no opposition would be tolerated.

A massive contingent of slaves and workers had built a mountain and set the foundation for Herod's palace upon it. It was less than an hour's walk from town. To the residents of Bethlehem, it felt like the dark shadow of this palace could reach out and touch them.

The last scroll Simeon had copied had come from the prophet Micah. It contained the hidden promise telling of the Messiah's coming birth in Bethlehem. As a result, Simeon monthly wandered to the town to speak to the old toothless rabbi. Had there been any boys born from David's line? Were any young women with child?

On his way back to Yerushalayim, Simeon decided to hike up Herod's hill to examine the fortress and palace. The peak provided a breathtaking view of the mountains of Moab to the east and Judean hills to the west. At the top he came to two hundred steps of hewn stone, leading to the double wall that circled the compound; it had four seven-storey towers and a gateway to the northeast. He was told the fortress contained storerooms and reservoirs, bathhouses, a huge theatre, banquet rooms, servant's quarters, and of course the massive palace still under construction.

"Herod's building a tomb for himself," one of the workers said. "He wants to rival the Egyptians with a tower no one can miss."

There were massive pools for collecting water and others for swimming. There were mosaics of grape vines and pomegranates plus dolphin fountains and richly woven Persian carpets. There were stables. Gardens were being planted among tiered levels on the side of the hill and an administrative centre was on the rise with dozens of support buildings.

Everything Herod had built so far was meant to impress and intimidate contenders for the throne.

Afterward Simeon changed his mind and decided to walk back into Bethlehem. Something about his visit to the Herodium had put him in the mood to stop for one last meal with the rabbi at the synagogue.

"If the Messiah is going to be born in your town, Herod isn't going to make it easy," Simeon said. "That is one massive fortress, and it seems that more and more of these fortresses are coming up around the country."

The old rabbi nodded. "You won't have to worry about any Messiah being born here. The young men and women leave Bethlehem only to move to one of Herod's great building projects. They marry those from other cities and never return. Apart from a few shepherds, this doesn't seem to be much of a place to raise a family. The legacy of Boaz, Obed, Jesse, and David will soon be little more than a dream from the ancient scrolls."

Simeon patted the old man's wrist. "Don't be surprised by what Ha'Shem can do. Look what he did for Abraham and Sarah. Consider what he did for Naomi and Ruth."

"May your dreams touch the heart of the Almighty," the rabbi said. "It's time for my nap. Right now, that's about the most important part of my day."

\* \* \*

To the north of the Temple court was a wall dividing Jews from Gentiles. It boasted a sign declaring death to all foreigners who would pass from the outer Gentiles' court into the inner forbidden court reserved for Jews. The wall wasn't high, but it was the most imposing barrier in the complex.

Hannah recoiled at her privileged status; she was able to walk past the desperate men and women who had been born elsewhere. The Gentiles' court was more of a marketplace with stalls operated by vendors who vied for the attention of anyone who hesitated for a moment to pray.

Hannah regularly wandered this court, looking for the return of Hiram the Phoenician. He had triumphed at his first games and returned regularly to seek her prayers before facing his next opponent. He would sit at her feet in the same way students sat at the feet of a rabbi. He absorbed her tales and teachings from the scrolls Simeon brought her way.

Dozens of students now sat before her when she perched on her stool. Some of the rabbis were growing increasingly caustic toward her.

"At least you know enough to keep your tribe outside the forbidden court," one of the rabbis told her. "You're wasting truth on dogs, on the feeble-minded and unworthy. Stick with your prayers and anointings and leave the real work to those who understand it."

The rabbi jutted his chin in the air, wrapped his robe around himself, and marched through the gate into the inner court.

She turned to those nearby. "Now, that's not what you want to be like when you choose to follow Ha'Shem. The Almighty inclines his heart toward the orphan, the widow, and the foreigner. He's done that for me... and he can do that for you."

Just then, Simeon sauntered up and leaned against the far wall facing her. His smirk and smile were distracting, even if his long grey beard and silver curls marked his advanced years.

"My good friend can tell you more about Messiah," she said to her students, gesturing toward Simeon. "He has the best-crafted manuscripts in all of Judea and a mind to match. Feel free to ask him anything you want."

Simeon clutched his scroll and stepped to the front.

"One day the Messiah will come for all of us," he said. "He may tear down this wall of hostility between the outer and inner courts and welcome you all into his family. Please be patient with those who don't know any better. Do what you need in order to become Ha'Shem's adopted sons. Get to know which gate you would like to enter, because there are thirteen gates in total. Four on the south, four on the north, one on the east, and one leading toward the west from the court of the women to the court still reserved for Jewish men." He suddenly turned and indicated the opening in the wall behind them. "This is the Nicanor Gate."

"What do you call the other gates?" a young man called out.

"On the south side, we have the Upper Gate. Then there's the Kindling Gate, where the wood is brought in. The Firstborn Gate is where people bring firstborn animals to sacrifice. Finally we come to the Water Gate, where the libation of water arrives during the Feast of Tabernacles."

"We have a gate for anything and everything," Hannah joked.

Simeon smirked. "On the north side, we have the Jeconiah Gate, where the kings from the line of David enter. Then the Offering Gate, where priests enter with the holy sacrifices. The Women's Gate is where women enter with their offerings and the Song Gate is where the Levites enter with their musical instruments."

A tall Ethiopian craned his neck forward. "What about the gate for foreigners who have sailed across the world to get here?"

"Any Jew, male or female, can walk into the court of the women," Simeon explained. "We even have a barber shop so those who have taken vows can get shaved. You'll see people singing, dancing, and enjoying themselves here. Deeper into the Temple there's another court for men to watch the priests perform sacrifices, and yet another court reserved for priests and Levites."

A tall Arab, his head wrapped with a white turban, stood at the back of the group. "I came from Yemen with a spice caravan to see this great wonder. Now I'm left outside like a dog."

"At least there's a space where we can gather together," Simeon said.

"I didn't come here to gather with you," the Arab said.

"You sure know how to keep people separate from your god," another man said. "Why do you even invite Gentiles when we get stuck in a market street with moneychangers who rob us blind? Then, when we donate money, we can't even get close enough to enjoy the music or the sacrifices. This seems like a moneymaking scheme to me." He stood up and backed away. "Herod worked with the Romans to get the bandits off the roads only to let them set up shop in here. Tell me when things change. Until then, I doubt I'll be back."

Simeon raised a hand. "Things will change when the Messiah comes."

"Is that another moneymaking scheme?" the man called out. "You keep promising everyone that one day we'll all be free in a perfect land. I've been hearing about this Messiah since I was a boy. But no worthy man has stepped up. I'm not telling my children lies anymore."

The man turned and walked away.

When the group had drifted off, Simeon slouched against the wall. Hannah came over and knelt beside him.

"Are these groups of visitors getting to be too much for you?" she asked. "I can get a younger man to handle them."

"No," Simeon said. "This was meant to be a house of prayer for all nations. I understand their frustration with having to stand behind walls in a market, trying to experience a God who seems locked away where no one can reach him. If only he would be the kind of God who walks and talks amongst us."

"We haven't had a recognized prophet for four hundred years. It's almost as if Ha'Shem is sending us back to Egypt where we had no hope. Perhaps we need to cry out for more of his mercy. Do you still believe the Messiah is the answer to our people's every need?"

Simeon nodded. "I'm more convinced than ever."

"And what are you learning these days?" Hannah asked.

He glanced back and forth along the corridor, then leaned forward. "I'm learning something so deep that it scares me," he whispered.

She knelt closer. "You can tell me."

"I've learned the sacred name for Ha'Shem, the one our priests are not to speak aloud. In fact, it's a name we say with every breath."

"What do you mean?"

Simeon sat up straighter. "Breathe out and then in again. In and then out." He waited as she did. "When a child takes his first full breath, he breathes in with *yah* and out with *weh*. Every completed breath is *Yah-weh*. This is the name our teachers forbid us to speak. It's our first breath as creations of Ha'Shem and our last sigh as elders." He struggled to his knees. "I see this embedded on almost every page of the scrolls I copy. Each time I set myself down to copy, I have to take a full bath and use a special pen. I am clean because he has made himself known everywhere."

Hannah helped him to his feet. "So every breath is his life moving through us. He fills us with life all day long. We are his witnesses, whether we realize it or not."

"Keep this to yourself," Simeon said. "There are so many hidden mysteries pulling me to explore them."

"I need to return to the place of sandals," Hannah said. "My girls will be tired after all these hours in the hot sun. They aren't used to the strain of kneeling so long. But please come again and tell me if you have any other insights into when the Messiah will come."

Slipping into the court of the women, Hannah took a moment to observe a circle of women singing and dancing as they moved in an ongoing rhythm of joy. What a difference it made to be one section closer to Ha'Shem's presence!

A young woman reached out, grabbed her hand, and drew her into the circle. For a moment, she felt young again.

When the dance was over, she found the two girls sitting against the foot-washing pool, shading their eyes from the sun. Dozens of sandals lay scattered around. Without a word, she knelt and brought the pairs back into order.

Within moments, the two girls joined her.

"We were thirsty," Phoebe said. "There were too many sandals and no one was leaving us any coins."

"We don't do this service for the coins," Hannah said. "We are the first chance for worshippers to understand that we come to a holy place to serve one greater than us. Many of these men are used to positions of power and influence and their spirits must be humbled before they sacrifice. We show them what humility looks like and don't expect them to give us anything. Whatever comes our way is a gift from Ha'Shem alone."

"Yes, Auntie," Phoebe said. "You are the prophetess. We live by your wisdom."

* * *

Outside the scriptorium, Simeon hesitated at the stall of an olive oil merchant. He needed a new supply for the lamps that burned constantly in the dark inner caves beneath the Temple complex. The cool air provided a good sanctuary for working on the scrolls. Synagogues from around the Great Sea continued to send representatives to claim the masterpieces being produced. The head rabbi from Alexandria had recently arrived to claim all that he could get his hands on.

"There is something about this land," the rabbi said as Simeon held out a tray of dates and figs. "The fruit is sweeter here. The honey creamier. The milk richer. Even your wine has a taste unique among the nations." The rotund man sat on a stool out of the sun and breathed deeply. "Even your air carries the scent of jasmine and orange. There is a reason our Cleopatra craved this land, a reason that Herod fought so hard to keep it out of her hands."

Simeon pulled up a stool across from the rabbi. "Some days it seems as though Herod is bent on choking us all on the dust of his projects. Masada, Antonia, and Herodium are all rising like the cedars of Lebanon—and we have to pay for them."

The rabbi chuckled. "If you think you're paying taxes now, wait until you get the bill for Caesarea. Its port, palace, and fortifications will drain your economy... and it's as pagan a place as you'd ever want to visit. There's a hippodrome for chariot races, not to mention bathhouses, an amphitheater, and a temple built to honor Augustus Caesar."

A younger man with a full dark beard, eyes blazing, stepped closer. "I heard you speak of that cursed place along the sea," he said. "A group of zealous are forming to fight for the Messiah when he comes. We're training with daggers and spears to contend with the Romans when they least expect it. We've heard how the tribes in Germanica ambushed the Roman legions through subterfuge, and we're ready to do our part."

The rabbi from Alexandria checked over his shoulder. "Watch your tongue, young man. Herod has recruited spies through the empire to root out loose lips like yours. You'll find yourself on a cross before you finish your first effort. We have enough rebels training in Alexandria. One day this will all be crushed by the emperor."

"We await the Messiah," the young rebel said. "If either of you hear rumor of his arrival, send for us. You can leave a message at the bakery in the upper city. We're ready at any time, day or night."

The rebel walked away with a swagger. An old beggar sitting on the side of the road fell in behind him.

"There's one of Herod's spies now," the rabbi said to Simeon. "That young zealot won't be free much longer."

"Herod acts like he's dragging us into a new age," Simeon said. "He wants us all to embrace the life, luxury, and thinking of the Greeks and Romans. Too many rabbis have been crucified for trying to stand up against his efforts. Corruption is seeping into the upper classes, even the Sanhedrin."

"If that is so, I'm glad to return to Alexandria," the rabbi said. "Gather the scrolls you have available and I'll leave you to your work. You have a special touch for copying and our library is pleased to have everything you produce."

* * *

The latest high priest, Simon ben Boethus, stood by the foot-washing pool as Hannah arranged his sandals.

"How many years have you served in the Temple now?" he asked.

"I've been here fifty-five years," Hannah said. "I've straightened more sandals than I can imagine counting. The smell of blood from men and animals has saturated the air from the beginning. I don't envy any man tasked with serving as high priest for this king, or these people."

Simon sat on the edge of the pool. "Being Herod's father-in-law hasn't been easy. My daughter's beauty wins his loyalty, but there are enemies who undermine her and the heirs she has produced. One day, people like the king's sister, Salome, will find an ally to end our favor."

"I know you're a supporter of the Sadducees," Hannah said. "I've been aligned with the Pharisees. Will we always be working to destroy each other in this place of peace?"

The high priest turned his back and dipped his feet in the cool waters. "You must understand. Although my school has common roots with the Sadducees, we are not the same. My ancestors taught that we are not to be like servants who serve our masters for the sake of wages; we need to serve without thought of wages." He wrapped his white robes tighter around his legs. "As for you and yours, you live a hard life here at the Temple, hoping for some distant reward. Somehow we must come not to depend on a resurrection or future afterlife. What riches we deserve are riches we must gather now."

"It seems to me that what you gather with one hand, Rome takes from your other hand," Hannah said. "What is this wailing I hear from the Romans these days?"

Simon adjusted his robes and swung his feet out of the pool. "Augustus has proclaimed a month of mourning for Agrippa. The two were agemates who built the empire together. Agrippa won land battles against Pompey and naval battles against Antony and Cleopatra. Without Agrippa, Augustus may not have become the emperor." He motioned for his sandals and waited as Hannah arranged them before him. "He was the best of architects and best of commanders. He served without seeking selfish glory. He fought Germanic tribes, Egyptian rebels, Gauls, and Romans. Anyone who opposed his friend felt the wrath of his spear. He alone modernized the city of Rome and brought water and services to all its citizens without discrimination." The high priest wriggled his feet into the sandals. "A magnificent parade has been organized in his honor and Augustus will place his remains in the emperor's own mausoleum. The emperor has already adopted Agrippa's own sons as his own."

"Wasn't Agrippa the one you sacrificed a hundred oxen for a few years ago?"

"Yes, at the emperor's request and expense," Simon said. "It's called a hecatomb and usually it's offered to the Greek gods. We were honored to be given that task."

"At the time, I thought you were compromising the purpose of our sacrifices," Hannah said. "Isn't he the same Agrippa who mapped out the Roman Empire from one end to the other? I saw a scroll in the hands of one trader who purchased it with his life savings. He vowed to travel to every part of Caesar's world to share its treasures and mysteries."

Simon stood and straightened his robes. "Such a man is free, but he is only free because we have an emperor who has built roads, conquered bandits, spread his mercenaries throughout every nation, and brought us together under one fist. Agrippa was behind so much of that..." He trailed off. "But he died from a winter fever. Even the greatest of men must pass away."

Hannah bowed low. "At such a moment, a man's future is determined by how others speak of his past. May Ha'Shem honor you with his peace as you serve him in humility and truth."

The high priest stepped away before turning back again. "Even though you loiter with the Pharisees, keep your ears open for dissenting voices so our nation can stand against the schemes of our enemies. If we learn to work together, perhaps we won't need to depend on some future Messiah to save us."

CHAPTER SEVENTEEN
# FEVER

*3 years before Messiah (9 BC)*

The scriptorium had become a triage center as fever swept through the Roman legionnaires. In an effort to save healthy soldiers, the centurions in Yerushalayim had taken over the cool underground chambers of the scribes and mandated them to care for the struggling men.

"More casualties!" yelled the centurion who barged towards Simeon. "Find more room at the back—hurry!"

Simeon was supervising the arrangement of supplies as others ferried cool cloths, ointments, herbs, and compresses to the suffering.

"There's room near the place we use for manuscript storage," Simeon said. "There's already forty-three in here. Isn't there another space? What about the hippodrome or the theatre?"

"We would use the Temple if your priests weren't threatening to revolt," the centurion said. "When this is over, we know who we'll be favoring around here."

A seasoned veteran was stretchered into the scriptorium and laid near Simeon.

"Help me!" the veteran croaked. "Water... I'm burning up..."

Simeon surveyed the room in order to assign someone the task of retrieving water, but every scribe was busy assisting someone who was moaning or groaning.

He knelt beside the man. "I'll get you some water. It's okay, you're safe here."

Simeon wandered over to the cupboard where mugs were usually stored, but he found it empty. Every mug had been taken to ferry water to others.

He stopped by the water barrel outside the kitchen area, but it was almost empty.

Motioning to the centurion, Simeon assumed an air of authority. "If your men are going to survive, we need some of your troops to keep this barrel refilled from the reservoir near the Temple. I also need someone to go to the marketplace and bring more mugs and plates. If we're going to save these men, we'll need as much help as you can spare."

"Done!" And with that, the centurion pivoted to address a legionnaire tying up horses nearby. A moment later, that soldier was off to fetch clay mugs and wooden plates.

Simeon snatched up a mug and filled it with water brought in by another soldier on the back of a donkey cart. He took the refreshment to the stricken veteran who had beseeched him only a few minutes ago.

"Here is your water," he said. "What is your name and why are you here?"

The veteran gulped the water greedily and held the mug out for more. After his second cup, he sighed and lay on his back, arm resting on his forehead.

"I am Claudius Tiberius, general of one of the seven legions under Nero Claudius Drusus Germanicus, politician and commander of Roman legions in Germanica. I was with him when we crossed the Rhine and was among the first to reach the Elbe River. We fought the Sicambri, and later the Chatti tribes." He rolled onto his side, groaning. "We were returning triumphant and wealthy from our victories when Drusus fell off his horse, caught a fever, and died. We thought his injuries were sustained from the fall, but when we boarded ship and were sent here I realized we were all becoming feverish." He made a motion for more water. "I'm sure it was those swamps we passed through. Thirty men died on the way here. We've been cursed by the gods of Germanica and need to find a god more powerful to cure us."

Simeon pulled up a stool and slouched down onto it. "The Temple you have come to doesn't contain a god you can appeal to on a whim. He's not like the gods of Germanica or Gaul, who you can defeat or placate. Neither is he like the gods of Rome or Greece, who you can appease with sacrifices and incense. He is the Creator of all the world and he demands complete loyalty to only himself."

"Right now I don't care what he demands," said Claudius. "If he's more powerful than other gods, I'm ready to obey. Only beseech him to release me from this fever."

"I have read the words of this god," Simeon continued. "He claims there is no god before him or after him. He claims to be the only true god who has ever been."

"That is ridiculous. We Romans have gods, the Greeks have gods, the Gauls have gods, the Germans have gods… everyone has gods and none of them claim to be the only one."

"The One who dwells in this Temple claims to be the only One," Simeon said. "He helps only those who put their hope in him. He is the true god of our people and the One who fights for us."

The general groaned. "If I wasn't burning up so bad, I would laugh in your face. Look at the Roman eagle mounted over your gate. The god of Rome, Caesar himself, has conquered your god and proven himself mightier. Your faceless deity is nothing more than the shapeless dreams of your insane prophets." He rolled onto his other side. "Water! I need water. Pay whatever you must, but beseech your god for all of us…"

Simeon retrieved another mug of water and set it near the general's head.

"If this Roman eagle representing the emperor is greater than the god of this Temple, I wouldn't dare insult you by praying to an inferior god," Simeon told him. "When you are well, search for a priest who will slaughter something to cover your own arrogance and curses."

He walked away, the feeble pleas of the general echoing off the walls. It mixed with the groans of a dying cohort of men who had fought so hard to live for the glory of Rome.

\* \* \*

The aging high priest leaned against the wall of the hall of marble pillars observing the worshippers doffing their sandals in front of the two girls who continued to scramble to put them in order. Meanwhile, Hannah stood beside the aging father of the people and waited.

"Our people have had a stormy past in recent years," said Simon ben Boethus. "I think the one lesson I've learned is that we cannot trust even those who worship with us. We entrust knives into the hands of priests because if we allowed them into the hands of those who bow with us, those knives would be used on our own necks. I remember when General Cassius came to this province to collect troops. He demanded such harsh tributes that whole cities were sold into slavery to pay the seven hundred talents he wanted from us."

"I remember those days," Hannah said. "So many of those people begged for relief from Ha'Shem on feast days. The priests here could do nothing to encourage them. The Temple guards had to pull double duty to preserve the few precious items we had left in case worshippers turned to thieving to save themselves."

"That's why we always keep one eye on the sacrifice and one eye on the sacrificer," Simon said.

"That must be a challenge. All I have to do is keep two eyes on their feet."

Simon stepped forward when he saw a worshipper deliberately kick his sandals out of reach of the girls.

"Did you see that?" Simon asked.

Hannah touched his elbow and he stepped back into the shadow. "They can handle it. They're learning humility."

"I cannot bear to see servants treated with indignity. I will remember that indolent soul when he comes to sacrifice again."

"It is gracious to forgive and forget," Hannah said. "Tell me more about the days of Antipater. I used to know him before he had such power."

"Those were the days I learned not to trust men," Simon said. "Antipater gave his sons, Herod and Phasael, the task of raising funds and they recruited a man named Malichus. That man hated Antipater and deliberately slowed his efforts so the king would feel the pressure of Rome. Antipater saved that man's life several times, but in return Malichus tried to assassinate him."

The high priest stepped forward again. A different young man had approached Fiona and began to flirt with her.

"Never trust a man." He shook his head. "Malichus eventually succeeded in bribing a cupbearer to poison and kill Antipater. It's those closest to you that you have to watch the most."

Simon stepped out of the shadows and walked toward the flirtatious young man, who upon seeing the high priest pivoted and walked quickly away from Fiona and toward the court for men.

* * *

The scriptorium had lost its coolness and sense of peace as the fevered men healed.

The centurion rubbed the sweat off his forehead with the back of his arm and let out a sigh. "We lost twenty-seven men, but you saved forty-three of the most desperate cases," he said to Simeon. "Rome should always be grateful for what you did. I'm not sure we'll convince General Claudius Tiberius of your heroic efforts, but at least he's quiet. It's sometimes surprising that men who face death day after day can be so greatly humbled when their own comes close."

"Let us know what else we can do to serve you," Simeon said. "My men are tired and ready to return to their families."

The centurion exchanged a few words with the recovering general before returning to Simeon.

"We'll be retrieving our horses and leaving you within the next few days," the centurion said. "I've asked the general to petition the governor for resources to compensate you for your efforts on our behalf. There are many things you can do to improve this space for your people. Perhaps you should have been a physician instead of hunching over manuscripts all day. Who do you expect to read these letters you write?"

Simeon pointed to a rostrum where readers usually shared the words of what had been written. "We fully expect that the Messiah, the anointed One, will someday soon walk into this place, or into any synagogue where we have prepared the scroll, and pick it up and read the very words of Ha'Shem to his people. I cannot describe to you what it would mean to have the One who embodies the hope of our people handle a scroll we have written."

"It's a dangerous time to be a Messiah in your country. Did you hear that Herod murdered the last two Hasmonean princes to avoid any rivalry for the throne? If you find your Messiah, it would be wise to warn him to establish himself somewhere other than Yerushalayim."

"I'm sure the Messiah will do what Ha'Shem calls him to do."

"So this Messiah… do you expect him to create trouble for us Romans?" The centurion raised a mug of wine to his lips, then held it high. "You do realize that my men are used to fighting barbarians and trained forces. I've seen nothing in this country that even comes close to the Parthians, Gauls, Germans, or Armenians. Your king is allied with the emperor to squash all discontent." He emptied the mug in one long guzzle before setting it down on a counter. "Your people make better healers and builders than fighters. I only have twenty years until my retirement and things will go much easier for both of us if you convince your people to live in peace."

"I need to prepare our table for Passover," Simeon said. "It's a sacred feast for our people at a time when the Messiah will one day appear. It celebrates our freedom and deliverance from tyrants and slavery. We do not wish to return to subservience with another nation like yours."

As the evening of Passover arrived, Simeon stood like a proud father at the head of a horseshoe-shaped table surrounded by dozens of scribes and students of the Torah. He waited while the candles were lit and then lifted a cup of wine.

"Blessed are you, Adonai our God, ruler of the universe, who has sanctified us with the commandment of lighting the holiday candles." Simeon lowered the cup only to lift it again. "Blessed are you, Adonai our God, ruler of the universe, who creates the fruit of the vine." He bowed his head. "Blessed are you, Adonai our God, ruler of the universe, who has kept us alive, sustained us, and brought us to this season."

The whole group drained their cups of wine and held them out for more.

Since bread was never cut, in keeping with tradition, Simeon took the loaves in hand and broke them. Although the poor were usually forced to satisfy themselves with barley, at this meal they had wheat. The usual strong millet had been eliminated. Goat's milk, cheese, and honey made the rounds, as did eggs. Bowls contained beans and lentils, cucumbers, onions, and lamb. Roasted walnuts, almonds, and pistachios sat alongside dates and figs.

"Why is there goat's milk and cheese at the same table as lamb?" one of the students asked. "In my hometown, we would never eat dairy and meat products at the same meal. It has something to do with boiling a kid in its mother's milk."

"Yes! I have heard of such practice," Simeon said. "We have not yet embraced it."

As in every Passover meal, the youngest attendee had the duty of asking the questions that brought meaning to the occasion.

"Why is there an empty seat at the table?" the appointed young scribe asked.

Simeon raised both hands, shrugged his shoulders, and scanned the group. "The extra chair is there because we are expecting…" He waited for a student to answer, but no one did. "Elijah! The prophet Malachi told us that the prophet Elijah would usher in the time of the Messiah in the great and dreadful day of the Lord. Perhaps he is at the door right now."

The young scribe paced dramatically to the door, then crouched, arched his eyebrows, and cupped a hand to his ear.

"I don't hear anything, but maybe…" The scribe listened very carefully. "Maybe someone is here."

He flung open the door and found the centurion crouched on the other side. The soldier looked startled and glared at Simeon.

"Welcome, centurion," Simeon said, walking toward the door. "The rabbis have told us that the Messiah will come at Passover and that the prophet Elijah will return to announce his coming. We are believers who act out our faith. Unfortunately, we cannot share this moment with you, so I will see you tomorrow."

He closed the door in the face of the Roman.

"Should we run and hide?" a student asked.

Simeon shook his head. "This is a sacred moment. We stay."

"Do you think the Messiah will kill the good Romans along with the bad ones?" asked the young scribe who had gone to the door. "If he calls us to fight, will we have to destroy the young and the old or just the ones who fight for Rome?"

"If we're going to have to fight with the Messiah, why don't we train ourselves on how to handle a sword?" another asked. "What is the good of praying for peace in Yerushalayim if we aren't able to help make it happen?"

Simeon held his hands up, palms out, in a call for quiet. The group stilled, but every eye looked at him expectantly.

"I pray for peace because I thirst for it like a stranger in a desert thirsts for water. We are focused tonight on another time and another place when Ha'Shem heard the cries of his people and acted on their behalf. We copy the scrolls because we believe that within these words our people will find their true hope and freedom." Simeon paced behind the students reclining at the elongated table. "Each of you has left home to chase this calling. You didn't leave to die by the sword. Although perhaps you still may."

He rested a hand on the shoulder of the young scribe, now kneeling as he prepared to take his place back at the table.

"I have shared with many of you my insights from copying the scroll of Isaiah at least thirty times," Simeon said. "This Messiah may be a suffering servant before he is a conquering king, or he may be far more than we imagine him to be. Every day I go to the Temple because the Messiah will be born and one day dedicated in the house of Ha'Shem." He raised his hands high in the air. "I will be there to greet him. This is my undying hope. If not this year, then next year in Yerushalayim."

The meal got back on track and finished without further incident.

Later that evening, however, Simeon paced around the outer walls of his home, eyeing the stars.

"Ha'Shem," he prayed, "you blessed Abraham with a promise that changed the course of our people. Promise once again that I too may see the glory of the One you will send to deliver us all."

The stars twinkled above but a fresh gust of warm wind blew over Simeon, and with the gentle touch of a breeze it felt as though the breath of God was confirming in his heart that he would not pass on until he had seen the anointed One.

The joy of a wedding dance surged through Simeon again and he broke into a new psalm from his lips to the heart of the Almighty. Alone on the roof, he felt immersed in an ocean of love and promise he had never known before.

CHAPTER EIGHTEEN

# THE CENSUS

*2 years before Messiah—(8 BC)*

The high priest was clearly agitated as he strolled along the lip of the cleansing pool. Barefooted, Simon stomped his way around the ledge five or six times before stepping off and sitting. He motioned to Hannah, who had been kneeling by the sandals.

"Come, share your thoughts with me," he said.

Hannah approached and stood before him. "Perhaps it is you who should share your thoughts with me."

Simon rested his bushy beard onto the knuckles of both fists and frowned. "A messenger warned me today that the emperor intends to conduct an imperial census and each person will have to return to their own homeland if it lies within Roman-controlled lands. That means I'll have to go back to Egypt."

"What would be the point of conducting a census so far from Rome?"

"It's Augustus's way of raising more taxes. It takes a lot of taxes to keep the army going in such a big empire. The slaves are building roads and wars have to be paid for. I don't know how it's going to affect the Temple, but people will be on the move all over the place."

"Maybe he'll change his mind," Hannah said. "It seems rather peaceful around here."

"He won't change his mind. He's recorded his intention in that wretched book of his."

"What book are you talking about?"

"The Deeds of the Divine Augustus." Simon stood and hissed into the breeze. "He fancies himself a god and the Senate has declared him Father of the Country. They've even changed the name of the sixth month from Sextilis to Augustus." How are we going to keep the people from revolting? Within a year, this place will be crawling with Romans preparing for the census. And with so many people coming and going, Herod will be anxious. After all, there are more than four million citizens. Of course not everyone will need to travel far. Maybe I'm worrying for nothing. Maybe I just don't want to go back to Egypt. I haven't been there for ten years. They almost took my head the last time. If it wasn't for my daughter being married to Herod, my life would probably still be at risk."

"It looks like you'll have to take this burden to Ha'Shem," Hannah said. "The time for evening sacrifice is near. Take a deep breath and release all your cares to the One who cares for you."

Simon nodded. "There's one more thing I need you to talk to your friend Simeon about. I hear a large number of Pharisees say they won't sign any registration document if it means acknowledging Caesar's divinity in any way."

"Why is that of concern to Simeon?"

"We don't need any more bloodshed in this place. I don't want any rebels hiding here if the Romans come. If they have to swear an oath to Caesar as Father of the Country, so be it. It's a small price to pay for Roman protection and provision. Of course no true believer in Ha'Shem can proclaim Caesar as a god, but—"

"These men aren't afraid to die for what they believe," Hannah said. "If you send a messenger to Simeon, I'll hear what's on his mind and heart. If you take care of the sacrifices, I'll try to take care of the people who come here."

Simeon arrived the next day, right after the morning sacrifice. Hannah knelt in her usual place as worshippers returned to claim their sandals. To an untrained eye, most of the leather shoes appeared too similar to differentiate. The key was placing the sandals in positions or angles that reminded her of who they belonged to.

Simeon stepped firmly into the gap, making his appearance as a pair of sandals just as was claimed. "Shalom, my friend. You called for me?"

He laid aside a cloth-covered scroll he had tucked under his arm.

"Shalom, rabbi," she replied. "Share with me the great revelations you are copying. And tell me what I should know about our Messiah and this Temple where I serve."

He pulled at his salt-and-pepper beard and sat on the edge of the pool. "You are always a student of truth," he said. "I am puzzled by something so simple that a child would understand it. The prophet Isaiah speaks of the Messiah as 'Mighty God, Everlasting Father, Prince of Peace,' but first he speaks about him as a son who will have the government on his shoulders. Is this Messiah like the Roman emperor, a deified man?"

"I'm sure you have given this more thought than I," she said. "I know he will be the hope of our people. He'll probably be more than most of us imagine, and likely less than most of us hope for. You have given me much to think of already… and I also have something for you to think on."

"What troubles your mind, my friend?"

"Simon, the high priest, has heard that at least six thousand of your Pharisees will resist the upcoming edict to register in the census. He is concerned about having this beautiful new space covered in blood again. How can you reassure him as we prepare for messengers from Rome?"

"I will encourage peace," Simeon said. "Perhaps some of these men need to go into hiding until this all settles down. Perhaps the caves in the desert, near the salt sea. You can assure the high priest that we will do all we can to keep his Temple unstained with anything but the blood of cows and sheep."

"Thank you," Hannah said. "Come and see me again when you encounter another mystery from the master prophet. I shall enjoy pondering this one and questioning the priests who think they know the mind of the Almighty."

Simeon picked up the scroll he had laid aside and extended it to her. "I know women don't usually keep scrolls for personal use, but you are a friend and I have copied this one for you. Guard it carefully. It has been declared to be the very words of Ha'Shem."

Hannah nodded. "It will be my life. Thank you for teaching me to read, and thank you for treating me with such dignity and respect. You are my greatest friend."

"And you mine."

* * *

Simeon motioned for quiet among the throng of shouting scribes and Pharisees.

"I'm sure we won't have to swear an oath that Caesar is lord," he said. "The emperor is trying to find ways to gain more taxes for his war machine. Possibly he needs money for roads. But so far more than six thousand of our number have taken an oath not to register. Do you realize what this could mean?"

"These politicians are bleeding us dry," yelled a stout young Pharisee at the edge of the gathering. "Taxes from Caesar, taxes from Herod, taxes from the Temple… how are we supposed to feed our children? Why should my son starve so someone can build roads and temples and fight wars?"

"Don't forget those tax collectors charging us for our donkeys, crops, carts, and even our coin purses!" called a tall scribe as he raised his closed fist. "We even have to pay for construction of a harbor on the Great Sea, even though most of us have never been near it."

Simeon raised his hands again and waited for the muttering to hush. "Caesar is attempting to do something no one has tried to do before. He is organizing one hundred twenty centers around the empire where all residents will be Roman citizens. His retired troops will be given land in these places. But all this costs money to accomplish."

The stout Pharisee stepped forward. "Are you saying that my son will starve because the soldiers who enslave us and pillage our nation need a place of peace to retire?"

"Those soldiers take a vow of loyalty at the start of each year," Simeon explained. "They lay down their lives for very small rewards. This is the emperor's way of showing his gratitude. Caesar is reducing the troops. Therefore, we won't be under pressure to give up our sons to serve anymore in this way. We should be glad to have the shalom we all desire."

"I've served Ha'Shem for fifteen years writing out manuscripts," a scribe upfront said. "How long do the Romans serve to get the promised reward of land?"

Simeon motioned to a robust man dressed in a leather vest and carrying a shield and spear. The vested man stepped forward and addressed the inquirer.

"Shalom," he said. "I'm Jonathan ben Isaac and I've been a praetorian guard serving sixteen years. The legionnaires you see around here will serve twenty years and their auxiliaries will serve twenty-five. The marines will serve twenty-eight."

He stepped back from the edge of the dais.

But the questionnaire had more to say. "What do they pay you for all that?"

Jonathan shifted his shield and spoke with authority. "Soldiers have different payscales, but in addition to our salary we receive shares of the booty… and then retirement bonuses. We earn what we are given." He raised his shield. "You realize that none of us who serve can marry, right? The troops on the frontlines are too busy fighting. Auxiliary units are locked up in forts along the frontier, far from any women. And the legionnaires live in camps."

"Then how do you explain all the children left behind?" an elderly Pharisee called out. "I've seen the swollen bellies of our women when your legionnaires finish looting. I'm one of the six thousand who refuse to make the pledge. I think Rome has taken enough from us already."

Jonathan nodded. "I'm here, with you, after serving my sixteen years keeping the peace. I plan to raise my family nearby. I've made friends of many of your countrymen and I've even converted to follow the faith of Ha'Shem." He handed his shield and spear to Simeon. "There! I give up my role as your conqueror. I will be taking on the role of postmaster for Yerushalayim, so any message you wish to send to the emperor can get to him in record time. If you want to travel, you'll be able to stay in secure lodges protected by soldiers who still keep the peace."

"Why should we care about your postal system or roads or wars?" the same elderly Pharisee demanded. "We keep to our villages and our Temple. The only messages we need to hear are proclaimed in our synagogues. What could you possibly offer us?"

The new postal officer stepped down from the dais and approached the old man, towering over him.

"You may not appreciate what we've done, but there are many who do," said Jonathan. "We've eliminated most of the pirates from the seas and bandits from the roads. We've kept trade routes open from the far east to the far west. We've welcomed travellers from the north and the south." He paced across the front of the group. "We've ensured supply lines so the goods you take for granted will be available in your shops next week and next year. We have a stable currency, allowing those from India or Persia to trade with those from Gaul or Britannia or Egypt. Roman art, as well as its athletic games, bring the world together in competition." He stepped back onto the dais. "You may not appreciate it, but the limits on personal freedoms in the empire also promote stability and security, establish peace, and build prosperity for all."

Simeon stepped in, splaying his hands. "Surely we can disagree without animosity. This man is our brother. That one truth overcomes everything that separates us." He handed the shield and spear back to Jonathan. "We may not like it, but we have the freedom to worship in a Temple that is admired by the world around us. We have the freedom to write out our scriptures and distribute them to synagogues so our children may read the very words of Ha'Shem. We can travel from afar without much worry on roads that draw our countrymen together."

"A man claiming the powers of a god can be nothing but a tyrant," the old man said, turning away. "All you have to do to find yourself on a cross now is to stand up with the words of the Almighty and claim you will love only Ha'Shem with all your heart and soul and mind. I don't want to be here when the wrath of Rome comes down on us."

"But we await the Messiah and his peace," Simeon called after the retreating man. "With the breath of his mouth, he will destroy his enemies."

"If things continue as they are, none of us may be here to ever see that happen!"

CHAPTER NINETEEN
# ZECHARIAH AND ELIZABETH

*1 year before Messiah (7 BC)*

Zechariah's beaming face said it all.

"I've been chosen," he said to Hannah. "Tomorrow the lot has fallen on me to offer the incense and prayer in the Temple. Can you imagine? A thousand years ago, the casting of a lot by King David created my division. Now, by the casting of another lot, I have been chosen for this once-in-a-lifetime honor."

Hannah accepted his sandals and arranged them neatly. "I'm sure you've prepared for this honor, but it seems that no one before you has had anything special happen. You and Elizabeth are so righteous that it doesn't make sense for Ha'Shem to keep her barren. I guess now she's too advanced in years to expect anything."

"I know Ha'Shem always hears the spoken and unspoken prayers of his people," Zechariah said. "For myself, I'm settled on serving the Almighty, but my Elizabeth feels such shame over the fact that everyone else in our family has children. She feels that the women whisper behind her back and question her conduct behind closed doors. If Sarah could bear children to Abraham, and Rebekah to Isaac, there's no reason Elizabeth should be left childless."

"Even I have seen your faithful service and your humble heart," Hannah said. "May the gracious and compassionate One do more than you could ask or imagine as you stand before the altar. May his peace guard your heart and mind. May he overshadow you with his presence and power."

Zechariah sighed. "It's been four hundred years since a prophet has spoken in our land. Perhaps you are the one to break through the curtain of silence to unleash the favor of Ha'Shem. I would praise him if even an angel would appear to confirm when Elijah is returning so we might prepare for the coming of the Messiah."

"I shall be one of those outside the court, praying for you while you're inside. I'll be waiting for you here tomorrow when you leave your sandals. Purify yourself and speak clearly to the One who hears the desires of your heart. Pray for our land and people and pray for the coming of the Messiah."

It was a slow day and Hannah left the care of the sandals to Phoebe and Fiona, who had become as efficient as she in their orderliness and recognition.

Her back and shoulders groaned with deep discomfort. Her knees complained. Her stomach growled. Her left eye filled with floaters that distracted her from worship.

Passover was only a week away and the garden she had planted outside the residence had released its first shoots. A row of blood-red poppies had sprouted early along with anemones, cyclamen, and irises. The garden needed her attention.

Samuel, leader of the Sanhedrin, approached Hannah later that day as she pulled weeds.

"What is wrong with that Pharisee you claim as a friend?" Samuel asked. "His men have gone crazy in their resistance of this latest edict of the emperor. The only way we all get ahead is by embracing the reforms of the world around us."

He marched out into the marble plaza before turning back.

"Why can't those sanctimonious peons admit there is no supernatural world for us to call out to?" he bellowed. "There is an emperor and a Senate to oversee this world. There is an economy and a world of wealth to sustain us."

Hannah picked a poppy and held it out to him. "It always amazes me how two groups of people so committed to what Ha'Shem has said can come to such a different understanding of the world. Does this flower exist in my garden? The Almighty lives in the supernatural, so it must exist."

"You're a prophetess, but clearly not a scholar of the Torah," Samuel said. "Who can imagine angels, demons, heaven, hell, and all things invisible? The writings of Moses guide us with all we need to know. The prophets were dreamers and visionaries, but they weren't in line with what we know to be true for the people of Ha'Shem."

"How do you find hope?" Hannah asked. "If there is nothing more than this life, as you say you believe, what about the desire for resurrection so many of us live with? What about an afterlife with blessing for the righteous and suffering for the unrighteous? Will not Ha'Shem prove to be a righteous judge beyond what happens here?"

Samuel turned his back on Hannah. "Do you realize that your friend and his colleagues spend so much time copying those scrolls that they take it all literally?

They spend so much time thinking of the promises of the afterlife that they have no time to invest in this current life. They are a drain on our society."

"Be realistic, now. Who are the people going to support when the Messiah comes? You Sadducees are so connected with the political machine and aristocrats that you don't understand how those of us who aren't wealthy hope for One to save us from our troubles. You're connected with the Roman government. We know the Messiah is going to overthrow those who oppress us."

"This idea of a Messiah is a dream, an illusion for those who cannot face the reality we live in," Samuel said. "If anyone tries to stand against Rome, they will stand against us and against the Temple. The Pharisees are merchants and small business owners, hardly influential with those who matter."

"Are you saying that common people don't matter?" Hannah asked.

"I've had enough of this," Samuel said. "Why don't you stick with flowers? At least you know how to care for something we can all see."

\* \* \*

Simeon bowed low with other worshippers as a priest entered the inner sanctum to offer incense on the altar. A loud murmuring echoed off the walls of the Temple as worshippers beseeched the Almighty with their memorized prayers.

"Hear, O King of the universe," he prayed. "Hear the prayers of your servants as we humble ourselves before you. You have given us this place to worship. You have promised your servant that you chose this city for your name to be exalted."

Simeon rocked back and forth, gaining a rhythm to the chant that gripped him.

"There is no other One like you in heaven or on the earth. You alone keep your covenant of love with your servants who follow you with their whole hearts. You promised you would always leave a descendant of David on the throne of this nation, and now I beseech you to fulfill your promise and bring us our Messiah."

The rocking continued.

"Almighty Lord, give attention to the cry of your servants. Open your eyes and ears toward us who bow before you. Hear from heaven, where you dwell, and forgive us where we have fallen short of your glory."

As he continued in prayer, the people's murmuring grew into a rumble—and at last to full-throated astonishment.

Simeon lifted his eyes to consider what might be happening. The priest who had offered the incense stood at the top of the Temple stairs, gesturing wildly.

"Zechariah has seen a vision!" someone yelled.

"He's seen an angel," a Pharisee nearby said.

"There are no such thing as angels," a Sadducee countered. "He's gone mad!"

"He can't speak," another priest said from the front. "He's seen something amazing!"

"Did he finish the prayers?" the Sadducee shouted. "Does the sacrifice even count if he didn't?"

A leader of the Sanhedrin stepped forward and gained the others' attention. "The prayers have been said, the incense has been offered, and all is well. Ha'Shem honors your presence. May the desires of your heart be heard and answered today." He turned toward Zechariah for a moment and then returned his attention to the crowd. "Zechariah is unwell and will return home to his wife. A once-in-a-lifetime honor can be overwhelming. You may all return home to your families in peace."

Confused by the commotion, Simeon turned to the worshipper next to him. "What happened?"

"The priest stumbled out of the sanctuary waving his arms. We all stopped praying to hear him," the man said. "He couldn't speak, but he made signs that seemed to imply he had seen an angel. If Ha'Shem has finally spoken to us after all these years, I want to find out what he had to say. It's not right that the priests get to keep the words of the Almighty to themselves."

"Perhaps this is the moment for us to learn of the coming of the Messiah."

The man's eyebrows raised and he stepped back with a stare. "There is no Messiah coming to this place! We are a forsaken and forgotten people. We are slaves to a new Pharaoh, and now our leaders are going mad."

As Simeon looked to the front, he watched Zechariah stumble his way down the stairs, where he was escorted toward the gate by another priest.

"This is not madness," Simeon said. "This is the answer to our prayers."

* * *

"Did you see what happened with Zechariah?" Simeon asked as Hannah set his sandals before him. It was the first time he had used a cane and he laid it aside to put on his footwear. He pressed a silver shekel into her hand and squeezed her fingers gently. "Did you understand that something miraculous is happening?"

"Some are saying he had a vision and others are saying he went mad," Hannah replied. "I spoke with him yesterday and he is not a man gone mad."

"What could be happening to him?" Simeon asked.

"The desire of his heart was for a child to bring honor and respect back to his wife. Perhaps he will be the father of the Messiah."

"No!" Simeon objected. "We haven't heard from Elijah yet. You don't think Elijah can be reborn, do you?"

Hannah sat back and smiled. "Here you are, student of the word, scholar of the scrolls, messenger of the Messiah, and you're asking me? We know that no one is reborn. It's appointed for man to live once and to die once."

"I for one am going to follow that priest home and find out what's going on," Simeon declared. "I'll come back and tell you when I find out."

"Why don't you wait a few months and stop by his home to find out if his old wife is with child? The gestures of Zechariah spoke of jubilation, and one thing I know could bring an old man like him so much joy."

"Do you think it could really have been an angel?" Simeon asked.

"If it was an angel, don't tell the Sadducees," Hannah said. "They would prefer to think Ha'Shem made us and then left us to find our own way in the world. If Ha'Shem is sending angels with messages, it means we're ready for something more amazing than we can imagine."

As Simeon hobbled away, Phoebe sidled up beside Hannah.

"Do you ever wonder if the two of you should have been a couple?" Phoebe asked.

Hannah reached out and tweaked the girl's chin. "Wouldn't you love to know the secrets of an old woman's heart?" She sat on the edge of the pool and watched Simeon slip out through the gate. "I wonder that very thing more days than you realize. We both had our chances with others. He focuses his love on the scrolls and I focus my love on the Temple." She patted the place beside her and Phoebe slumped down close. "If you don't find your love soon, you may find yourself vulnerable to the desires of those you may not love. There is protection and provision in a good man. Ha'Shem has proved to be the best provider and protector for me and I'm satisfied that this is where I belong."

"How will I know if I have found a man worthy of love?" Phoebe asked.

"Usually that would be the task of your mother and father," Hannah replied. "But since you don't have a parent, we'll have to find someone else to arrange that for you. Do you see someone you like? Is it one of the young worshippers?"

The girl giggled. "A son of one of the Levites keeps looking my way. We're both too young, but I'd like to talk with him to find out why he smiles so much."

"Next time he shows up, point him out to me. What's his name?"

"Reuben. I heard his father calling him. He comes every day right after Torah studies and before the evening sacrifice."

"And when did you first notice that he might like you?"

"He stood in his sandals while I waited for him to step out of them," Phoebe answered. "When I finally looked at his face, he was smiling at me. He stepped away and kept looking back the whole time he followed his father into the court-yard."

"So what have you done to show him you've noticed him?"

Phoebe giggled again. "I hid his sandals and ignored him when he asked me about them."

"That's exactly what I would have done," Hannah said. "May Ha'Shem guard you until we can find an advocate to arrange the next steps."

\* \* \*

The scrolls stretched across the length of the wooden table. Simeon hovered over the passage that vibrated into his dreams on a nightly basis.

> Nevertheless, there will be no more gloom for those who were in distress. In the past he humbled the land of Zebulun and the land of Naphtali, but in the future he will honor Galilee of the nations, by the Way of the Sea, beyond the Jordan—the people walking in darkness have seen a great light; on those living in the land of deep darkness a light has dawned.[4]

His eyes raced ahead.

> For to us a child is born, to us a son is given, and the govern-ment will be on his shoulders. And he will be called Wonderful Counselor, Mighty God, Everlasting Father, Prince of Peace. Of the greatness of his government and peace there will be no end. He will reign on David's throne and over his kingdom, estab-lishing and upholding it with justice and righteousness from that time on and forever. The zeal of the Lord Almighty will accomplish this.[5]

What did Galilee have to do with a child who had godlike titles? The Mes-siah was to be born in Bethlehem, the homeland of the great king David. And Yerushalayim was the place of David's throne.

---

[4] Isaiah 9:1–2.

[5] Isaiah 9:6–7.

He scanned the scroll again. How would such a child rise to overthrow Herod and Rome?

Images of Zechariah burned into his mind. It was time to pay a visit to the old priest and his wife at Ein-Karem, although it would require an hour and a half walk to the west. Well, it would actually require him to hire a carriage now that his knee bothered him so much. He could combine the visit with another ride out to Bethlehem and the Herodium.

The trip happened the day after the Sabbath with the sun glistening off the fresh dew hanging on the grapevines. The birdsong provided a symphony of celebration, as if somehow the world was a better place today. Getting away from the noise and bustle of the city was a tonic of life for his heart and mind.

The Temple towered above him as he looked back on the place he had come to know as home. The thick walls assured him that Hannah was safe, the Temple worship would continue, and the scrolls would be written and prepared for when the Messiah came to take his place.

"What brings you out on this fine day?" the carriage driver asked him. "Most of my passengers going to Ein-Karem are priests. You don't appear to be a priest."

"My name is Simeon and I'm a scribe working in the scriptorium under the Temple," he said. "I was attending a service where an old priest offered incense and then was stricken speechless. I want to find out what happened to him. I also want to visit a rabbi in Bethlehem to see if there has been any news of the Messiah."

"I know this priest," the driver said. "Zechariah, right? Three full moons ago, near Passover, I took him home and he was beaming like the sun. But he couldn't speak. The last I heard, he still wasn't speaking. Strange things are happening."

"What have you heard from Bethlehem?"

"The rabbi there died last week. The innkeepers are expecting a lot of bookings over the next year as the census takes effect. Far too many Romans are setting up shop in our towns and villages to manage the emperor's latest edict. Well, I pay my fair share of taxes and don't want any more reasons to have to starve my children."

"Perhaps I've been thinking about this all wrong," Simeon said. "I assumed the Messiah's birth would come from someone residing in Bethlehem, but the rabbi told me that every young person is on the move to their homelands. Perhaps the census will bring a young couple home... perhaps they'll give birth while they're here..." He thought a moment. "Perhaps they'll come from the Galil as descendants of David."

The carriage driver frowned. "Nothing good comes from the Galil. I think most people have given up on the idea of a Messiah. I can't imagine Ha'Shem would disrupt the entire world with a census to move someone to a place like Bethlehem."

"Ha'Shem doesn't think like men. In the scroll I'm copying, it says, "'For my thoughts are not your thoughts, neither are your ways my ways,' declares the Lord. 'As the heavens are higher than the earth, so are my ways higher than your ways and my thoughts than your thoughts.'"[6]

The driver shook his head. "Rearranging the whole world to get one child born in a tiny village? No, it definitely doesn't seem like a smart way to bring about a Messiah to overthrow Rome. If I were you, I'd be looking to the Herodium for a new child. It's close to Bethlehem and would be the kind of place where a king should be born."

"Perhaps by the end of our tour, we will both have answers," Simeon said. "I won't be long at this first stop. I'm ready to be amazed at what Ha'Shem does among us."

The path to Zechariah's home was well-worn and easy for the driver to find. And when they arrived, Simeon stepped slowly off the cart, grabbed his cane, and hobbled to the gate.

"Shalom, my friends," he called out.

An elderly woman peeked out the door. Her scarlet head covering and royal blue robe spoke of wealth and status.

"Shalom," she said.

Simeon stepped into the yard. "I've come to talk with Zechariah."

"I'm his wife Elizabeth," the woman said, tucking a strand of gray under her scarf. "Zechariah can't talk."

"Is he away?"

She glanced at the driver and then rubbed her own shoulders against the cold. "No! he had a vision and hasn't been able to talk since."

Simeon stepped closer. "Do you know what the vision was about?"

Her brows furrowed. "It seems to have been a promise for a child."

"Are you with child? Is it a son?"

She smiled. "No one knows yet."

"Will he be the Messiah?"

She shook her head vigorously. "No, he's just a child."

At that moment, an elderly man opened the door fully behind her and stepped into the yard. Zechariah held a piece of vellum and a quill in his hand.

---

[6] Isaiah 55:8–9.

# CHAPTER TWENTY

# ĴOHΠ

*Months to the Messiah (6 BC)*

Yerushalayim and its surrounding villages bulged at the seams when enforcement of Caesar's edict took hold. Quirinius, governor of Syria, had rallied his census takers and bargained with Herod over his take of the proceeds.

Simeon unrolled the missive he had copied from Zechariah, who had written out his story for all to see:

> While I burned the incense, an angel of the Lord appeared to me, standing at the right side of the altar of incense.

He had been very precise in his notation.

> I was startled and gripped with fear, but the angel told me, "Don't be afraid, Zechariah." He knew me by name.

There was no question that such an encounter would terrify a man.

> The angel told me that my prayers had been heard, that my wife Elizabeth would bear a son, and that his name would be John.

Such a strange name when no one in the family carried that moniker.

> The angel said that the boy will be a joy and delight to us and that many will rejoice because of his birth. He will be great in the sight of the Lord. He is to be a Nazarite, not taking any wine or fermented drink. He will have been filled with the Holy

Spirit even before his birth. He will fulfill the final words of the prophet Malachi. He will go on before the Lord in the spirit and power of Elijah.[7]

Simeon unrolled the words of the final prophetic voice before the great silence, words spoken to Malachi:

> See, I will send the prophet Elijah to you before that great and dreadful day of the Lord comes. He will turn the hearts of the parents to their children, and the hearts of the children to their parents; or else I will come and strike the land with total destruction.[8]

"What's got you shaking your head, old man?" a voice sounded behind him. It was the carriage driver he had met the year before while on the way to Bethlehem.

Simeon embraced the man like an old friend, then pointed toward the scrolls. "These words from Malachi seem to say that Ha'Shem will draw families and loved ones together in a way people will notice before he brings a great judgment on our people. Do you remember the words I read to you from Zechariah's hand? They align perfectly with the last prophecy we were given before the great silence."

"I'm still not sure why you scholars think we're in the middle of some big silence. You should try living at my house while the sun is up!" But then the driver grew serious. "I thought you might be interested to know that Zechariah and Elizabeth have a visitor from the Galil. A young woman. You mentioned that you had some question as to whether the census might be used to bring someone back to Bethlehem."

Simeon grasped the driver by his wrists. "Did she bring her husband? Are they staying in Ein-Karem or moving on to Bethlehem? Are they relatives of King David?"

"Whoa! My friend, it was one young girl by herself," the driver said. "She's a relative of Elizabeth's who has come to help with the baby."

Simeon nodded. "Thank you for keeping your eyes open. I'm looking for a young Galilean couple who are ready to have a child and have come to Bethle-

---

[7] Paraphrased from Luke 1:5–17.

[8] Malachi 4:5–6.

hem for the census. I could be wrong. This mystery lies just beyond my ability to understand." He gestured to the scroll. "The words are here, but they dance in the shadows."

"There are thousands of Galileans moving around at the moment," the driver mused. "I don't know how you hope to find just one."

"Very well," Simeon said. "Perhaps this newcomer knows someone in the Galil who is from Bethlehem. I will go with you tomorrow and ask her. Do you know her name?"

"I think the name was Mariam."

"A common enough name." Simeon sighed to himself. "Elisabeth's pregnancy is in its ninth month, so let's go see what Ha'Shem might do when this child is born. I'll talk to this Mariam for myself to see what she knows."

When Simeon awoke the next morning, the skies were unleashing a torrential downpour. The streets had transformed into rivers as the sewers overflowed and emptied their stinking contents over the rims of doorsteps and garden beds. Soil from neatly planted flowerbeds eroded and joined the flood rushing down into the valley. A stream had even found its way into the scriptorium and men were scrambling to dam off the flow.

This would not be a good travel day. Simeon sent his regrets to the driver at the stable through one of the younger scribes.

For three days, the rains unleashed their cleansing devastation over the land. By the time the first rays of sunlight returned, Simeon was huddled in bed, covered in blankets, his teeth chattering. The journey to Ein-Karem would have to wait.

\* \* \*

Hannah would never forget the day Zechariah returned to the Temple, finally able to speak again. The old man stood in the middle of the plaza, hands held high, twirling, dancing, and singing.

"Praise be to the Lord, the God of Israel, because he has come to his people and redeemed them," Zechariah prophesied. "He has raised up a horn of salvation for us in the house of his servant David (as he said through his holy prophets of long ago), salvation from our enemies and from the hand of all who hate us—to show mercy to our ancestors and to remember his holy covenant, the oath he swore to our father Abraham…"[9]

Upon his exit, having spent a considerable time in the Temple, Zechariah moved to retrieve his sandals.

[9] Luke 1:68–73.

Hannah was waiting for him.

"It's nice you got your voice back," she said. "How is Elizabeth doing?"

The priest outbeamed the sun. "We are like youth again! Our son has been born. Your prayers, God's angels, our dreams… Ha'shem has given us a prophet for a son."

"It will be good to have a prophet around again. I've never heard one," Hannah said. "I heard you say that Ha'Shem has raised up a horn of salvation for us in the house of his servant David."

"That's right. He has answered the prayers of our nation for a Messiah."

"But you and your wife are from the house of Aaron, not from David."

"Yes, we have seen the mother of our Lord," he said. "The Messiah is coming and our son shall announce his arrival. I must hurry. My wife isn't sleeping and we have to be back to dedicate our boy tomorrow."

He walked away, without his sandals. Suddenly remembering, though, he returned and slipped into them.

"Who is the father of the Messiah?" Hannah asked.

Zechariah shrugged. "I've never met the man. Praise be to the Lord, the God of Israel, because he has come to his people and redeemed them."

He walked away with a spring in his step that belied his age.

Hannah watched him go, realizing that this was news Simeon would want to hear immediately. She sent a messenger to call her friend to the Temple.

The old man arrived the next day at the morning sacrifice, leaning heavily on his cane and walking with a limp.

"Shalom, friend," Hannah said. "It looks like the rooster has disturbed you too early."

"Shalom, friend. Although it wasn't the rooster who roused me too early today."

"It looks like Ha'Shem's promise to you will come true." Hannah helped him out of his sandals. "Zechariah is back at the Temple, talking and singing and dancing. It was an angel who spoke to him. Apparently he has seen the mother of the Messiah."

Simeon's face brightened. "I had arranged to go and visit the old priest and his family, but I've been ill after the rains. What is the Messiah's father's name?"

"He doesn't know."

"He's met the mother but not the father?"

"It seems that way."

"What's the mother's name?"

"Mariam."

"Every other girl in this nation is called Mariam," Simeon said. "It's probably the same young woman who visited Elizabeth to help her with the birth of John." He looked off into the distance, musing to himself. "I probably set off a rumor by telling that carriage driver I thought the parents of the Messiah might be from the Galil and come down for the census..."

Hannah patted him on the back. "You may have missed the Messiah's mother, but you're in time for the dedication of the firstborn son of Zechariah and Elizabeth. Look behind you."

Simeon pivoted slowly and gazed at the elderly couple working their way gingerly past the glut of sandals strewn about.

"Looks like you better call the girls for help," Simeon said. "There will be too many worshippers this morning for you to keep up."

"If I didn't get into conversations with people like you, maybe I would keep up," she retorted with a smirk. "This babe and his parents will need a prayer. Let's go see the happy parents. You can ask your questions about the Messiah."

A priest stepped in to do the honors and ensure the sacrifice of a lamb was conducted according to tradition. The ceremony wasn't long.

Afterward Simeon laid his hand on the boy. "What will be his name?"

"It will be John, in line with what the angel told me," Zechariah said. "He is our gift from Ha'Shem and will shine a light on the One who will lead us all out of darkness."

"So let it be," Simeon said. "This child will be great among the prophets of Ha'Shem. He will draw generations toward each other and toward their Creator and Redeemer. He will be a leader who calls our nation back to repentance and away from judgment." He hesitated, disturbed at the images playing in his mind. "Hear, O Israel, the Lord your God, the Lord is one."

Simeon suddenly released the baby and stood back as Hannah stepped forward to share her own prayers.

When the last of the priests had accepted the offering of five shekels, chanted his blessing, and patted the head of the boy, Simeon stepped forward again.

"Zechariah, a word if you please," he said. "I've heard that you encountered the mother of the Messiah but that you don't know his father or family name. Please tell me where I can meet this child so I can bless him. Is he still in Bethlehem?"

Zechariah seemed surprised. "The child isn't born yet."

"What do you mean? How can you know his mother?"

"His mother is a relative who came to visit us."

"Every mother in this land thinks her child will be the Messiah," Simeon said, backing away.

"You don't understand," Zechariah gently rocked his whimpering son. "The same angel who promised that my son would be the forerunner of the Messiah also met this girl in the Galil, proclaiming that she would give birth to the Messiah."

"Where is her husband?" Simeon persisted. "What family does he come from?"

"She has no husband yet, but she is betrothed." Zechariah handed his son to Elizabeth.

"Are you saying that the mother of the Messiah is with child but unmarried?"

"Yes! It is a miraculous birth, just like ours. She has returned to the Galil to prepare."

"How can this be the Messiah?" Simeon asked. "The Messiah will be born in Bethlehem, not the Galil. He will be a royal person from the line of David. How do we know that some peasant girl has even seen an angel?"

"How do you know I saw an angel?" Zechariah pointed toward his son with one hand and toward his own mouth with another. "He cries and I speak. Why is everyone around here talking about this miracle? What do you think Ha'Shem is preparing us for?"

A nearby priest broke in, having overheard. "What is this child going to be?"

"Why don't you go back to searching your scrolls and I'll go back to raising a prophet," Zechariah said. "Keep your eyes open—the Messiah is coming soon."

* * *

The change in Simeon was clear to Hannah. A few days later, she spotted him arriving at the Temple plaza walking around with a renewed zest for life. He seemed to have set aside his work on the scrolls, opting instead to spend his time strolling around the Temple grounds examining closely every child brought forward for dedication. Hannah watched as his eyes glazed over with each one, focusing. Every time, he shook his head slightly and backed away from the parents.

His disappointment never lasted for more than a few moments, though. He kept rallying himself to approach the next child.

Hannah caught up to him as he sat on a bench near the gate. "You'll wear yourself out if you keep up this intensity," she whispered.

"You'll have to speak up," Simeon said. "Have you ever been one heartbeat from a promise fulfilled? Have you ever taken a breath knowing it could be the last one before you see what you have waited your whole life to see? Have you ever looked into the face of a child and wondered whether Ha'Shem had broken through the veil of our world to meet with us again?"

"Ha'Shem meets with us here in the Temple every day," Hannah said, louder.

"This will be different, somehow." Simeon fidgeted in place. "This Temple cannot contain the Almighty. His thoughts and his ways are higher than ours. The prophets have seen enough to woo us into dreaming of something beyond what we can know."

"You're scaring me. I've been with you from the beginning and have never heard you talk this way. What did you see in the scrolls? Have you also met with an angel?"

Simeon gazed up and smiled. "I have knowledge inside me as sure as the breath I breathe. My waiting is almost over. I will see him, here. We shall see him together."

"What if he comes when you are away?" Hannah asked.

"I will be here every day. Ha'Shem has given me a new strength. I haven't even needed my cane the last few days."

"Stay close then. If you fall asleep from exhaustion, I'll wake you myself when the little one comes. Elizabeth told me the babe would be born at Passover."

"Why at Passover?" Simeon said. "The city will be crowded. The Temple will be packed with people. There will be no place for a child to stay." He rubbed his forehead. "What if I miss him among all the people?"

"It will be okay," Hannah said. "He won't be dedicated until forty days after Passover. This will allow time to learn whether a new boy has been born in Bethlehem."

Simeon nodded, relaxing somewhat. "If all this is so, maybe I should get some rest while I can. I have wearied myself thinking that each day might be the day I see him."

"You will see him soon enough. His time is near."

# CHAPTER TWENTY-ONE

# THE MESSİAH

*Time of the Messiah (6 BC)*

Quirinius was applying pressure to finalize the census registration throughout Syria, and those who had moved far from Yerushalayim since being born there were taking advantage of the Passover festival to take care of business.

Simeon had made two trips to Ein-Karem to satisfy himself, through Zechariah and Elizabeth, in the matter of Hannah's prediction of the Messiah being born at Passover.

With the rabbi in Bethlehem having died, Simeon befriended a local shepherd who could alert him to the events there. He had been waiting patiently, but so far the only news spoke of too many people flocking into the village to discern who might be with child. Besides, the shepherd didn't understand why anyone this close to giving birth would risk such a long journey.

However, a few days after Passover, the shepherd hiked up to Yerushalayim and met Simeon outside the Temple courtyard to share some news: the Messiah had been born in Bethlehem, just as promised.

"Tell me everything," Simeon said, visibly shaking as he slumped onto a bench.

"Two days before Passover, we were camped out on a field," the shepherd said. "The next day we intended to herd the last of the lambs to Yerushalayim for Temple sacrifices. From our camp, we could see the bright lights of the city. People were celebrating. We also could see the lights of the Herodium. Most of us sat by the fire sharing the kind of stories only shepherds share with each other." He laughed to himself. "We were also talking about how bright the moon was, and how the stars seemed to be more numerous than even Abraham could have imagined…"

"What about the Messiah?" Simeon prompted. His heart pounded in his chest and he forced himself to take a breath.

"Yes, yes. Anyway, it was like a star suddenly exploded in front of us. An angel appeared out of the flash and grew brighter than the sun at midday. I can't explain it any other way! He stood in front of us like you're standing in front of me now."

Simeon eagerly leaned toward the shepherd. "And then?"

"The angel talked with us. I can tell you that I was so afraid that I nearly lost my bowels."

"And what did he say?"

"He said, 'Don't be afraid.'"

"What else?"

The shepherd laid a hand on Simeon's shoulder and nodded. "Peace, my friend. I'll get to it. You're talking with a shepherd. We usually have all night to get through a story." He found a stool and sat across from Simeon. "The angel said that he was bringing good news that would bring great joy to all the people. He said that in Bethlehem, in the town of David, a Savior had been born and that he was the Messiah.[10] We would find the baby wrapped in cloths and lying in a manger. Our manger? We could see Yerushalayim and Herodium, where anyone would expect a king to be born, but here he was—in our own manger!"

"That's quite a story! So you went to see him?"

The shepherd held out his hand. "There's more to it. First, the whole sky lit up. So many angels appeared that we never could have counted them all. We couldn't see the moon or the stars… that's how bright the sky was. The angels said, 'Glory to God in the highest heaven, and on earth peace to those on whom his favor rests.'" He crossed his arms and stared upward, remembering the moment with great reverence. "That's all I can remember. They left us and the night became dark again, with the full moon and the infinite stars. We talked together and decided we had to go and see this baby for ourselves."

"So you were the first ones in the whole world to see the new Messiah?"

"Yes, so it seems." The shepherd stood up. "We raced around, telling everyone about what we experienced. I remembered how interested you were in all this, so thought I needed to come and tell you in person. The other shepherds are taking the lambs to the Temple. What a strange night!"

Simeon looked contemplative. "Was anyone with the mother when you tracked down the child?"

---

[10] Paraphrased from Luke 2:1–20.

"Of course!" The man's eyebrows knit together. "Her husband Yosef was with her, although we saw no one else. They are both descendants of King David. After they register in Bethlehem, they'll be looking for a place to live."

Simeon couldn't believe what he was hearing. "Tell me again. You say the baby was born three days ago?"

The shepherd rubbed his forehead with the back of his wrist. "I've been running around so much… sharing the news, bringing lambs to the Temple… that the time has passed quickly. I came as soon as I remembered you."

"Thank you. Yosef and Mariam… those are their names." Simeon nodded to himself. "I'll be in the Temple courtyards, waiting." He raised his hands, smiling. "The Messiah is here."

\* \* \*

Hannah found the news from Zechariah to be mind-numbing.

"Tell me one more time," she urged the priest. "So I can share this with Simeon."

Zechariah sat beside her on the lip of the foot-washing pool. "I was called a week ago to provide circumcision services for an eight-day-old boy. It was Elizabeth's cousin Mariam and her new husband, Yosef. They had found a small home on the edge of Bethlehem on property he claims as his ancestral legacy…"

The old man trailed off as he fell into deep thought.

Hannah gently touched his hand to draw him back. "Tell me more."

"Yes!" he said, smiling. "I circumcised the boy and they called him Yeshua. They told me about the angel that had appeared to both of them separately, explaining that this was to be the child's name. After what happened to me, I had no doubt that it was the same angel. He called himself Gabriel."

"I thought this woman was alone when she came to your place," Hannah said. "She was pregnant and unmarried?"

Zechariah nodded. "Yes. Apparently the angel told this young woman, Mariam, that she would conceive by the power of the Holy Spirit, without a human partner. And she did. During her pregnancy, she came to stay with me and Elizabeth, and we encouraged her. And of course she encouraged us! Afterward Mariam went back to Nazareth and told the news to her betrothed, Yosef. At first he was going to divorce her, but the angel met him in a dream. Yosef completed the marriage and made the journey with her down to Bethlehem."

"She was almost to term and still came all this way?" Hannah asked.

"She is a brave young woman. Yosef is from the line of David through his son Solomon, and Mariam is from the line of David through his son Nathan. They have a strong case to establish a new legacy on their ancestral lands."

Hannah gave this some careful thought. "They'll be here to dedicate their son in two weeks then. Simeon will want to know so he can be here." She smiled to herself. "I almost feel like we're the great grandparents of this Messiah. Eighty-four years is a long time to wait for the fulfillment of a promise!"

The next day, Hannah heard the steady clicking of Simeon's cane across the marble plaza. Even the slither of his sandals as he shuffled along was familiar and a comfort.

Without looking up, she greeted him. "Shalom, my friend. So you've heard."

"Shalom, my friend," he said, stepping out of his sandals. "Everything we've been waiting for is happening. The Messiah is here."

"Tell me what you know so far. I've heard from Zechariah about his circumcision and naming day."

"I can tell you about his birth from a shepherd who was told by angels."

"Yes, some of the worshippers have been whispering about angels and a baby," she said. "They were afraid to speak up because of the Sadducees and the high priest, who don't believe in angels or Messiahs."

"This is one time I'm glad to be a Pharisee and student of the scrolls, so I can believe without hesitation."

Simeon turned and motioned for another man to catch up with him. Nicodemus hurried up, occupying himself with the task of unrolling a large scroll. He placed it on a dry spot along the edge of the pool.

Simeon bent over it. "I've been studying the words of the prophets Isaiah and Malachi. What the shepherds tell me is making more sense now. A young woman, possibly a virgin, will conceive and give birth to a son. So it says."

Hannah hunched over the scroll as he pointed to a passage of text.

"Zechariah told me that Yosef is descended from David through his son Solomon and Mariam is descended from David through his son Nathan," Simeon continued. "The Messiah is of royal lineage in the line of kings."

He unrolled the scroll a little more and pointed at another line of text.

"What we're hearing makes sense of what the prophet wrote about a son being given, one who will have the government on his shoulders. He says, 'Of the greatness of his government and peace there will be no end. He will reign on

David's throne and over his kingdom, establishing and upholding it with justice and righteousness from that time on and forever.'"[11]

"A king is coming here," Hannah said. "How do we declare this without unleashing the wrath of Herod?"

"We don't!" Simeon said. "Herod isn't ready to release his throne and this child is too young to claim it. That will be for a future day. So we will worship in silence, waiting for Ha'Shem to reveal all things in his time."

Hannah nodded solemnly. "The time is near for all your hopes to come true. You never doubted, not from the first time you told me about the Messiah. Your faith brought healing and hope to my life again. I know you'll be here every day waiting to see him for yourself."

"This scroll of Isaiah tells me that his work will be for more than just our people," Simeon said. "I read that he will be a light for all the nations, that he will open blind eyes, free captives, and release those trapped in darkness."

"Do you think that is literal or figurative?" Hannah asked. "Will he open the eyes of blind people or will he help those of other nations to understand who he is?"

"Perhaps he'll do both." Simeon's forehead creased. "One thing disturbs me still. The same prophet who predicted the Messiah's birth and future reign also predicts a role of great suffering. I have always hoped that Isaiah spoke of yet another. But the more I read, the more I am convinced that life will not be easy for this child, or those who raise him."

"Let's focus on today. The child is a child. We live in a time of peace. What good will it do to disturb others with the things we know?"

"You may be right." Simeon motioned to Nicodemus, who rolled up the scroll again and tucked it under his arm. "I'll be back each day for the morning sacrifice. Soon we will see our hope together."

Two weeks passed before the morning finally arrived. Simeon trembled with certainty as he rose from his reed mat just before dawn. The past eighty-six years had brought so much hope and pain.

The rooster crowed long after he'd washed and dressed and taken some tea. Three times he changed the head covering he would wear for this special moment.

He sat on the bench outside his garden when Nicodemus arrived to escort him up the hill to the Temple plaza. Fresh energy drove him to conquer this hill he had walked a thousand times or more. His eyes vibrated with renewed clarity.

---

[11] Isaiah 9:6–7.

As the time of sacrifice arrived, he looked for Hannah and found her kneeling in her familiar place. By this time Phoebe and Fiona had been betrothed, but a new girl stood watching and learning.

When Hannah looked up, he motioned for her to join him.

"Today is the day," Simeon said to Hannah. "I have calculated it over and over and I am certain. It has been forty days and the time of the mother's purification is here. The child will be dedicated and a sacrifice will be offered. They will be here."

"They are young and from the north," Hannah reminded him. "What if they decide not to follow the traditions we have been raised with?"

"They will be here," Simeon said. "Now, the sacrifice is over. Keep your eyes open."

A few moments later, a young man stepped through the gate, his eyes wide at the awesome scene before him. Thousands of pilgrims jostled for space in the courtyard as the sun glistened off the marble pillars. His well-groomed beard was offset by the bleary eyes of a new parent. A young woman cradling a newborn sheltered behind him, holding onto the crook of his arm.

Simeon shuffled forward and held out his arms.

In response, the woman looked up at her husband, who nodded. She gently handed over her baby.

"The sacrifice is done?" Simeon asked.

"We offered two turtledoves, in accordance with the law," the man said. "And the five shekels as the price of the firstborn."

The shofar blasted and Simeon looked up at the priests holding the ram's horns to their lips. It was as if the heavens were declaring this moment despite the numerous times those horns had been blown before. The noise of bleating lambs, lowing cattle, chanting priests, praying worshippers, coins being offered, and vendors hawking their wares all faded away as Simeon looked into the face of his hopes.

"Yeshua," he said.

"Yes," the man said. "I am Yosef and this is my wife, Mariam. We have come from Nazareth to Bethlehem for the census. My son is forty days old and the time for purification has come."

"A blessing for a firstborn son." Simeon lifted the child higher than it seemed his feeble arms could manage. The chanted hymn flowed from his lips without effort: "Sovereign Lord, as you have promised, you may now dismiss your servant in peace. For my eyes have seen your salvation, which you have prepared in the sight of all nations: a light for revelation to the Gentiles, and the glory of your people Israel."

It was as if the angels who had heralded the moment of the child's birth to the shepherds now stood as invisible witnesses to the dedication.

A deeper prompting seized Simeon and he frowned at its implications. He pulled the child close and stepped toward Mariam, peering into her eyes.

"This child is destined to cause the falling and rising of many in Israel, and to be a sign that will be spoken against, so that the thoughts of many hearts will be revealed. And a sword will pierce your own soul too."[12]

As Simeon handed the child back to Mariam, Hannah stepped forward and placed her hand on the child.

"A shoot will come up from the stump of Jesse; from his roots a Branch will bear fruit. The Spirit of the Lord will rest on him—the Spirit of wisdom and of understanding, the Spirit of counsel and of might, the Spirit of the knowledge and fear of the Lord—and he will delight in the fear of the Lord." Hannah's voice rose as she focused her pronouncement. "He will not judge by what he sees with his eyes, or decide by what he hears with his ears; but with righteousness he will judge the needy, with justice he will give decisions for the poor of the earth. He will strike the earth with the rod of his mouth; with the breath of his lips he will slay the wicked. Righteousness will be his belt and faithfulness the sash around his waist.."[13]

The pronouncement seemed to startle Yosef and the crowd pressing close all around them only seemed to add to his clear discomfort; he was a man from the country, used to open spaces.

Yosef nodded several times as he pulled his wife away.

"I think you frightened them," Simeon said to Hannah once they were alone again. "The words of Isaiah are strong medicine for those who haven't had the chance to lean on them."

"They are strong medicine for those of us who do lean on them," Hannah said. "Was it worth it for you? You've waited your whole life for that one brief encounter. Was it enough?"

"Like I said to them, now I can depart in peace. Besides, I know where they live." Simeon turned towards the collection of sandals by the pool. "My scrolls are more precious than ever. I see that the words I've copied for so long are words of truth and hope for a nation that has lost its way."

---

[12] Luke 2:34–35.

[13] Isaiah 11:1–5.

Simeon sat on the edge of the pool and allowed Nicodemus to slide his sandals onto his feet.

He turned to Hannah. "We started our journey together at a time of death. We are nearing the completion of our journey with a focus on life. You and I have shared a moment that will eclipse the ages."

"Why do you say that?" she asked.

A shudder rippled through his body. "Somehow this child will know sacrifice like no other before him and no one after him."

# ABOUT THE AUTHOR

Jack A. Taylor (PhD) grounds his novels in solid historical research and real-life characters. His eighteen years in Kenya, current work in Rwanda, and twenty-five years in cross-cultural ministry keep him globally aware and connected. He and his wife Gayle live outside Vancouver, Canada and have been married for forty-seven years. They have four children and eleven grandchildren. Jack is an award-winning author with Faithwriters and writes monthly for Light Magazine and other publications (www.jackataylor.com). He has helped found nine organizations, including the New Hope Community Services Society, which has provided housing for more than eight hundred fifty refugees from sixty countries. He is a credentialed marriage coach and focuses on helping leadership couples when he isn't writing (www.1heartcoaching.com). He has master's degrees in leadership, counseling, and theology, plus his PhD in counseling. Jack's hobbies include raising tropical fish and reading.

ONE LAST WAVE

Katrina [Katie] Joy Delancey has staked her life on keeping the past and future away from her heart. But she is no master of fate or captain of her own journey. A near fatal race with a wild stallion, an unexpected discovery of lost African journals, and a chance encounter with a tae kwon do master, leads Katie through love, grief, faith and terror like she's never known it.

*One Last Wave* is a story about being discovered by faith and love no matter where you are, no matter where you've been, and no matter what you think may lie ahead.

NO PLACE TO RUN

Pushed to her limits, Katie Delancey stands at the pinnacle of a bridge. Growing up as a missionary kid changes nothing now. Witness protection has failed her. The determined human trafficking ring has tracked her down. A continent away from her fiancé, she is wooed by a 'wolf in sheep's clothing' and trapped. Weary and vulnerable from losing her mother to cancer, the upcoming wedding of her sister, the loss of her horse, the needs of the refugees she loves, and the constant surveillance of the police, she has no place to run. When you haven't got a prayer where do you turn? Katie is about to find out.

*No Place to Run* is the second novel in an adventure about rediscovering faith, hope and love when the maze of life seems to close all exits. It is a story about how the whispers of the past can be keys to our future. It is a tale about how the illusions of the obvious may be sinister traps designed to destroy us.

STRETCHING FOR HOME

A blissful love nest amidst a brutal Minnesota winter turns into a fiery ordeal of grief and terror as Katie is caught up in the never-ending pursuit of human traffickers who want to eliminate her from their deadly game. Isolated and forced to go undercover with the RCMP, the gambit almost backfires. Escaping to Africa doesn't release her from the trail of death relentlessly pursuing her.

*Stretching for Home* is an education into the heart of missionary kids searching for healing as life tumbles in around them. Their quest for home can be as elusive as a rainbow's pot of gold. Finding old roots and spreading new wings can be a challenge.

THE CROSS MAKER

First-century Palestine is a hotbed of political, cultural, and religious intrigue. Caleb ben Samson, a carpenter from Nazareth, and Sestus Aurelius, a Roman centurion, both want peace. Can this unlikely partnership accomplish what nothing else has accomplished before? Can they bring about peace through the power of the cross? And what role will Caleb's childhood friend Yeshi play in a land that longs for hope?

In *The Cross Maker*, Jack Taylor weaves a tapestry of creative history, powerful characters, and dynamic dialogue to bring to life a shadowy world. In a land where tragedy is as common as dust, triumph is about to make itself known.

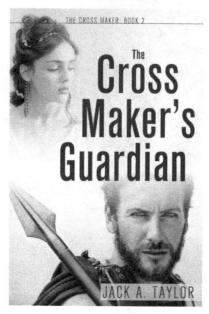

## THE CROSS MAKER'S GUARDIAN

Roman legions thunder across first-century Palestine, seeking to use the power of the cross to crush the lightning strikes of the zealots led by Barabbas. Behind the scenes, a secret squad of thespian assassins are being trained—and Titius Marcus Julianus is caught up in this silent whirlwind, conscripted to be the new guardian of the cross maker, Caleb ben Samson.

Titius is fuelled by vengeance and love as he seeks to regain his stolen Roman estate and the young Jewish slave who once captured his heart. Meanwhile, voices from his past and present wrestle for control of his heart and mind.

In *The Cross Maker's Guardian*, Jack A. Taylor unveils the clash between the Roman and Jewish civilizations as they battle for life in a world suffused with international intrigue. Descriptive narrative, biblical history, and powerful characters all come alive in this thrilling read where death and love are only a blink away.

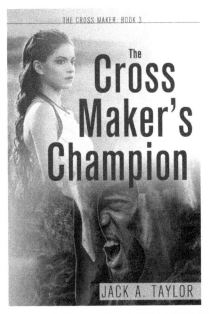

## THE CROSS MAKER'S CHAMPION

Persian slaves who fight for their lives in gladiator arenas rarely rise to be anyone's champion. But the wounded Nabonidus is soon wooed by two women—a priestess at the Temple of Artemis and a humble follower of Yeshua, Daphne. Soon he must learn the truth about himself—is he a missing Persian prince or simply an unwanted orphan?

The arena claims whatever soul may venture there, and Demetrius, a silversmith, joins forces with a giant German giant gladiator, Selsus, to confront the followers of the Way.

Meanwhile, Caleb, Suzanna, Titius, and Abigail fight through their own life-threatening challenges to join the apostle John and Nabonidus in time. Soon the arena will be packed with chanting patrons. Who will still remain standing when the final blood is spilt?

Jack A. Taylor weaves his readers through a maze of Ephesian mysticism and terror as Roman and pagan powers combine to destroy the infant movement of the Way before it takes its first steps out of its birthplace.

JACK A. TAYLOR

WHEN *Ministry* AND *Marriage* COLLIDE

Honest Conversations on Thriving through Conflict

## WHEN MINISTRY AND MARRIAGE COLLIDE

Over twenty-five percent of marriages among today's ministry leaders face significant struggle and strain. The demands and temptations of our public and private worlds often create a tension that pushes our love relationships to the breaking point. Through honest conversations with seven couples, Jack A. Taylor reveals five quagmires that can capture the souls of dedicated leaders.

Areas like Identity, Attachment, Calling, Family, and Intimacy can seem straightforward until you're stuck in the challenges they present. *When Ministry and Marriage Collide* provides over fifty practical tools to help strugglers move from striving to thriving. Ideally, this work is designed to be paired with a relationship coach (see 1heartcoaching.com), but it is sufficient on its own to produce significant conversations with anyone willing to delve into the roots of their challenges.

Based on crucial training from the Thriving Relationship Center, readers will discover the five stages of thriving relationship growth and six foundational pillars for healthy intimacy and communication. After the vows—in the middle of real life—investing in your most important earthly relationship is vital to avoid becoming another statistic. While the couples described here are fictional composites, the issues they deal with are anything but imaginary.